HINDSIGHT

CHRIS MCKIERNAN

Chris McKiernan

COUNTRY BOOKS

Published by Country Books/Ashridge Press
Courtyard Cottage, Little Longstone, Bakewell, Derbyshire DE45 1NN
Tel: 01629 640670
e-mail: dickrichardson@country-books.co.uk
www.countrybooks.biz

ISBN 978-1-910489-03-1

British Library Cataloguing in Publication Data.
A catalogue record for this book is available from the British Library.

Disclaimer:
All of the characters in this book are fictitious,
and any resemblance to actual persons, living or dead,
is purely coincidental.

COVER IMAGE
Red deer hind at sunset
© 2014 Ian MacLeod, Nevispix
www.nevispix.com

Printed and bound in England by 4edge Ltd. Hockley, Essex
Tel: 01702 200243

DEDICATION

To my family.

ACKNOWLEDGEMENTS

With thanks to crosswaite.plus.com for allowing me to quote
and to Erlin Toong for all her help.

And special thanks to Ian MacLeod for permitting the use of
'Red deer hind at sunset' on the cover.
www.nevispix.com

CHAPTER 1

"And so what are we suggesting here?"

I noticed the professor was very careful to say 'we' so we were all somehow involved in discovering and accepting the astonishing idea that was being broached.

"That... but wait, there are more Allington Castle papers to be investigated and deciphered before I can go any further. But we must now, in the light of my findings..."

He was clearly building to a crescendo. The lights seemed to perceptibly dim in the hall at the very idea.

"... consider at least the possibility that Elizabeth the First of England was not perhaps the daughter of..."

Pause. Wild applause. Light bulbs flashed and popped, all the audience were on their feet and journalists were already dashing out of the hall, mobiles to their mouths. Common sense seemed to have left too!

How I wished that Joe, who had invited me to share this moment with him, had actually appeared. But still no sign. He had, inexplicably, missed it all. Still, he would come, he had my car and I needed to drive back to London – that was the deal.

It was a famous night, perhaps the most famous night the relatively new University of Surrey had hosted. The great Cambridge Tudor scholar, Professor Dove-Kemp, choosing this moment to suggest such a dramatic re-writing of sixteenth century history.

But that wouldn't get me home, whereas my car would. The crush was easing as I manoeuvred out of the hall and reached the steps leading down to the car park where I still expected to see him, late and shame-faced. After all not only was it his idea, it was his University (well, he was actually a visiting lecture/tutor there) and his subject (well, not quite, I suppose, his was literature but near enough). As a scientist myself, these Humanity type subjects all blended into one rather hazy mass. And then of course he had suggested that the talk would be exciting, even implied he would have a hand in making it even more exciting (how, I couldn't imagine).

Glancing at his watch, as the car park emptied, and a gentle drizzle began to fall, I felt some alarm. It was nearly eleven o'clock on a rainy night in late October in Guildford and I had to be at work in London tomorrow. I rang his mobile yet again – nothing. Not even switched on. It had been the same throughout the talk, as I surreptitiously grovelled in my bag, hoping the bleep wouldn't disturb anyone. Where was he? More to the point where was my car!

At 11.30 I rang his wife – no answer. Then, reluctantly, I rang my sister, Sonia, who groaned but agreed to drive down from Marlow (rotten journey, M4, M25, very tired, etc. etc.) and pick up her stranded younger brother.

I would have to spend the night in Marlow at her house and phone work in the morning with toothache or whatever.

The M25 and the M4 weren't too bad, my sister chatted on about her children, what a trial our dad was (he lived with them) and thought that Joe (who she never liked, "a bit of a ladies' man" she said in that very old-fashioned way of hers) was probably off chasing some skirt somewhere.

It was gone one when we arrived at 'The Finches', too dark to see the river and the lights on the bridge had gone out.

2

Everyone was asleep so I thanked Sonia and crept up to the attic – and spent a restless night, half-worried, half-angry at what had happened.

Worry replaced anger completely as a police car pulled into the drive early in the morning. Whether worry about Joe or my BMW was uppermost I couldn't say. By now the whole family – Sonia, her husband Gerald, the kids and Dad were staring at the car. I had gone out to meet the police on the drive.

"I wonder if you could come down to the police station in Marlow with us, sir?"

"What's happened? Why? Is it Joe? Where's my car?"

The burly constable wasn't giving anything away. "Just get your things, sir, and come with us, if you would."

I left the family gaping out of the window. Dad, frailer than I'd seen him for a while, came out and held my hand and said "Are you in any sort of trouble, Stephen?"

"No" I said "none at all. It's just about my car, it's probably been stolen, then found, I expect."

But inside Marlow Police Station, it was nothing like I expected. First of all a man introduced himself as Detective Inspector Williams from Mid Surrey C.I.D. The **Mid** Surrey thing seemed very important to him, he was very disparaging of South Surrey CID, West Surrey CID etc. A young constable later told me he was jealous because the other four branches of Surrey CID were all so successful! A large gloomy man with a permanent scowl, he didn't seem too happy in alien surroundings, Buckinghamshire not Surrey! In a world-weary voice he said:

"If I could just check a few details before we start. Let me get them up on the screen. Now, let's see. Tell me if any of this is not correct. Stephen Johnson, age 35, address Spitalfields Market. Very nice! Unmarried, no children, with one sister and a father in his nineties!"

He raised his eyebrows, implying there was something not

right, even suspicious, about men fathering children in their fifties. I didn't rise to it. He seemed very keen on my details, pernickety even, pointing out that I was six foot tall, had fair hair and blue eyes which I already knew, thanks very much. Then I realised with alarm that he was looking at a photograph of me and that I was being treated as some sort of suspect!

"Are you the owner of a blue BMW 318 SE registration HY56 RKE?"

"Yes" I replied, already fearing the worst.

"Your car has been found on the Hascombe Road by the Arboretum. It's been involved in an accident, were you driving it, last night, by any chance?"

"No", flustered and frightened "what about Joe, my friend? I'd lent it to him. Is he alright?"

"There was no one in the car, sir."

"Thank God" I stuttered, "thank God."

"But" remorselessly Williams went on "we found a young woman, unconscious several yards from the car. She is now in The Royal Surrey County Hospital. She hasn't recovered consciousness yet. The car was badly smashed up and caught fire. We were able to use the address in the service booklet to find you. We phoned and visited your flat in London and then managed to contact your sister."

I was astonished. What had happened? A young woman set alarm bells ringing. I knew Joseph, of old. He had an eye for the undergraduates in his classes as his wife well knew. He was only a visiting lecturer at Surrey and the English department members, renowned for their integrity in the treatment of their students, were desperately trying to terminate his 'visit', having realised they had a Casanova in their midst. Was she one of his students? Poor girl. But where was Joe – had he run off? Of course, I wasn't going to share all this with Williams. But the consequence of this was suspicion, on his part.

"Can you confirm your whereabouts to us for yesterday, Mr

Johnson?"

It soon became clear as I went through the events of Monday, October 17, 2011 that I had spent a large part of the day alone with no one to vouch for me until I arrived for the talk at the University.

Williams was non-committal. His slab-like face which I was beginning to dislike immensely didn't betray anything. His young sergeant was busy taking notes including the address of Joe and his wife Ella, which I supplied.

"Well, sir, we'll make sure you get back to 'The Finches', safe and sound." (a hint of irony, was Williams capable of irony?) "If you go back to London, please ring and let us know. As yet your car remains with us, I'm afraid. Should you hear from your friend, likewise ring us at once. You can keep the documents from the car for now."

Bewildered, as the police car raced along by the side of the Thames, the green of the opposite bank waving in a stiff breeze, I couldn't make any sense of it. Idly I thumbed my car documents – as I did, something seemed to have been slipped in between the booklet and the plastic folder, hidden almost, maybe the police hadn't bothered to take everything out of the wallet. I eased it out – the two constables in the front were chatting about the Arsenal – it was a thin piece of paper and in handwriting I didn't recognise at all, it certainly wasn't mine or Joe's as far as I could tell, was written:

'Whoso list to hunt'

that was all. What was it doing there? Before I could speculate further, one of the constables turned to me and asked me about the Arsenal. As a kid who had been taken regularly by his fanatical father to White Hart Lane I just grunted. Then I pushed the paper back in its place and said nothing about it.

The kids were agog, the adults aghast, at the turn of events. Gerald reckoned, cruelly, "the floozy would be one of his

students. Done a runner, probably pissed, and left the girl."
Sonia was more worried about "the poor girl. Should we go
and visit her, take some flowers, would they let us see her?"
The kids just wanted to know how wrecked the car was and
how burnt. "Could we go and see that?", never mind the girl!
Dad was worried about me. Bless them, at least they all
believed me, unlike Williams!

The most sensible course of action was to go to see Joe's
wife, since she still wasn't answering land-line or mobile. But
then I thought, I was going to drive up to Hascombe, but in
what? And Sonia and Gerald needed the car – it was half-term
and both of them had taken time off to be with the kids.
Hascombe was impossible to reach by public transport from
Marlow – so until I figured something out, I was sort of stuck.

Dad set off for a stroll along the riverbank to his beloved
boat. A converted narrow boat named 'Greavsie' after Dad's
hero. Gerald had splashed out (as he jokingly put it) a lot of
cash for it. I think it was actually to keep Dad out of the house
as much as possible.

Once a sailor, always a sailor. Though not firing torpedoes
at the Hun anymore! I said I would join him later for some air
but there was something I had to do first. Gerald agreed to let
me have the use of his computer, so after a quick phone call
to work, mumbling and making tooth-achey sort of noises and
promising to be in by Thursday (it was now Tuesday), I
settled down at the computer. Gerald had said, with a smirk,
"if you fancy looking at any particular websites (nudge,
nudge, wink, wink) then make sure they vanish before we get
back".

I used Google on the cryptic phrase to find out almost
immediately there was nothing cryptic about it, it was the
opening of a well-known poem. This is what I read:

> *'Whoso list to hunt, I know where is an hind*
> *But as for me, helas, I may no more…*

The vain travail hath wearied me so sore,
I am of them that farthest come behind.
Yet may I by no means my wearied mind
Draw from the Deer, but as she fleeth afore
Fainting I follow. I leave off therefore,
Since in a net I seek to hold the wind.
Who list her hunt (I put him out of doubt)
As well as I may spend his time in vain.
And graven with diamonds in letters plain
There is written, her fair neck round about:
Noli me tangere for Caesar's I am
And wild for to hold, though I seem tame.'

I didn't understand it but I knew it was a sonnet (I had counted the lines and remembered from dim and distant English Lit lessons that sonnets had 14 of them). It was by someone called Sir Thomas Wyatt. I wouldn't say I was crestfallen, but it was hardly the stuff of James Bond. I hadn't the faintest idea what the first few words were doing in my service booklet wallet. Could some love-lorn mechanic have left it there, inadvertently, after changing my oil filter? On the face of it, unlikely. Could it have been blown in by the wind? There weren't many scenarios which led to half a line of a sonnet by Sir Thomas Wyatt ending up in my plastic service booklet wallet. Actually there weren't any. So, for the time being I dismissed it as being one of these unexplained and bizarre things that happened some time. Of no relevance to the case in hand. How wrong can you be?

I decided to look for Dad and set off along the riverbank.

Marlow was looking exceptionally pretty, dare I say 'twee', on that fine sunny October afternoon. But not for long. It was Williams on my mobile. "Is that Mr Stephen Johnson?" I resisted the impulse to say "just call me Mr Johnson" – "Would it be okay if I came round to see you, I presume you are still at your sister's and we happen to be dealing with another case in Marlow?" I wondered what he would have said if I'd replied "Well, no, actually, it isn't okay. I have nothing to do with it." But in spite of all these hypothetical replies, all I said was meekly "Yes, of course." I just had time before his arrival to ferret out Dad from the bilges and gunwale or whatever the innards of the boat that he was crouched in, were called.

"Not exactly HMS Whatnot." I said. "Not quite what you were used to." As always, whenever any of us made the slightest reference to the War, he was off on one of his stories about some pal of his on another ship. Long ago, we'd all noticed how he was careful not to talk about his own ship or anything about what **he** did in the war. Most of my friends said the same; their fathers would talk endlessly about others' exploits. As if what they actually saw and did was too real and too harrowing to discuss. We never bothered to explore further, clearly it hurt too much thinking of dead comrades.

I had hoped never to see Williams again but there he was large as life and twice as lugubrious, waiting for me outside the house, scowling at the river. "Water!" he said "why do people like to live near water? Full of rats I reckon. Posh as well. Pooh!

Now then, Mr Johnson, it's time we had a longer chat. Maybe you've remembered something about where you were, who saw you and whether you were driving your car after all?"

"No" I replied.

CHAPTER 2

I felt obliged to make the Detective Inspector a cup of tea. I wanted a stiffer drink but that didn't seem at all wise. So tea all round – I didn't suppose there was any chance it would choke him!

"Now, Stephen, I can call you that, can't I?"

"Okay" (I'd prefer Mr Johnson, sir).

"We've been to see Mrs Lief, Mrs Ella Lief, odd name that, odd spelling. Anyway, she had no idea that her husband was driving your car."

"What!" I was astonished "She must have known."

"Why?"

"Because… because, I assumed that Joe would have told her. Besides she must have known his car was out of action. She would have seen it in the garage!"

"According to Mrs Lief" his voice not rising or falling but inexorably monotone "she assumed he was getting the train to London. He got a taxi to Guildford Station or was it Godalming? I'll have to check with Sergeant Wilson later. Apparently said he had some research to do, would be away a few days. She didn't know anything about his using your car. Which incidentally, of course, she does know quite a bit about." Eye-brows raised quizzically.

"She works at the garage where I got the car. She's a receptionist there – she was working there when I bought it several years ago."

"The BMW garage in Hindhead. I'm told it has a very good reputation."

"No. 'The Orangery Garage' it's called, it sells all makes and models. It's the other side of the National Trust car park from the one you mean."

"Cheaper, I expect, but, of course, unwise in the end not to use the main dealer" was his reply.

Who was he to lecture me on where I bought my car. Cheapskate I may be but I didn't want him calling me one.

"Mrs Lief gave us almost a perfect description of the car," he said "not, of course (a lot of 'of courses') of the state it's in now. Useless for forensics. Charred wreck".

He was enjoying this. A hint of a smile playing on his lips.

"I'm afraid we still need the car. But soon you can have it back." he almost chortled "Mrs Lief's explanation doesn't help you very much, does it Stephen?"

Only Williams could somehow make using my Christian name, rather than my surname, sound like an insult. Sarcasm at best. I was tired of this silly game-playing.

"Look, inspector…"

"Detective Inspector."

"Look, I am telling the truth. I had nothing to do with any of this. If you think otherwise, then say so!"

"Easy, tiger" (the man was insufferable) "nobody is accusing you of anything yet. It would, of course" (there we go again!) "help if Mr Lief turned up to corroborate your story. By the way, the young lady has not come round yet, in fact the doctors think she may not do so for a while. We haven't been able to trace her, nothing in the car was of any use for that. You wouldn't be able to help us there, would you? Been to see her yet, have you?

So what exactly was the arrangement between your good self and Mr Lief? Perhaps you could give me some details?"

I had been ransacking my mind for those very details. The

trouble was, it was very hazy and that would soon be apparent even to a buffoon like Williams.

"Well, he emailed me about a week ago. He said his car had packed up and he badly needed wheels to pursue this important research – he said he was 'on to something'. Now I don't see how poetry and stuff could ever be described like that, but he's been my best friend for ever. So I rang him and said he could. He said he'd come up to London and pick it up, then return it a few days later. I said that I fancied going down to Marlow to see Sis and maybe look up some friends in Surrey, so I'd get the train down and meet him at Hascombe, I could catch up with Ella. Then he suggested we meet at the University – there was this big important cheese giving a spiel and that his research (Joe's that is) was connected to it. He emailed me a ticket. He also said there was someone he wanted me to meet, I knew what he was like and guessed it was his latest girl. He also said he had a lot of exciting news to tell me but (and he stressed this) he'd rather I didn't speak to Ella. He'd run me back to London after the talk – that was a bit odd, it`s more than a 'run' all the way to the East End."

"Spittlefields, isn't it?"

"Spitalfields." Why did I just know he would deliberately mispronounce it.

"The email will still be on your computer?"

"Of course!"

"Then be so good as to supply us with a copy as soon as possible."

When Williams had gone, having given me permission to go up to London and sort out work and flat before being back down in Guildford for 'further questions', I decided to go and see Ella. But first, I had to get to Guildford, The Royal Surrey County Hospital to be precise. The clattering in the kitchen told me the children were home and that meant Gerald's car might be available.

"Off to see the floozy, hey? And then the lonely wife?"

More smirking, Gerald was enjoying my predicament. Still, with my sister looking on clearly concerned and with Dad due home soon, to put more pressure on him, he gave in about the car, albeit ungraciously.

The Royal Surrey County Hospital is close to the university and the cathedral up on Stag Hill. Like all hospitals, it was almost de rigueur to get lost in it. I had asked at the desk and this is where it all started to go wrong.

"A young woman, you say. Well that narrows it down a bit. To about three hundred. Might there be a name? Or even a ward? A condition?"

It was a day for sarcasm. Was there something in the air? Was it Guildford-speak? Was it me? Well, it was, I suppose, truth is I didn't know anything about her.

"She's been involved in a road accident, is in a coma, the police don't know who she is."

"Ah" said the receptionist "that young lady. And have you got permission to see her?"

I explained that DI Williams had suggested I come. "My car was involved, you see."

Suddenly, she was all ears, as were all the other receptionists. Typing stopped. Phones rang unanswered. Patients' relatives ignored. Juicy gossip at two o'clock!

Directions to the private suite followed and it was these I was sadly struggling with until a helpful porter virtually took me there.

When I explained who I was and why I was there to the Ward Sister, she agreed to let me see the girl. Sadly, still no name!

I was ushered into a side room and there she was. Lying still as stone, peaceful, serene even, pale as pale could be. Utterly beautiful and achingly young. How old was she – eighteen? I was sure she was one of his students. I knew the pattern and she fitted the bill perfectly. I could have described her, in a way she was what I expected to see. But not so beautiful. I stared at her a long time; ignoring all the equipment around her, busy monitoring with buzzes and bleeps.

"Lovely, isn't she?"

I started, caught in a reverie, almost guiltily. A nurse had come in unnoticed.

"I only started on this ward today and she's my first patient. She was in a car accident, still I expect you know that, Mr...?"

"Johnson, Stephen Johnson. It was my car... But I wasn't in it, a friend had borrowed it."

"Yes, I heard something like that. I'm Nurse Helen by the way. I'm glad someone's come to see her, it makes her seem more real, more of a person than a mystery."

Just then a voice called and Nurse Helen turned to go.

"I hope you come back" she blushed. Just briefly I was being made aware that it wasn't just because she wanted the mysterious patient to seem 'more real'. I smiled, Helen was someone I wouldn't mind coming back to see too.

"I'll be back, I'm sure."

And then it was just me with the ice-maiden. Somehow, that's how I thought of her. What was the secret – locked up in her mind? Who was she? Surely someone should have missed her by now? Especially if she was a student. Surely, even Williams wasn't stupid enough not to have explored that angle. I made a mental note to check unexplained students absences – especially from English Lit classes taken by Mr Lief.

I stayed longer than I intended but if I hoped my presence would rouse her – why should it? – it didn't. On my way out I made a point of looking for Nurse Helen again. I met the Ward Sister and asked where she was. I made the excuse of wanting to thank her. The Sister looked at me pointedly, helped by her gimlet eyes and pointed nose. She said dismissively "She's only been here a day or two and everyone's looking for Nurse Helen! Another young man who came to see the road accident patient seemed quite taken with her too."

Despite the slight frisson of jealousy I felt (why – I had only just set eyes on Helen) I was more concerned that someone else was visiting her patient.

"Do you recall his name?"

The Sister clearly busy, said as she set off down a corridor "Goodness me, I haven't got time to remember the names of all the nurses' admirers. Lake was it or Land? – something like that – a bit more foreign sounding." And with that she bustled off.

To get to Hascombe, I had to drive the few miles from Guildford to Godalming, courtesy of my brother-in-law's car of course, which was very swish and sleek. His Aston Martin Vantage was top of the range and reminded me of what a tip-top solicitor Gerald must be. Not that he'd offered me any help or advice. But then, we'd never been close. I think Gerald wanted Sonia to himself and Dad and I, especially Dad, were a nuisance at best. To be fair, having a nonagenar-ian living with you must be a trial, even one as spry and ship-shape as my father!

At Godalming I took the route I was dreading – up to Hascombe past the Winkworth Arboretum where the accident had happened. It's a tricky road initially, narrow and lots of parked cars but the country section is easy enough – it was hard to see how anyone driving could have had problems, though in the dark it was pretty pitch I imagined. Joe knew it well of course, so did I. But the ice-maiden? So who **was** driving? The police had offered no thoughts on that. Joe wasn't the sort to run off even if he was over the limit. So if Joe wasn't driving, why was the ice-maiden driving up here **in my car**? She certainly wouldn't be a hapless pedestrian out there at that time of night. A selfish thought intervened – was she insured? Was my car insured for any driver – I hadn't a clue. Did she have a licence? – oh no!

The car caught fire. Why? Out there – late at night? Did she hit another car, (another blank from Williams) a wall, a tree? Everything about this accident was bizarre and simply didn't add up.

I was still musing on this when Ella answered the door.

"Oh, it's you. I suppose I always knew you'd turn up, sooner or later." Charming!

Ella and I go back a long way – a long stormy way. She has always been one feisty lady and we did have a fling back in the days. It was through me she met Joe and I was best man at the wedding.

Lately she has blamed me for Joe's various infidelities, because "I supported him" – all I did was stay out of it. But she also uses me for information and that was about to happen now.

Their house at Hascombe is huge – Ella inherited a lot – and I mean a lot of money – from her parents. We trooped through all the rooms to the conservatory – which gave out onto a scene of autumnal splendour worthy of the Arboretum down the road. Blazing reds lit up the woods at the bottom of their garden – estate might be a better word. Not that I'm jealous you understand, I have my flat in Spitalfields but when your sister overlooks the Thames at Marlow and your best friend lives like this – well it does make you wonder where you went wrong.

Ella went on the attack right away.

"I suppose you knew about this latest girl – one of his students I expect. The Inspector who was here thought as much. Apparently one has not turned up for any lectures since – not that that means much, I never did! Joe hasn't rung you yet, has he? He usually does when he goes off like this and you never tell me. Still he doesn't usually leave quite such mayhem behind. Probably boozed up and ran, always a coward my husband. Could never face the consequences of his stupid actions."

On and on she ranted, bitter and angry. But still hoping to

hear from him and by the looks of it, still ready to take him back.

"No, he hasn't been in touch. Truly. And no, I've never seen the girl before. I've just been to see her now."

"Rat!"

"Williams told me to, virtually" I defended myself. "Look, would it be any use trying to find out where he was actually doing this research of his in **my** car?"

Ella frowned "What research? He never told me about it. Oh and his car's still on the drive – fine as far as it seems. The police had a look at it and couldn't find anything wrong with it. Another lie – the reason for which escapes me." Another hard stare!

"No idea about the research. But I thought that maybe if I could have a glance at his desk or computer, something might give us a clue as to what he was up to?"

"I know what he was up to" stormed Ella "same as always! Anyway there's nothing, I've looked. So no point."

Just then the front door bell rang and Ella disappeared, I could hear an altercation at the door which sounded typical Ella and likely to last. So, quick as a flash, I knew where the study was, I was in there and at the computer. Wham – to the email. Sounds still from below, I took a chance and clicked the most recent message – there was just time to skim it and memorise what I could before the door closed. I got out of the emails and dashed to the bathroom – noisily splashing about and flushing the loo. All the while hanging onto the details of the extraordinary message I had seen.

Back with Ella, we agreed to stay in touch. She made me promise to tell her the minute Joe phoned. We also said we would swap notes about Williams. She was pretty scathing about him. I left hurriedly, claiming (rightly) I had to be back in Marlow to deliver the AM Vantage and get a train to London.

Once on the drive I gave Joe's Vauxhall the once over – it

looked okay from the outside. Ella's BMW (courtesy of where she worked) was also there. I roared off into the darkening lanes – but once past the Arboretum gates and well away, I stopped and wrote down what I remembered. This is what I wrote:

'... followed his car... only the girl... pay for what happened in Crete... swear with your help. Darling...'

This was all. But this was enough. If only I had had time to read the whole thing or better still, print a copy.

All the way back to Marlow and on the train to London these fragments went round and round in my head. As I let myself into the flat above the market they were still with me. Emailing Williams as promised, leaving a message at work explaining I would be away even longer than I thought – vinyl testing would go on without me – I kept trying to make the words mean something to me.

Later that night, at a table for one, below in Spitalfields Market in my favourite Greek restaurant (irony!) I tried to recall anything that Joe had said. But to no avail. Joe and Ella had holidayed on Crete at some time, so had I for that matter. So had most people. Crete was an island famed for its vendettas but what had any of that got to do with any of us?

As the waiter brought my dolmades and I absently said 'efaristo', I knew I had to contact Williams and tell him what I'd seen. Would he think I was crazy? When I opened my phone, he had forestalled me – his text read:

'Stephen, you will be glad to know that the girl was one of Mr Lief's English students as you seemed to realise (I didn't like that!). *Her name is Maria Kyriakos.'*

"And I bet she's from Crete" – I said aloud.

CHAPTER 3

"Portsmouth, actually."

It was confirmed by Williams in his lair. I had been summoned from London after a fitful night's sleep. My sister wasn't best pleased to see me again; Gerald had been moaning, but Dad was delighted. At least I had a roof over my head for the night – I didn't fancy this commuting – how did people do it? Up and down from Surrey to central London (or in my case the East End) every day! I would have to look for somewhere else to stay.

But for the time being it was Mid Surrey CID who called the shots and here I was in Guildford police station – the home of the illustrious Detective Inspector, which to his probable chagrin he shared with the super-successful East Surrey CID.

So it wasn't Crete. It wasn't even Greece. The ice-maiden, very un-Greek sounding (and looking) for that matter, was from Portsmouth!

"She was a first year student, doing a degree in English Lit at the University here. Mr Lief was her personal tutor. Her boyfriend is also a first year Lit student, his room was across from hers in the Halls of Residence. Handy that" said with a salacious grin.

"He supplied the details that enabled us to contact mum and dad in Portsmouth. They're currently all by her bedside. Father **is** Greek by the way, no surprise given the surname.

Oh and it looks like you're in the clear" spoken very grudgingly. "Not only is it more than likely she was with Mr Lief, because she knew him well, but also because said boyfriend saw her getting into your BMW on several occasions last week, tallying with your sketchy apology for an alibi." More than grudging, downright hostile.

"Why should she be from Crete, incidentally?"

Now I had a decision to make. Tell him about Ella's email? Drop her in it? Show myself to be a snoop? Open a can of worms or not? I decided to pause rather than fast-forward on that one. For reasons, in the end, I was far from clear on myself.

"No special reason. About the only part of Greece I know. So am I free to go for good?" changing the subject quickly.

"I suppose so" more grudgingly "but we will need to stay in touch. And of course if you hear from Mr Lief, let us know at once."

"Before I go, can you tell me any more details about the accident? And about my car – like when I can get the insurance onto it?"

Williams, who thought he would now see the back of me, was abrupt where this was concerned:

"No, the enquiry is ongoing. Miss Kyriakos is still critical. Mr Lief is still missing. The details of the accident are not yet in the public domain. Your car is part of the enquiry. I'm sure your insurance company can supply you with a courtesy car" said with the utmost lack of courtesy.

I walked up Stag Hill to the hospital. "No change, I'm afraid" said the Sister on the ward. But Helen was waiting for me outside the room.

"A student at the University here. Maria, she's got a Greek surname and parents. Oh and a boyfriend – he's still here."

It was nice to talk to someone so open and friendly and clearly pleased to see me. We chatted about 'the case', whether Maria had shown any signs of recovery (none), whether the parents were distraught and/or angry (both), whether the boyfriend was upset (definitely) and whether the mysterious young man who came to visit Maria and stayed to chat to Nurse Helen was her boyfriend? To which final question the answer was – "oh that was a reporter from the local paper – he'd smart talk anyone for a story – I sent him away with a flea in his ear and haven't seen him since. I haven`t actually got a current boyfriend."

But all the time I was circling towards a very different question, being led by the twinkle in her deep blue eyes. I got there in the end (I always do) and she agreed to meet me that very evening in Guildford in front of the theatre. Then Sister called once again, rather disapprovingly.

As I went into the room, at first all seemed the same. Stillness, sadness, lifeless almost. But a young man was standing at the window and it was clear he was crying. I apologised for my entrance saying if he wanted to be alone I would leave. But he gave me a warm smile and introduced himself. I explained who I was and why I was there and we spent a long time staring at Maria – willing her to open her eyes. The hospital cafeteria, no sign of Helen, was busy when we lunched together.

I enjoyed lunch with Rydal. We got on well. He may have been half my age but we seemed to click. He commiserated with me about 'vinyl testing' which I was impressed by. I envied him his student days but not the Literature – all that reading – which he accepted. He talked of his strong feelings for Maria – which amused me since term was about a month old and he'd only just met her. But I could tell he was genuine. I said he was very lucky to have found someone so beautiful at the start of his university career and studying the same subject as him.

He told me about his name – Rydal. His parents were obsessed with the Lake District though they lived in London. I laughed, asked him if he had brothers and sisters called Elter or Ulls or Crummock. No, he said, but the dog was called Bassenthwaite. Our guffaws caused quite a stir in the cafeteria.

Then I asked him about Joe and the car:

"Yes, I saw her getting into and out of the BMW several times. I was a bit jealous. She seemed to have a bit of a crush on him – but that's all it was, I'm sure. He's a married man. I don't know how she ended up outside the wrecked car but I believe in her."

His passionate defence was touching. The odd thing was, I believed in her too.

He went on:

"I think it was only this Wyatt thing that she was fascinated by."

I nearly missed it, busy picturing my wrecked car.

"What did you say? Wyatt? Would this be Sir Thomas Wyatt who wrote – hang on…?"

I still had the Internet printout in my pocket. God knows why. *"Whoso list to hunt, I know…"*

"That's the one. In fact, that was Maria's all-time favourite poem. She thought the references to Ann Boleyn were so clear:

> *"And graven with diamonds in letters plain*
> *There is written, her fair neck round about:*
> *Noli me tangere, for Caesar's I am,*
> *And wild for to hold, though I seem tame."*

Poor Wyatt had the hots for her but Henry bought her with diamonds and a crown. The message is clear: 'Don't touch me, I'm the king's now.' A bit ironic about the fair neck – given what happened to it."

Double-take number Two!

"Wyatt was in love with Ann Boleyn?"

"The poems suggest they were lovers but once Henry VIII got interested Wyatt probably backed off. Why?"

"Probably backed off?"

My mind was racing. Joe said he had some significant contribution to make to the meeting. He had been researching poetry (with Maria in tow, a student fascinated by him and/or by Sir Thomas Wyatt) and Dove-Kemp had left us all at that meeting with the distinct impression that Henry VIII may not have been Elizabeth I's father. Now I was no hot-shot at history, but even I remember Elizabeth's mother was Ann Boleyn. There was one way to clinch it.

"This Wyatt guy, has he any connection with Allington Castle?"

"It was his house" said Rydal immediately.

Bingo! Two and two making five, six, seven in my head.

I shared what I knew with Rydal. He was as eager as I was to find out more about what Joe was looking for. The puzzle was whether historical research had anything to do with his disappearance. Surely not – that was Robert Goddard stuff, wasn't it?

"Look, Rydal, I've no access to Joe's papers or computer anymore but what about Maria's?"

"Don't you know? The police went into her room soon after they spoke to me. It had been turned over, ransacked!"

"Good God! When? Why? What were they looking for? I ought to tell the Surrey CID about Wyatt. On the other hand, knowing Williams they'll dismiss me as a crank or worse start investigating me just when I'm in the clear. Is her room still out of bounds?"

Rydal was pretty sure it was. But then he made me an offer I couldn't refuse. His mate, James, who lived on the same landing as he did, had gone off to Bolivia 'to find himself'. I would have thought finding Bolivia would be tricky enough having seen a programme about the hair-raising roads in Latin America! Rydal had the key of his room and since I had already told him I was looking for somewhere to stay other than my sister's, he suggested I bunk down in James' room. Finding yourself in Bolivia could be a long job and probably not cheap – he could do with the rent!

Brilliant! I had just landed myself at the heart of things on the University of Surrey campus. Yards away from Maria's flat and for that matter from Maria. Relatively close to Ella. And presumably, an added bonus, closer to Helen too!

"Rydal, I'm glad our paths crossed. Consider it a deal. I'll give you the rent for James. Oh and get your road atlas out, when my wheels arrive we're off to Allington, wherever that is."

Chapter 4

More calls. Sonia couldn't hide the relief in her voice when I said I had found somewhere to stay. Dad came on briefly. "Is everything okay, Stephen?" I answered him it was.

"How's the boat, Dad?" It was like a joke between us, I asked so many times over the years.

I was right about Williams. I told him all about the poem, the research, even the Dove-Kemp talk. Stony silence. "Well I'll see if this Whynot fellow is on file" was his only response.

"Wyatt" I said "and he's sixteenth century – so he won't be on file. It looked like I was on my own (or at least Rydal and I were) on this one. Then I told him about Ella's email – I knew I had to in the end – but his reply was surprising. "Oh yes, we examined Mr Lief's computer and found all their messages, even the deleted ones. One did mention Crete but she confirmed that they were planning a holiday – nothing sinister there." Which was odd because a lot of that email was sinister to me.

"What about following cars and vendettas?"

I could tell Williams was struggling with 'vendetta'.

"No, nothing like that" was his terse reply.

And that was it. "How not to spot clues" I thought. But then I had to admit Sir Thomas Wyatt and/or Cretan vendettas were all a bit far-fetched and the truth was, no doubt, much more mundane.

"Norbert Dent. How may I help you?"

My final call was to my insurance company. I tried to explain to Norbert that the police had my car, it was a burned out wreck and that I would need a courtesy car. I even supplied a police reference.

"Near Arboretum, you say, where's that? It's not coming up on my computer."

"It wouldn't, it's a sort of tree garden. Winkworth." My exasperation was showing.

"I beg your pardon?"

"Winkworth is the name of the arboretum, tree place. Look what does it matter where it happened?"

But Norbert, a stickler for procedure, was having none of it. Eventually we got there and I was told I could pick up a car in Guildford that afternoon and keep it until the police investigation was sorted out. But then it all went pear-shaped again when we got to the other named drivers.

"Rydell, like Rydell High?"

"No" I said, "Rydal – I suppose it is quite high up, the dog's called Bassenthwaite". I couldn't resist.

Long silence. Had I offended Norbert? Did he have the faintest idea what I was talking about?

Finally, Rydal or possibly 'Rydell' was a named driver on my courtesy car and I bade Norbert a fond farewell. I could imagine what he told his colleagues in the call-centre about me.

I collected the car mid-afternoon, a zippy little Ford Fiesta and was heading back up Stag Hill to my new home. Turning into the campus I was confronted by the huge metal stag sculpture – the figure soon to become such a common a sight that often it was invisible to me. I suppose the Surrey hills once were home to huge herds of deer rather like Scotland or the New Forest.

Room 303 was small but serviceable – after all it wasn't for long (it won't take long to crack this case, Watson!). Was that really what I was doing, playing at detectives? No, it was much more serious than that, a good friend was missing, an innocent student's life on hold and mine had certainly taken a detour, if not a new direction.

The block was right at the top of the hill and a little cut-through brought you to the cathedral car park (out of bounds for student cars) and the cathedral itself. I would pop in there soon. And it was very tempting to use the car park, rather than walk some distance from the block to my parking space.

By seven I was spruced up and not a little nervous. By eight I was outside The Yvonne Arnaud Theatre watching the muddy waters of the usually sedate Wey swirl by, we had had a lot of rain in the last few weeks. Helen looked very striking in boots, jeans and a clearly expensive designer black leather top and leather coat. The meal in the theatre restaurant was tasty and later we strolled by the river getting to know one another.

She was from 'up North'.

"Just outside Watford then?" was my inane attempt at wit. "Well, I'm not racist, so don't worry. We can't all hail from the home counties." More attempts at wit!

She brought the subject of Maria Kyriakos up, showing interest in my situation, which was an indirect way of showing interest in me. Not being vain, she was clearly happy to be out with me. It was so seductive almost, that I began to unload the whole saga so far. She listened patiently, offered a few theories of her own and made me promise to keep her up to speed. It was a delicious feeling to matter to someone again.

She could also keep me up to speed with Maria's progress in turn. Not sure she was quite so happy with this. A hint of jealousy evident in her?

"She's got a boyfriend, you know." Don't forget poor Rydal!

I had told her about my new living arrangements. She was oddly reluctant to fill me in on hers. She was cagey about her background and flatly refused to discuss home.

But it was good to kiss her goodnight outside the Nurses' home and arrange to meet again very soon.

Thursday, October 20, dawned grey and soon became wet. Not auspicious for our journey to Kent. Rydal was going to skip lectures – "it's only Restoration dramatists – all bosoms and cuckolds" – and we were setting off to Allington at 10. The first night in my new, very narrow bed, in my little room had been far from restful, partly because of the loud music coming from next door till 2 am but then, I had a place to stay, not quite trendy Spitalfields, but it would do.

Allington Castle, near Maidstone, was not open to the public we had discovered on the internet via Rydal's iPhone. But we hoped somehow to persuade the owners to at least talk to us. How do you contact the owner of a castle? Well by phone it turns out.

The owner was delightful, very helpful and friendly and soon put us on to the research team. Rydal was brilliant, whilst I would have stuttered and stammered unconvincingly, plausible as you like he said:

"Part of Professor Dove-Kemp's team. Just a few loose ends to tidy up. Hope you don't mind. Needn't disturb you. Just point us in the direction of the Wyatt papers that Prof has been using."

And it worked. We made an appointment for midday and a secretary would show us the relevant office and leave us to it. It all seemed a bit too easy for my liking. But with the confidence born of youth Rydal pronounced it:

"No problem. We're in!"

On the way, as we sped and alternatively crawled along the

M25, M26 and M20, Rydal brought me up to speed (our current in-phrase it seemed) with all the Wyatt/Boleyn carry-on.

"Ann and Wyatt, Henry's court poet, probably had a fling in the late 1520s or early 1530s. This petered out or was put a stop to by the king, a friend of Wyatt as well as his employer. But in November 1532 she went to France and Wyatt went too on some embassy or other. Wyatt even wrote about this.

'And now I follow the coals that be quent from Dover to Calais against my mind'

Quent means quenched, fire of passion out – but it could also be a pun on 'queynt' which", here Rydal blushed profusely "which might mean…er… something…"

"I get the picture" I put him out of his misery, "pronounced with a c not a q."

"Yes, well, it could mean the fire was reignited."

I began to sing Take That's 'Relight my Fire…'

He couldn't stop laughing. We really did share the same sense of humour!

Rydal went on: "Now on January 25th 1533 Henry married Ann, their daughter Elizabeth was born September 7th – so she was conceived December 1532."

"So," I said "Wyatt and Ann might have relit their fire, so to speak, in France in November, and possibly kept the flame alive back in England during December. Ann got herself pregnant and somehow passed it off as Henry's? That's what Dove-Kemp has proof of? God, historically it's a kind of bombshell, I suppose, and probably will make Dove-Kemp famous."

"And rich" said Rydal very cynically.

We were ushered into a side door by a-sort-of steward person, having marvelled initially at the towers and battlements dominating the waters of the Medway. The sort-of-steward person then gave way to a-sort-of secretary person who informed us brusquely that his instructions were that we were to be shown into the library. And we were, super-brusquely.

Astonishingly, Rydal and I were in the vast library of an ancient castle all on our own. The trouble was, we didn't have a clue! We had been sort-of-pointed at some papers and abandoned. I had been quaking in my boots, expecting to be grilled and discovered as frauds. What next?

Rydal was already scanning the documents – heaps of them. When I joined him it became clear this would take a long time since we didn't know where to begin. What made it worse was they were all impossible to read.

"Secretary hand" said Rydal helpfully "Can you read it?"

"Nope. What exactly is it? We need an expert."

"And here I am" came a booming voice from a deep recess of the library. A very distinguished looking grey-haired gentleman was the owner of said voice.

"Forsyth, Ballantyne, at your service."

The thing was, which name was which? I reckoned later his Christian name was Forsyth, Rydal plumped for Ballantyne. We never did find out. But what we did discover was that he was a whizz at secretary hand and had been helping the Professor with his researches.

"Odd, he never mentioned anyone else would be here today" boomed Ballantyne (or was it Forsyth).

With his help, we made a start on understanding the latest documents Dove-Kemp had been working on – they were in French anyway, something else I couldn't read. But he was happy to translate that too:

'Sir Thomas Wyatt visited the chateau at Vilmy near Calais. The Lady Ann was present and her ladies in waiting. There was much surprise to see Sir Thomas and everyone was well pleased. Particularly the Lady Ann...'

This was promising. It would be a stroke of luck if the vital document was this one – if only our luck would hold.

Our luck ran out as Professor Dove-Kemp strode into the room.

"Well, well, Ballantyne. And who have we here? Some of my team, I believe. Come on team, you seem a little tongue-tied?"

The eminent professor, darling of the press, was not above a little sarcasm. His manner was intimidating and threatening even. Large, powerful, more bruiser than professor, I sensed his controlled anger.

Rydal to the rescue. He managed a decent explanation about being so impressed by the talk, so thrilled (he laid it on thick) that we had used a little subterfuge admittedly to see 'history in the making' for ourselves. Hoped he would understand, apologies all round. With that we scuttled out. Leaving a bemused, though still booming Ballantyne "Who were they?" and a professor far from fooled, I suspected.

The most telling moment had been when Rydal mentioned how as a student of Mr Lief's he had had an extra incentive to visit the castle. I saw Dove-Kemp's face register real alarm at that point.

We beat our ignominious retreat to the car, watched all the while by the pair of them from the vantage point of a window in the tower.

The M25 signs warned us it was closed due to an incident and so we were forced onto side roads. The A25 is about as different from the M25 as it is possible to be. One narrow single lane road as opposed to an eight lane highway, narrow, twisty and busy as a result of the closure, in the developing twilight. I think I was still in shock from our Allington debacle. I was aware the car behind was close on my tail, flashing his lights angrily and anxious to get past. He took his chance with a gap in the oncoming traffic, even though there was a bend coming up. He just made it but pulled back in far too sharply and suddenly, he caught the front of my car – pushing us into the side where there was just a stone wall, we smashed into that and bounced across into oncoming traffic, buffeted by that and the fast moving car behind, I lost control and thought that was it. Rydal was slumped in the passenger seat. But somehow I got control back, and after much flashing of lights, swearing and cursing, I pulled very gingerly onto the side. Fortunately, no one, except us, had sustained much damage and no one fancied staying around to swap insurance details. I tried to rouse Rydal. He groaned, he had a bruise but otherwise seemed unhurt, if stunned.

"Sorry" I said "I think the whole Dove-Kemp thing rattled me and I lost concentration for a minute. Are you alright?"

"It wasn't an accident" he said in between groans "I was concentrating. That wasn't just bad overtaking. He meant to do it. He waited until the bend and the wall, knowing we had nowhere to go but into it! It was an arranged accident."

The enormity of this hit us, as we sat shocked on the side of the darkening A25. Surely Dove-Kemp wouldn't? Couldn't? We had not been gone from Allington long. And why? Was it so important what we had seen?

"I got a look at the driver" said Rydal "he was dark-haired and I reckon he was wearing a track suit with a logo or something similar. That's really all."

When we got back to the relative safety of our block on campus we began to speculate on the traumatic events of the past few hours.

CHAPTER 5

Rydal and I agreed that if thugs were on our trail we had better be very careful. The only thing to link us to Guildford was the mention of Joe by Rydal. I'm sure the Professor would never have noticed me in the crowd on the night of his great triumph here. But why was Joe involved at all? If he was! All questions; no answers.

Rydal was going to spend the evening by Maria's bedside catching up on work he had missed at the same time. After a quick meal in the University refectory I drove across to the Nurses' home, I needed to see Helen, not just to go over the day's events but for some female company. We had only kissed but then we had only known each other a few days.

It wasn't that easy getting into the nurses' halls of residence, our block back up at the University was free and easy, anyone could come and go (alarming in a way, anything could happen and someone had ransacked Maria's room); this place was more like a prison with cameras and wardens everywhere. I managed to avoid detection and knocked on her door – she answered, but was startled when she saw it was me, and none too pleased.

"Oh, it's you, Stephen, just hang on will you, my place is a mess." And I was left standing outside feeling far from welcome. How different from her previous attitude. Was there a man in there? But when she opened the door again, the smile and the eagerness had returned. Perhaps she just didn't like surprises or callers when the room was a tip.

I was keen to tell her what had happened. She put her arm around me as I told her about the accident.

"I think Rydal was probably being a bit melodramatic. It sounds like just reckless driving to me. I'm always being cut up on the A3 and that's a big wide road. Are you okay? Do you want me to check you out?"

I liked the sound of that. And soon I'd forgotten all about the crash as we got closer. The mood slightly cooled when she suggested we go out, into the town for something to eat. Whilst she was in the bathroom I had a brief look at her book shelves – always a good way to judge how compatible someone is. It looked good – Dexter, Goddard, Rankin, we shared the same taste in thrillers. A book, still open, had fallen down behind the chair probably in the clean up earlier and I retrieved it – just as she came in, looking terrific in a short tight dress. There was a hint of irritation as she grabbed the book.

"God, what am I like? So untidy" and placed it in the shelves, "come on, let's eat."

Over the meal in a cosy little Italian by the river, I tried again to find out about who Helen really was and failed. She resolutely refused to go there, apart from her nursing career. She was entertaining about her training though – the old story about taking out all the patients' false teeth to wash and mixing them up I had heard before – but lurid tales of stuffing intestines or enormous hernias back into patients made me laugh!

When we got back to the room, it was, I thought, to get even closer. But after coffee the shutters came down again when she claimed to be tired. As she was looking for her work shifts so we could plan to meet again, I glanced at the book shelves. Odd, the book I had retrieved, quite noticeable in that it was a big hardback amongst the paperbacks, wasn't there. Had it fallen again? No, I looked. The title had surprised me anyway: 'Warfare at Sea World War II' – an odd choice. Then in a sort of flashback I saw myself picking it up earlier and noticing that it had fallen open at 'Crete 1941: The Evacuation to Egypt' Somehow this had stuck in my mind without my being fully conscious of it. Oh well, I had always found World War II interesting to read about. But as we parted, when I said:

"like I mentioned in the restaurant, we share the same interests: Goddard, Dexter, Rankin and even World War II."

"That's not mine, that's my…" she stopped, and with a slight adjustment "friend's."

Unsettled, we parted without even kissing. As I drove back up Stag Hill I mused on her moodiness even saying to the welcoming silver stag – "Women!"

The heavy metal began right on cue as I hit my pillow. Throb, throb, throb! Was that the music or my head? I stormed round to 305 and banged on the door – predictably no reply. How could they hear? So I opened the door and stormed in. I was in a green sea – lurid luminous creatures floated by, the surf was pounding above my head. A strange creature undulated its locks before me. Then it stopped – the music that is, the strange creature reassembled itself as a very large, very Caribbean student. Off went the lurid green lights and on came soft gentle ones. Just as a soft gentle hand held mine and said "Peace."

"At last" I replied. "I can't sleep. I'm next door."

"Yow can't sleep, well neither can oy, so I ploy music." came the helpful reply.

Osbert, I know the names at the University of Surrey take some believing, was a Maths student. He loved heavy metal, he told me over green leaf tea, and he loved peace. When I pointed out the two were perhaps incompatible he laughed.

34

Would he stop or at least lower the volume of his music? He shrugged, I gave up, drank the green tea and wished him good night.

I slept like a baby in the silence that followed. And in the morning I invited Osbert for coffee. He was from that well known outpost of the Caribbean – Brum. His Brummy accent seemed stronger in normal room 303. He called me 'Stoyvin' – which I loved or 'yow'.

"Yow see thees" or "yow loyk thees…" Now that was music. He knew Maria, was so sorry for her and dedicated his music to her. To be honest it could have woken her up in the Royal Surrey quite easily.

I thought the reasons I was there were far too complex to go into, so just stuck with the stunning cover story Rydal had invented: "I'm a friend of Rydal's" and left it at that.

But it was nice to have such a big strong albeit lunatic Brummy next door, just in case hired thugs came calling.

Rydal was out, perhaps by Maria's bedside again. So I had time to think. It was a bright, sunny and mild morning for late October and I strolled past the lake on campus, lost in thought. I was confused on many counts and couldn't pull all the disparate threads together to make a whole – not even 'string theory' was more complex or baffling than all this. I needed a plan of action – why? – none of it mattered that much to me – why not 'do nothing' and 'go away'. But somehow I couldn't. If all this was left to Williams where would we be?

So, I did what I always do. When I got back to 303 I made a to-do list and determined to tackle it one by one and tick things off as I did.

Here is my list:
Friday, October 21, 2011   *Room 303*   *10 am*

To-do list
> • *Phone work – no, text work – no phone work
> (the to-do list was a work in progress) and tell
> them I wouldn't be in until October 24.*
> • *Go and see Maria – how she drew us to her!*
> • *Go and see Dad – it was his birthday.*

So far I didn't quite seem to be penetrating the heart of the mystery.

> • *Is there a mystery with a heart to penetrate?*

Not much better. At this point Rydal joined me and brought some focus to the list after telling me, sadly, Maria was still the same.

> • *If the accident was no accident then find out
> more about Dove-Kemp at Cambridge.*
> • *If Ella's email was suspicious then go and see
> her again.*
> • *Could we tie any of the threads together – how
> ever tenuously? Common sense suggests there
> is no connection between Wyatt and Crete at all.*

End of to-do list.

We started at the end, as you do. It was Rydal, who had a talent for summing things up, who pieced it all together as far as it could be pieced.

"Someone crashed into your BMW with Maria in it. Presumably they were after Joe Lief – was he driving? Find out if the driver's seat was pushed back or not? Joe is a tall guy, Maria is small. Someone crashed into your courtesy car, with us in it."

"They don't like my choice of cars!" I suggested helpfully!

"Both staged crashes were an attempt to kill or injure. But such a haphazard and inefficient way to do either. Both 'accidents' were Dove-Kemp's way (or his hired thug's way) of warning Joe and us off the Wyatt thing. Not sure why but

Dove-Kemp's reputation and future riches are behind it. We need to find out more and since Allington seems off limits at the moment, then it's got to be Cambridge. As for Mrs Lief, she has a curious email which mentions following a car and some kind of Cretan vendetta from someone who calls her 'Darling'. My guess, and it's only a guess, is that the email, she has since explained away was from... her husband! That's why it said 'Darling' and mentioned the car and, stay with me here... the Cretan thing is some kind of secret message or code or ..."

"God" I shouted out loud "He's in Crete!"

"Well, I wasn't actually going to go that far but..."

Just then there was an enormous banging at the door and Osbert burst in.

"Stoivyn, are you alroit?"

He calmed down when he saw Rydal. I apologised for shouting. He asked about Maria and then hurried away to a lecture on "probabeeleetee." Probably!

I phoned Ella, texted and emailed. No reply. Soon I was gunning, well heavily revving, the Ford up the road to Hascombe. We fell silent as we passed Winkworth. The house looked empty. A neighbour, well she lived in the next house which was about 100 yards down the road, said she thought Mrs Lief had gone away. She saw her with suitcases getting into a taxi about two hours ago.

I have a penchant for making huge numbers out of two plus two and did it again. "Crete!"

Another interminable jam on the M25 meant Gatwick took a desperately long hour and a half. We took one terminal each. I drew a blank but Rydal had a Kwikjet flight to Heraklion departing in about half an hour. I rushed over and we dashed around the terminal – no sign.

The departure lounge was beyond us without a reservation.

But we could see a Kwikjet plane on the tarmac, as it happened, and with binoculars borrowed from a surprised plane-spotter we checked passengers getting onto the plane. I knew Ella well and spotted her immediately!

After that we watched with mingled satisfaction (at our powers of detection) and frustration (we were helpless in the airport lounge) as the plane roared down the runway and lifted off into the blue, well grey actually. Was Ella on her way to a Greek island to rendezvous with her "darling" husband?

Williams had not actually forbidden any of us to leave the country but I thought it might be a little difficult. He knew about Ella's holiday email and presumably had okayed it. So I could go too! Rydal had some studying and catching up to do and on a student grant, Greece was not an ideal destination cash-wise. Glastonbury mud in August maybe, but Greek sun, albeit in October, no.

I dropped Rydal back at the University, zoomed into Guildford and found a flight to Heraklion for the following day. How big can an island be? I was about to find out! That just left time to pop up to Marlow and wish Dad many happy returns.

Who was I kidding? "Popping up" to Marlow involved the usual soul-wrenching crawl through endless traffic jams. Why did we all want to live in this desperate tangle of motorways?

"Happy Birthday to you, Happy Birthday to you,
Happy Birthday dear Granpops..."

At least Sonia hadn't managed to fit 90+ candles on the cake. Dad wouldn't have had the puff. The children were ready to light the candles and sing again, for the 5th time, but Gerald had had enough and put a stop to it rather rudely, I felt.

"Now that's enough. Granpops is a bit tired; he doesn't want any more fuss or NOISE."

Rubbish – Granpops was having a whale of a time! Funny

how nautical metaphors cling around Dad – talk about old sea-dog or is it sea-salt!

"Alright for some" moaned Gerald later "off to the beaches on the Med. All those ladies bouncing past, hey?"

I put Gerald straight on that one – in October the beaches would be quiet and quite possibly wind-swept. I was going walking – Samarian Gorge, Profitas Ilias, I'd done my homework! I also threw in a few archaeological sites too, in case he wasn't persuaded by my sudden desire to go hiking. It wasn't all lies – I would really like to see Knossos, I had read about Evans' remodelling of it.

Later up in Dad's room I toasted him properly with the nice single malt I had bought him. When he went searching for the glasses for that, I'd had a look at his memorabilia – always in the same drawer. Details of all his fellow sailors, then later his men when he was captain. But all peace-time or at least Cold War. Nothing of World War II at all.

I poked about behind the stuff at the front of the drawer and came upon some old press cuttings. The date was faded but looked like 1940's, '41 possibly. There was a picture of a warship – again faded; the name of the ship was hard to make out though.

"Stephen! Leave that stuff alone!"

Dad was almost always calm; I hadn't seen him that angry for years. He was trembling and suddenly looked very frail. I closed the drawer and got busy with the malt. It was wrong of me to pry; he clearly had bad memories of World War II, why should I dig them up?

By the time we parted, he was my dad again. Calm and quiet and looking forward to sailing to Henley on the following day. As a boy I had done that trip so many times. Marlow to Henley. I knew virtually every stretch and had often helped Dad at the tiller. I used to enjoy dodging the rowers. They treated boats like ours the way lorry drivers treat cyclists on the road – like they're not there.

I left 'The Finches' around ten and was snuggled up in my bed in 303 by midnight, all quiet on the Osbert front, I drifted off. Dreaming of Arsenal losing to Spurs in the Cup Final. I woke with a start, the alarm rattling. I had to be at Gatwick for ten and it was already seven.

I just made it before they closed the flight – budget airlines are irritating when they do that. But still, Crete in October for £27 one way was astonishing! Rydal had got up early to wish me bon voyage – bon wild goose chase more like – and had promised to phone with any news – providing I could get a signal on the island.

Heraklion airport wasn't quiet at all, although it was October 22, it was rammed. Clearly tourists were still keen to see the island, sun or no sun. No sun in fact, a nasty rainstorm was blowing outside. This made the optimistic Brits in tight shorts and t-shirts look even more ridiculous than usual. The lot returning from Crete to Gatwick did look very brown – so it looked like we'd got here just in time to miss the Indian summer!

The plan was to try all the car hire firms. Rydal, who else, had devised it. If Joe was on the island and waiting for Ella then he would have a car – of course he may have got it days ago – but still there was a chance. I was to say that my friend Mr Joseph Lief from England was supposed to be picking me up – he had hired a car from car hire firm 'x' – but I couldn't find him. Could you confirm blah-blah-blah...?

The car hire firms, as in most small airports, were all next to each other – often sharing one office. There were a handful of them. Some famous world-wide organisations, some

Greek which I had never heard of. The latter looked a bit dubious, run on a shoe-string from what I could judge. There were queues but fairly soon I had got the hang of it. Most assistants looked quizzical or hostile until they saw the 50 euro note sliding out of my wallet. This was Greece after all and money was in short supply – given the horrendous debt problems the country was facing. Virtually all checked their records – but nothing. Only one left. Autoquick – the biggest and busiest.

The 50 euro note was joined by a 20 then another 20.

"Ah yes. Mrs Lief picked up her car yesterday. According to the document she signed (another 20) she is staying at the Hotel Euro "(how appropriate)" here in Heraklion before going on to Elounda, Hotel Acropolis."

Fortunately, his English had not been sharp enough to distinguish between Mr Lief which is what I said and Mrs Lief, what he thought he had heard.

I hired a car from them, why not, and having made the assistant's day with all that cash, was soon following his directions to the Hotel Euro. Driving on the right is never easy at first and I had several close shaves before I got utterly lost. The problem with Greece, as I recalled from earlier holidays, is that four- lane highways can turn into cart-tracks just round the bend. You need to hold your nerve and assume you are still on the right road. Tricky when you find yourself in a gypsy encampment . More €20's put me on the right road out of town and finally into the car park of the Hotel Euro. So far so okay, but now I had to be circumspect. Joe was my friend but he and Ella would not want me barging in on their secret just yet. So sun-hat and glasses (in the drizzle) I inspected the car park – I had the registration, courtesy of another note back at Autoquick.

I found it almost immediately and as I approached the hotel I saw Ella waiting in the reception area. She looked good – obviously she had made an effort for Joe. I got the impression he would be down any minute. So I stood there, out of sight, but where I could see them. Should I announce myself to them right now or wait. The question was answered for me as he appeared from the lift – only he wasn't Joe. Whoever he was, he embraced her warmly and they set off hand-in-hand. I had never seen him before, big, dark, broad-shouldered, swarthy almost, handsome in a Lothario sort of way. Was he Greek?

What else could I do but follow them? My mind was racing. The pace was slow as they frequently stopped to kiss one another. I couldn't go all moral, Joe had been womanising for years. His latest flame might be lying in a hospital bed in a coma but that's what she was, his latest. Ella was showing 'what's sauce for the goose'. But somehow, with Joe missing, it seemed callous, even vindictive.

I'm no private detective and I soon found out that following someone is far from easy. There seemed a distinct lack of shady trees, buildings or anything to hide discreetly behind. Every time they stopped, I froze, which was probably the last thing I should have done. It was like playing that childhood game called 'pins and needles' or was it 'giant strides' where you only moved when the person 'on' wasn't looking. What you should do is, of course, stroll nonchalantly onwards until you come up to them... Ah no! What would I do if Ella turned round? But she was absorbed.

Then they stopped at the bus stop. Panic. I couldn't just stand there, I couldn't join the bus queue, this being Greece more of a formless group who would all invade the bus at once. Luckily, it arrived almost immediately and those continental buses with entrances at front, middle and back suddenly seemed such a good idea. They got in the front, I got in the back. With not the faintest idea where we were going. Or worse, how to pay! As usual, in this situation every-one else flashed passes. So I pretended to do the same and sat down. But some busybody, actually a charmingly helpful Greek lady, said, in almost perfect English (how do they know you're English even before you open your mouth? Do I look English? Why couldn't I be German or Bulgarian or Serbian or whatever?):

"You must have your ticket activated in the machine. If you don't they will fine you many euro."

Lamely, I replied:

"I haven't got a ticket. I didn't know what to do."

"You may have mine; I have another one I can activate."

And she got it punched in the machine.

All this 'activating' was a bad distraction as I tried to keep an eye on my quarry.

I could just about see them at the front and kept a wary eye. The bus was heading for the centre of Heraklion judging by the steady increase of grander, more formal looking buildings.

At the next stop, the whole of Heraklion tried to get on the bus and very nearly succeeded. I could just see boyfriend's head above the crush. Then boyfriend's head moved, so I tried. Hemmed in by old ladies with huge shopping bags and girls with hockey sticks (hockey on Crete?) I tried to push my way out. But the stop came and went without me. I glimpsed them through the window as they crossed the road and entered a building. I memorised the frontage, hoping one day I would see it again.

The next stop seemed about 5 miles away but in reality was about 200 yards along a very busy but very straight main street. Off at last I ran back, not as fit as I used to be, I was panting desperately when I arrived outside the building. The rain had gone, the sun was out and for October, to me, it was boiling. I was sweating profusely for all sorts of reasons. Should I go in and risk being seen? Imagine the conversation:

"Hi Stephen, what a surprise to find you in the same obscure building in the middle of Heraklion as my Greek boyfriend and me. Small world!"

However, in I went. I was in a museum. Not the one I hoped one day to visit where the finds from Knossos (I do have some culture) were displayed.

But the one you always dread on holiday – the local museum where they keep all the morris dancing costumes from the last century, or whatever was the equivalent on Crete. Or the enormous trade union banners which people carried barefoot from coal-mine to Town Hall, or whatever was the equivalent... The Museum of Heraklion. I couldn't find them in any of the crowded galleries. But as I rounded a corner I saw them shaking hands with a big bearded man in black – Rasputin? Archbishop Makarios? – a striking figure you would not easily forget. They were leaving his office and heading down the stairs to the exit.

Think! Follow them or stay with the Archbishop. It was 50/50. I chose the third option – dithering on the stairs till both other options had virtually disappeared. I knew where they would be later – the hotel. So I took heart and knocked on the office door.

The bearded gentleman, whose name tag, the Roman alphabet bit anyway, said he was Georgios Soudakis, shook my hand and welcomed me in. He spoke very good English and without me saying a word said:

"Ah, Mr Smith, you are early. Allow me to clear away the material my last client was looking at. I won't be a moment then we can get down to your grandmother's teapots. He went into a storeroom and in seconds I absorbed what I could. The newspapers in front of me were all in Greek but there were photographs of warships.

As he tidied it away, making conversation, he outlined what it all was:

"Interesting, isn't it? These are photographs of British war-ships evacuating the defeated troops to Egypt in 1941. A sad time for your countrymen. We, in Crete, have never forgotten the valiant efforts of the British to help our resistance. That is why I was so pleased to help the couple who have just gone. Now, teapots…"

But the teapots would have to wait for the grandson to arrive, I had gone. But not before I had noted with perplexity that one of the warships looked very similar to the one I had seen in the photo in Dad's room.

I spent a thoughtful evening keeping out of their way. I saw them at a distance in the hotel restaurant, on the terrace in the moonlight, romantically entwined. I also found their room and managed to squash myself into a broom cupboard across the corridor and peep through the door as they both went in and didn't come out – this was late at night. I was distressed for Joe, could believe it of Ella and puzzled by the boyfriend.

The following day I was determined to get close to them, it wasn't easy, but luckily he was alone in reception so I was safe enough but even so, I kept out of sight but within earshot. The voice I heard was English with just a hint of an accent. I had heard that trace of an accent before somewhere but I couldn't place it. So, no Greek boyfriend. This made their curiosity about the evacuation in 1941 all the more odd. Still that would have to wait until I was back in Surrey and could discuss it all with Rydal. I had texted the details but had no reply.

The other thing I needed to do was also tricky. I needed at least one decent photograph and preferred to use camera rather than mobile phone. In the end I hid behind a lorry delivering at the entrance as they emerged and got the pair of them arm in arm.

What next? They were off to Elounda soon and I hadn't the time, money or inclination to follow them. I had a flight booked anyway for Monday. I decided nothing could be gained by following them and risking being seen. I sensed the information they had been seeking had been found and now it was holiday time! Perhaps I wanted to believe that. I was heartily sick of skulking round the Hotel Euro and never wanted to see Heraklion again. So I spent the day at Knossos, just out of town. I found it, perhaps it was my jaded mood, supremely disappointing. Arthur Evans' famed reconstructions to me were faintly ridiculous and not a little Hollywood.

CHAPTER 6

I woke early on Monday morning. Very early because the flight left at 6 am. So following the instructions of the airline I had to be at the airport for 4 in the morning. I don't think so! Of course, as usual, it became a mad dash to get there before the check-in desk closed.

At Heraklion airport it was bedlam at 5 am! Why were all these people up and where were they going? Where was that pasty-faced young man going? Where was that Orthodox priest going? Where was that big dark broad-shouldered...?

It was my turn next at the check-in desk but I no longer wanted to check-in. Surely boyfriend wasn't flying by himself? There wasn't an airport anywhere near Elounda anyway. But Ella's boyfriend it certainly was.

"Reservation please and passport, sir."

"Oh, sorry" I mumbled "I'm not flying just yet."

"I beg your pardon, sir, but the flight leaves at 6 am – in fact the captain hopes to take off earlier, he has a better slot" she snapped.

I stumbled back through the queue, resisting the temptation to tell her what the pilot could do with his better slot. I was missing my flight, but what else could I do? I had been partly reluctant to leave anyway.

I prowled around Heraklion airport, slowly realising that **he** might not have missed his flight and was gone.

The departure hall isn't that big at Heraklion and I had soon exhausted it. He was gone. And so was my flight. Or was it?

I raced back to check-in. Snappy woman was still there and she was getting her things together. But the screen above her head still said 'London Gatwick' so I presented myself in front of her.

"Sorry," I said "bit of a problem, but here I am after all. Here's my reservation and passport."

I tried an ingratiating smile.

"Check-in is closed. It closed at 5.30 sharp."

"But it's only 5.29" I said looking at my watch "There's still a minute to go."

"Your watch is wrong, I'm afraid." Snap! Snap!

With that parting shot she disappeared through a door and the screen went horribly blank. I thought of complaining. But who to? All signs of the budget airline had vanished like it never was.

Forlornly, I trudged around Departures and the various eating establishments. The next flight, for which I didn't have a reservation, was in the evening. What was I to do?

I wandered out disconsolately through Arrivals and there he was, sitting reading a newspaper in front of that glass corridor/entrance that people appear almost magically from. He wasn't going anywhere, he was waiting. So I would wait with him.

Was he waiting for Joe? It was just possible even though he was Ella's lover. He might be waiting for his mum and dad for all I knew. I just sensed that whoever it was up there in the skies (or perhaps even now in the baggage hall) mattered. I was in a bar close by where he was sitting, trying to make a Greek coffee last a long time – not easy given the thimbleful of extremely thick dark liquid I had been presented with.

Did he look on edge? Not especially. Eager? Not really. In fact he looked just like someone waiting to pick up their mum and dad. Just then he stirred as people began emerging. As always, the new arrivals looked slightly bemused, looking around them expectantly, or scanning the signs (especially unfamiliar in Greece), but trying to look like they knew where they were and what they were doing, especially that they were not Billy no-mates.

Then Ella's boyfriend strode forward confidently and shook hands with a much older man, oh God he was meeting his dad. But would you shake hands with your father?

Not that the man looked remotely like a dad. I think the kindest description would be hippy. Ageing hippy. He was wearing a flowered t-shirt and battered jeans. His hair was long, lank and unkempt. Thinning on top. But his biggest give-away was the guitar case on his luggage trolley.

I got as close as I dared and heard:

"Benjamin! Benjamin, welcome to Crete. I've been looking forward to meeting you. Let's get you back to the hotel for a rest before we set off for Elounda."

Benjamin's reply was indistinct. And they moved off where I couldn't really follow without being spotted. All I had gleaned so far was that they hadn't met before, yet Benjamin was going with them. Why? At least I knew where they were going in the very near future. Back to the Hotel Euro. The trouble was how did I get there, not to mention Elounda, when I had dropped my hire car off only an hour ago?

"I'm sorry, Mr Johnson, you have already dropped your car off" said the very puzzled Greek lady at my favourite place, the Autoquick car-hire office!

"I know. The thing is. I want it back. I'm not leaving after all."

"But you do not need to see it again. There is nothing more to do. It is okay. Spiros has checked the car and it is in good condition and there is Benzene in it."

Leaving aside the bizarre idea of a car full of Benzene, I tried desperately to make her understand that I wanted the car back to drive away, not just to see it again, as if I was missing it or something!

"No. I want to drive the car. I want to hire it again. I..."

It was no good. Bafflement was writ large on her face. Fortunately, a growing number of people in the back-office had been listening (and laughing) and one belatedly came to our rescue. He understood what I wanted and politely didn't refer to the strangeness of the request. He even organised the same car – newly washed and full to the brim with Benzene (Benzini is the Greek for petrol I discovered).

Back at the hotel car park, I was on the watch. I dreaded the thought of re-booking my room. Luckily, almost immediately on cue, the three of them came out with suitcases, Ella and boyfriend with the oldest swinger in town in tow.

Just then the hotel receptionist ran out and shouted in halting English:

"Mrs Lief, the Hotel Acropolis will be expecting you."

What imaginative names all these hotels had. It was if in London all the hotels were called 'Marble Arch' or 'King's Cross'... wait a minute. Anyway I was very grateful for the information because I had forgotten the name of the hotel. Tailing them all the way to Elounda, a good 75 miles, would not have been easy.

As it was, an hour and a half later I was waiting for them outside the Hotel Acropolis which was easily found slap-bang in the middle of the smart, slightly up-market resort. When I saw them safely inside, I nipped across the road and booked myself into the far less swankier Hotel Aphrodite (don't!). From its terrace and even from my room I had a superb view of the entrance of the Acropolis.

Whatever they were up to with Benjamin, I would be along for the ride, if possible.

Incredibly it still wasn't noon; I had been up since 4 am and was dozing. It was lucky that as I got up to go to the bathroom

I glanced across the road – they were on their way out. I threw on some clothes and dashed. Tracking them in the car on fairly deserted October roads – it was still warm but there were few tourists left – would not be easy. Tracking them in a boat, which was what they were soon clambering into, was impossible. I could only watch in frustration as they headed out to sea in this fishing boat of all things. I thought they might be on their way to Spinalonga, the haunting ex-leper colony island, but no, I could see the boat breasting the waves beyond it. All I could do was wait. That seemed all I ever did on this wretched island!

An hour later as I sat harbour-side sipping my coffee, the fishing boat appeared skirting Spinalonga and was soon tying up on the quayside. I watched as they shook hands with the captain or fisherman or owner – who could tell? Had they been fishing? It was hardly one of Ella's pastimes. I thought she looked distinctly green as I scanned her through the new binoculars I had acquired that morning.

Keeping out of sight of Ella was becoming increasingly difficult and I knew I couldn't do it for a week. There was a plane home in the evening and I wanted badly to be on it. But I couldn't leave without knowing what on earth they were all doing here.

So I took a chance and when they were safely in the hotel, I strolled past the boat and smiled at the captain, who was doing whatever it was that fishermen do with nets and pots. He was very grizzled, an old sea dog he would have been called in Portsmouth.

"Do you speak English?" I said.

"A little."

"I was thinking about a fishing trip," here I did a rather hopeless fishing mime. "I saw you took some people earlier fishing?"

"Oxi, no, no. They did not want the fishes. They want to know about my father in the…."

"War" I supplied, taking yet another chance.

"Nai, war. My father was on a ship in Iraklio. He saw some bad things. I tell them what."

"But why did you sail out to sea **here**?"

"They want private. I give them trip."

Private? From who? Surely they hadn't seen me? Why was what they were doing so secret? And what was Benjamin there for? The old man was disappointed when I left without booking a fishing trip or even a quick ride across the water to Spinalonga.

I sensed I had discovered about as much as I could and decided to cut my losses and leave Elounda. I had parked the car down a cobbled side street and was loading it when I heard a peculiar noise. The best I can describe it as was strumming. And it was getting louder. Before I could move, the strumming came round the corner. Benjamin, guitar in hand, smile on his face. Blank look in his eyes. I had seen that look before on my teenage friends way back when. *Stoned*!

"Hi" I said, as he passed, still strumming.

"Yeah, I guess I am." He replied.

He wouldn't remember me or anything, I suspected, when he came back to earth. Nor was there any point in going after him.

So I left him to sun, sea, Spinalonga and the famous Ferryman restaurant he was heading for. He was back in the Seventies by now! He was certainly a long way from home, given his Antipodean accent.

I was on the plane by early evening – what an exhausting day, would it ever end?

I arrived at Gatwick on a very chilly night. My phone call from the airport to Vinyl Testers – they always work till late, was abrupt. My announcement that I was still suffering from the after effects of the road accident, whiplash, etc. was met with incredulity and a demand of proof. Which I promised would be with them within 48 hours. "How?" I screamed to myself as I heard myself say it.

My phone buzzed as I grabbed a bite to eat in the airport lounge. The text was brief but heartening:

'Maria coming round. Rydal'!

I did the journey from Gatwick to the hospital in record time and hurtled up the steps to the ward. The Sister smiled at me, Helen was not on shift that day as I recalled, and said "Good news, at last. Go on in. Her boyfriend is there already."

My heart leapt as I opened the door and saw Maria, pale and tired but with eyes OPEN! Rydal beamed at me from her bedside. In a way it was awkward, I felt I knew her so well but of course, she didn't know me at all. Though I was eager to discover the truth of it all, I knew that these things take time.

"Isn't it wonderful?" said Rydal "She's suffered no lasting damage! She's finding it hard to speak and to focus. But she's said a few words." He beamed at her.

Her blank if sympathetic look worried me. And before he said it, I sensed it. She didn't know me, of course, but it was clear she didn't know who he was either!

We were asked to leave her bedside fairly soon afterwards, she had smiled sadly and been polite. We hadn't mentioned the accident. But she did say she wanted to get back to her studies soon. We both knew that at the moment she had no recollection of what had happened that fateful night. But she did know she was a student. We knew we had to be patient and hope something would return.

Williams had been informed and before long he came into the ward waiting-room together with two uniformed policemen. His face fell when he saw me.

"Oh! I didn't expect you. I was told you were on holiday. Not the only one, Mrs Lief took herself off too. Same Greek island I believe. Odd that. Did you come across Mr Lief by any chance?"

The sarcasm was heavy and my explanation of coincidence, both liking the same sort of holiday, didn't wash. Surrey Police kept an eye on us it seemed and the fact that we were both in the Hotel Euro had obviously sent alarm bells ringing even in Williams' clouded mind! But I stuck to coincidence. What on earth Ella would say when he challenged her on her return about me being there, I couldn't imagine!

Williams was primarily here to see Maria. Even he realised it was too early to question her but he felt he had to put in an appearance. He stayed in her room a few minutes, and then spent a long time with a consultant. We were still sitting disconsolately in the waiting room when he came back in.

"Well, that was no use" he said callously "as far as I can see she can't remember a thing. Even Mr Lief's name didn't register on her radar.

The doc says she has amnesia which could be temporary or permanent. He advised us to come back in a couple of days. Says she will remember everything fine up to a certain point. She'll know she's a student and what she is studying and her family but not the last few days or weeks. Her parents have been and she knows them okay, which is something I suppose. But Rydal here (still the old familiar Williams) she doesn't remember. Exactly how long had she been your girl-friend?"

"About three weeks to a month." said Rydal.

"Well, then, since she does remember coming to Surrey and her course and she only began the end of September – it looks like about the first week of term and that's it – a blank from then on. The doc guy said amnesia can be selective – so she might remember bits from last week and the week before not connected to what's happened. We'll have to wait and see. In the meantime, the case is being downgraded and I'm being taken off it" he said with clear relief "after all Mr Lief's disappearance is hardly a surprise, he's done it before after his wife has found out about his philandering. I expect he'll reappear with his tail between his legs. Miss Kyriakos (at least he didn't call her Maria) will make a full recovery – if three weeks of her life will always be a blank. So where's the crime? I'll say cheerio then."

And to my astonishment, he shook our hands as if we had been great friends. He hadn't the wit to make it an ironic gesture. Maybe he led such a lonely unloved life that even people/suspects he didn't like were better than nothing? I almost felt sorry for him. I wouldn't have done if I'd known he would come back into our lives ere long!

CHAPTER 7

It was just over one week – seemed like a year – since it all kicked off. One week it was a Surrey Police investigation given its own high-profile (well, ugly profile) detective. Now it was not even yesterday's news, but last week's. Williams' 'downgraded' was a euphemism for 'forget all about it'. "There was no crime" he said. But there was – in fact there were two deliberate attempts to kill or injure and my good friend had vanished. Rydal and I both agreed that we would, rather dramatically he said, "keep the flame alive."

His spirits were not diminished by the love of his life's inability to recognise or remember him at all. He would be beside her for as long as. There was just time to show him the photo – more for interest than anything else. "That's Ella", I said "Joe's wife."

"Never mind her" he said, rather dismissively "is this the boyfriend?"

"Yes" I replied "he looks Greek, but he isn't. He's English with a faint accent of something. He's interested in ships from World War II."

"And he's a very bad driver" said Rydal enigmatically.

"What?"

"A very bad driver, he's fond of steering cars into walls on the A25! That's the man at the wheel, I'm sure" Rydal asserted "the one wearing the logo thing. He tried to injure us!"

Too many coincidences to be coincidences. My mind was a tangle of fake car accidents, Tudor poets and World War II ships. None of it seemed to fit. Like pieces from two separate jigsaws that had to fit together and yet couldn't possibly.

Time to revisit the to-do list:

But it wasn't much help. It did remind me to contact work again – still bad whiplash. Another week. I could hear open laughter in the office. So what? "There were more important things in the world than the relative strength of vinyls." Did I really say that? It wouldn't be long before I heard from the big boss. Or as we called him in the office 'Big Vynyl'!

Ella was still dipping her toes in the Aegean or was it the Med? Assuming it was still warm enough down there.

Dad's birthday had come and gone. Though soon I would have to do something I was dreading and ask him about the War.

That left Cambridge and Dove-Kemp. But before that I had to go and see Helen, mostly because I missed her company **and** kissing but also to tie up the odd incident of the book on the evacuation to Egypt. That was a coincidence! I was sure Helen was just a lovely nurse I'd met. But the friend with the interest in history, who was that?

Rydal knocked. Maria was getting stronger and would soon be going home to Portsmouth to recuperate. With a view to resuming her studies later in the term. Rydal, who was carless, hinted at being able to use mine to nip down the A3 as he put it: "you know: Guildford, Hindhead, Liphook, Petersfield and all stations west!"

"Okay" I said "it'd be a pleasure."

"Oh and Osbert's having a party" he announced and then to my groans he added "and we're invited."

I could take Helen. Perfect. I rang her – no answer, probably working. So I texted – *'come to 303. I need you! Next door are having a party tonight. Say nine-ish. Love Stephen x'*

It took me so long to text the message that Rydal promised to teach me text-speak.

He said he was free for much of the day; he'd been working early morning. So what about a jaunt to Cambridge? Hardly a jaunt, more a nasty cross-country drive: A3, M25, M11 with potential for all sorts of traffic jams.

"And accidents" he added, chillingly.

We arrived at Cambridge, hauntingly silver in the October sunlight, without any mishaps. Virtually all the way there Rydal had been searching the net on his iPhone. He discovered that Dove-Kemp was a fellow of St Simon's and that would be where his rooms were. We found St Simon's fairly easily, central but in a quiet part of town and asked the chap on the door if Professor Dove-Kemp was available. But it wasn't that simple. The doorman or whatever grandiose title he had, turned his nose up, almost literally, at us. When was our appointment? What was our college and all sorts of other whatnots? We beat a hasty retreat. And waited. And waited. At length we saw the man leave and we tried again, this time his underling was easy for Rydal.

"Appointment at two, from Sidney Sussex, Dove-Kemp, find our own way, cheers." And we strode in, despite his rather feeble protests.

Rydal asked the first Fellow i.e. the first person he came across in a gown who was middle-aged, where Dove-Kemp's rooms were and he pointed across the immaculately cut lawn to some medieval tower affair – at the top of which apparently, resided the illustrious Professor. And up we went. At the top, handily, was a brass plaque saying Professor Dove-Kemp.

"This must be it, Watson" said Rydal, laughing.

I was quaking. Any minute he could come out and find the two bogus researchers of Allington! But all was quiet. Rydal tried the handle – the door opened and we found ourselves in a medieval chamber-like room. Behind the desk was a huge floor-to-ceiling, wall-to-wall bookcase – it looked like it contained every book ever written on Tudor history including plenty on Sir Thomas Wyatt. In the desk drawer we found a folder labelled 'Translations of French documents at Allington Castle' – this was too easy. We even found the bit that Ballantyne Forsyth had translated for us and when we read on we found:

"Sir Thomas had been previously a paramour of Ann Bullen but since the King Henry turned his affections to her the love had cooled. Sir Thomas was all courtesy and gentleness with her but nothing more during their stay."

That wasn't very helpful. In fact, deflating. "A pity it didn't say and the randy pair got at it in the chateau," said Rydal.

Then we heard voices, including, unmistakably, the voice of the dreaded Dove-Kemp. We stuffed the file back in the drawer and opened the nearest door – broom cupboard, the next – toilet. There was no time to do more and we squeezed into the toilet and crazily Rydal locked the door.

The Professor came into the room with several others, the voices sounded young and eager for knowledge – students. A tutorial! (In Cambridge it's called a supervision, Rydal informed me later.) We prayed they all had strong bladders. What followed was a tedious hour where Dove-Kemp, who clearly loved the sound of his own voice, jawed at them incessantly. This wasn't education, it was telling them what to think. After an hour the students, full to the brim with facts, staggered, we guessed, down the stairs. Did he need a pee? What would we do when he found the door locked? We soon found out when he rattled it and rattled it, then swore and strode out of his room, shouting "blasted door stuck again – how many more f...ing times!" We heard his steps retreat down the turret, presumably in search of somewhere else to relieve himself and of the person who fixed toilet doors. We ran helter-skelter down the stairs, across the manicured lawns and out into the city streets.

We had got nowhere twice on our trail of the Professor. Except we had found a document which fairly clearly suggested no shenanigans at all between Ann and the poet. "One document doesn't make a summer" Rydal said, cryptically. It was unexpected though. Here was a man proselytising the greatest upset in Tudor studies since, well since the Tudors, and yet he had in his possession at least one document which belied it altogether!

As we pulled into the University of Surrey, we waved ironically at the stag, all shining steel, the huge beast that greets all visitors (well by car anyway) to the University. Rydal said the students in his block called it 'Stig' implying, ironically I'm sure, a certain amount of disrespect for their university. It was a refreshing world away from the nightmare that was St Simon's.

"Who is Sidney Essex anyway?" I said, "A cousin of David?"

"No, Sidney Sussex, and he's not a he, he's an it. A college in Cambridge in fact, the only one I could think of."

I had a text from Helen:

'Looking forward to it. C U at 9 Lover x'

That sounded promising. We grabbed a bite to eat at the student refectory and as students do, 'chilled' for a while.
Osbert was already cranking up the volume and we could hear people arriving. I hadn't been to a student party in years and wasn't quite sure what to expect. Helen arrived, demure and lovely, in a little black dress. She was also full of trepidation,

she admitted.

"When I was a student nurse I went to a lot of parties. They were wild, drunken orgies full of grass and cocaine and the floor swimming in beer and fags."

"Let's hope, then" I said jokingly.

The three of us, Rydal lived more in 303 now than his own room, went into the corridor. Or rather we tried to but the door of 303 wouldn't open. We pushed and pushed and eventually dislodged a drunken student who had been sitting propped up against it. There were people everywhere – the party had very soon burst its banks as it were and was spilling out all over Stag Hill. We could hear a riotous group caterwauling in the cathedral car park. And it was only 9.15! Osbert had been forced out of 305 by the crush and was harassing some Asian guy in the corridor about the merits of The Veela.

"What's a Veela?" Rydal said.

"Search me" said Helen.

It was only when he mentioned West Brom that I cottoned on – football talk – Aston Villa!

Helen and I went outside the block – it was a bit chilly – I was hoping for a cuddle. But first I said casually:

"That book, I saw, you know, the one about World War II and Crete whose was it?"

She froze – it wasn't that cold – for a few seconds and then:

"Oh, Emily, a student friend of mine. She's into that sort of thing. God knows why she left it in my room."

Then she got closer and it was very pleasant and very distracting to find at last I was getting somewhere. I suggested 303 – she said she didn't know that position and we scampered up the stairs. But Rydal had invited Osbert's over-spill into my room and the place was jammed. Ditto Rydal's room. I would have gone on looking but Helen seemed cooler now – there was that mood swing again – and excused herself with a headache and a busy day. She said there was no need to walk her back – it was only across the road.

So, a bit non-plussed I joined Osbert and becoming steadily more glazed as the wine flowed told him 'The Veela' were rubbish and began to sing "Spurs are on their way to Wembley, Tottenham have gone and done it again" at the top of my voice!

I woke on my sofa (rather grand word for the student double-chair thing) with a bad head. Rydal was busy clattering coffee cups and generally being Rydal. Was he a friend or my major-domo? Wooster and Jeeves? Wimsey and Bunter? Ant and Dec? Anyway the coffee was welcome.

"Who's Cyril?" he said as he handed me a cup.

"God knows" I said "why?"

"Because you were singing about him all night. Nice one or something."

All the Tottenham football songs must have come out last night, they often do when I drink too much. I turn into Chas or Dave.

"Never mind" I said "it's Emily we need to discuss."

"Emeli Sande?" Rydal's favourite singer.

"No, Emily, she of the fascination with Crete and the evacuation to Egypt."

"Sure you don't mean the 'flight into Egypt'?" laughed Rydal going all Biblical on me.

"I just wanted to make sure it was Emily's book. I'm sure it was…"

"What was it Ronald Reagan said 'trust but verify'" said Rydal.

"Exactly."

At that point my phone rang:

"Hello old sport."

Big Vinyl!

He read 'The Great Gatsby' years ago and ever since then he fancied himself as Gatsby.

"How's the car?" I replied.

The standard response to any phone call from him. With most people it's 'How are you?' but with him you always asked about the car. If you wanted something, as I did now, you knew you had half-an-hour of information about the car to come. But it would be worth it. And you needn't listen much of the time.

"Well, guess what, you remember that slightly rusty letter R. I found a lovely shiny one. It's not a Jensen one but it really looks like it is. No one would know the difference..."

And on, and on...

When he wasn't Gatsby he was some bloke called Jason King from an ancient TV series who drove a Jensen Interceptor Mark III. It had to be a Mark III.

Finally, I got in about accidents, whiplash and work and begged for more leave.

"Of course, old sport, nasty thing whiplash – did I ever tell you about when Maureen and I were taking the Jensen to Brighton?"

"Sorry, someone's at the door, got to go. Thanks – I'll phone soon."

It was done. Free for a while longer to solve the mystery. Rydal had already said we should write a book one day – it would be a best-selling thriller called 'The Cretan Wyatt' or 'Boleyns and Battleships'.

I knew that Helen was working that day so I decided to 'trust but verify' in the words of Ronald Ray-gun! I went round to the nurse's home and hung about outside her door – if anyone saw me, they would assume I was waiting for Helen, most of them knew me by now. Whenever a neighbour came by or a cleaner – I chatted a bit and casually asked them where Emily, Helen's mate lived. I soon established it was a room in the next block, number 24. So I went over to 24 and knocked – I had my story ready, I was confused and thought Helen was off work and after a bit of chat would lead up casually to the book.

Emily opened the door; at least I assumed it was her.

"Hi" she said "you're Helen's boyfriend Stephen, aren't you? Come on in. She's working I think. Fancy a brew?"

Emily was very tall and thin but had a lovely smile. In fact, she was Emili from Egypt. She chatted happily about Alexandria, Cairo and The Nile, she also loved Greece, especially Crete. This gave me my opening. I was relieved her interest in the subject was virtually explained.

"That's why your book about the evacuation from Crete by sea in 1941 was in Helen's flat." I said.

"Sorry? What book? No, I've never heard of – what was it? Crete in 1941."

Her bafflement was obvious. No less obvious was the fact that Helen had been lying about the book. I was struggling to come to terms with this but I knew there had to be a simple explanation. The fact that I couldn't see what it was, didn't mean it didn't exist.

I thanked Emili for the tea and left.

By 2 pm I was exiting the M4 on my way to Marlow to see Dad. The rush hour was pretty dreadful on the A404 but there was no alternative. It took me an hour to cover a few miles. It was dark when I got to 'The Finches'. The evening meal was in full swing. I had some of Sonia's utterly delicious lasagne and had a glass of wine or two with Dad and Gerald whilst the kids watched TV prior to bed. We left poor Sonia to do the washing up – well not quite alone, the new au pair Isabel had arrived from Spain. I knew what was coming:

"What do you think of old Isabel then, hey?" Gerald was clearly full of her. I had watched him at dinner, his eyes sinking from her face to her admittedly enormous bosoms. Sonia was glaring. Dad was embarrassed and I just wanted to laugh. I could see already Isabel's days were numbered.

"Very nice." I said.

"Oh, come on, Stephen, I bet you had your eye on her. Good job old Joe's not here, nudge, nudge, wink, wink."

It was going to be that kind of evening. Voices were raised in the kitchen. When I went in, there was an argument going on between Sonia, "not acceptable", "cover them up" and Isabel "I am proud of my busties. In Sevilla we are not ashamed."

Too stormy for me, I took another bottle of wine and got out. Gerald was looking pie-eyed by now so Dad and I went upstairs and left him to what was probably certain disaster.

I knew the war was a touchy subject, so started quite generally about the jungle, the desert, D-day and so on and approached the Med that way. As we got closer to talking ships in the Med, I could see panic in his eyes. Was he reliving something awful? It wasn't fair to torture him like this. But I had to ask – "I saw some pictures last time I was here of warships taking the remains of the defeated British army from Crete to Egypt and I wanted to ask…"

"Stop it, Stephen! Don't. I don't want to talk about the War. I realised last time you were here you had been poking about in my things. He was so very agitated, my guilt was immense. How could I upset my father like this?

I stopped. I would have to find out what Ella and boyfriend were looking for another way. When he went to the bathroom, he took so long these days, I had plenty of time to look at the photo again – but it had gone. He didn't want me to see it! There was little else either – more guilt as I rifled through the drawer – why had every reference to his ship in World War II been got rid of? I did find a letter from a mate of his, dated 1941 congratulating Dad on getting a promotion to LTO (leading torpedo operator) on a new ship and saying "I know you'll like the name – right up your street!" But that was all – could be anything. So I gave it up.

I was late, I was a bit drunk, Gerald was snoring on the sofa, precious Isabel-watching time being wasted. If I knew Sonia the au pair wouldn't be around very long. So I got a bed there for the night. Just before I went to sleep – I checked my phone. The text was simple but it stopped me sleeping and sobered me instantly:

'Meet me market at noon – don't reply, delete. Tell no one. J'

CHAPTER 8

I took the train up from Guildford. Squashed into a scrubby looking train with hundreds of bored looking commuters – 'crumpled, grubby, dazed and late' and that was in the morning! You see I do read poetry occasionally, or have it thrust upon me anyway.

I arrived with plenty of time and checked out the flat – Joe hadn't been there, though he did have a key. I didn't ask what he sometimes used it for when I was away. I had a pretty good idea though.

I love Spitalfields Market – yes, it's not a market really now, just a lot of restaurants tucked inside a market hall – so you're neither outside nor inside but it's very trendy and smart and the area though shabby is moving upmarket rapidly.

I knew where he would be. We both love Greek food and I spotted him at a table 'outside' 'The Real Greek'. Ludicrously he had scarf, glasses and hood, in fact you couldn't see anything of his face. Not to mention a copy of the Daily Telegraph, which hid him too. That's why I knew it was him, it was how he escaped from outraged husbands or mistresses.

I sat down opposite. "Morning."

"Afternoon actually, you're late."

"About a minute. And I have just come from Guildford."

"Well, never mind your travels, have you been followed?"

"Do you mean how's Maria?"

"Well, yes, of course" he said shamefaced. Well I expect he was underneath all that disguise.

I let him have it, then. All the angst watching the sad ice-maiden turn into the lovely, charming yet lost Maria and all he cared about was himself. No change there then. Then I let him have it about my car, what was left of it. Then I asked him what all this Wyatt stuff was about?

At that, he looked up, removed his ridiculous spectacles in genuine astonishment and said "You know about that! How, if Maria can't remember?"

What followed was a long detailed account from me of what exactly had been happening – Williams, the quotation from Wyatt, Rydal and Maria, Dove-Kemp, Allington, the staged accident, Ella and lover boy, Crete, warships, Cambridge and on and on until I had somehow got it all out of my system.

"Golly" he said "you have been having a busy time. Who is this jerk in Crete?"

"Don't tell me, you're **jealous**, I don't believe it after all…"

"Well, she didn't waste much time, did she?" he whined. Still the same self-centred old Joe.

Then he told me 'his' story.

Ella had been neglecting him. He felt lonely. He met this astonishing student – Maria – astonishingly clever and astonishingly beautiful. There was a tedious boyfriend buzzing about, but he was soon swatted away. I was so angry at this dismissal of Rydal.

She loved his lectures on Tudor poetry and the Wyatt/Ann Boleyn thing intrigued her. He took her on his researches to Allington and Calais, following in the footsteps of Professor Dove-Kemp. All he found was evidence that Wyatt and Ann were not lovers any more.

"I couldn't find anything that he had found to support the theory he was going to present at Surrey, of all places. I found plenty to disprove it.

One day at Allington I came across a locked drawer in the

desk that old D K used. Well, as you know, I'm quite handy with the old credit card trick, so I had a go at his locked drawer – no go. So I got a big iron crowbar from the car and smashed it open."

Only Joe could manage to do something so crass and stupid.

"Well, I found a letter from Cromwell to Wyatt which seemed like the equivalent of the crown jewels, suggesting Ann Boleyn's trial was a set-up. What was it doing there? I suspected it was a fake, which had somehow become detached from the Prof's other 'documents' by accident. Maria was with me – this was the day before the talk and of course we'd borrowed your BM, if you recall."

If I recalled!

"Anyway, I had to get that letter out of there fast and take it to be checked by experts. I texted you about making a splash at the meeting. But I couldn't organise any check for forgery in time realistically. So that evening we stayed at a swanky hotel near Leeds castle and had a very romantic night, I played Wyatt and she played Boleyn!"

I just looked disgusted.

"The following day I told her to take the letter and drive back to Surrey and hide it somewhere. I would go on searching then join her at the talk in Guildford and you, of course. She texted me about 6 to say when she got back she found her room had been ransacked! Someone rather nasty was looking for the letter. I was scared. So I did one. And given what happened that night to Maria, I was right to be scared, so I laid low."

"And left Maria to her fate." I said caustically.

"Well, I didn't think they would harm her. Anyway, I don't suppose you or that creep, her boyfriend, have any idea where she hid the letter, have you? It could be worth a lot of spondulicks!"

I couldn't believe what I was hearing. "What were you going to do with it, sell it or use it to blackmail Dove-Kemp?

You're mad. Maria's well rid of you. Ella too, to be honest. And I've had enough."

He looked pained. He always did during our rows about his behaviour. And he always got to me. But I knew I had to tell him about the poem.

"I found the first opening words of Wyatt's poem about Ann Boleyn scribbled on a piece of paper in my service booklet. I don't suppose you put it there?"

"What, the *'Whoso list to hunt'* sonnet? Well, blow me, Maria must have written it. Let's have a dekko?"

I took it out of my wallet. "I know it wasn't there before I gave you the car because I checked the service details."

He looked at it a long time before handing it back.

"I think it's her handwriting. I couldn't be sure. But who else would pick that line? It must be a clue for me. Damned if I can understand it though. I'll have to have a think."

"Do!"

He didn't deserve it but I found myself saying "What are you going to do now?"

"Can I have the keys to your flat, I've lost the ones you gave me. Oh and can you find out who this jerk in Crete is and what he's doing with Ella? Warships and Crete mean nothing to me at all. Very weird! And can you try and jog Maria's memory about where she hid the letter? Clever girl Maria, it will be a fiendishly clever place. Brilliant mind... and body."

He was lost in a reverie for several moments.

"Is that all?" I said with heavy sarcasm.

"Oh, and can you pay, I haven't got a bean. Ella's stopped all the cards – how ungrateful can you get!"

We went up to the flat. I looked at the huge pile of mail, found the two or three real letters and sorted them. Binned the rest. Joe was helping himself to the cans of beer in the fridge. On top of the wine we had already imbibed, this meant he was getting squiffy. Once his tongue was loosened he was perfectly capable of ruining even the most basic of plans. I

70

could see him picking up the phone and contacting his mates, former girlfriends et al, at my expense. And announcing to everyone where he was, clearly aided and abetted by me. So I warned him to leave the booze and phones alone. When he was sober, I would let him decide whether he wanted me to let Surrey police know he was alive and well. Though that might mean Williams would want to see him.

I slept on the sofa, he in the bed. How does he do it?

My dad used to tell me about a programme called 'The Likely Lads' where the sensible one kept bailing out the wild one who had all the fun. We were very like them, I thought.

I made him rack his brains about warships – but it was no good. He was being straight for once, and knew nothing about them. They plainly had nothing to do with Wyatt. He assumed it was Ella's new boyfriend (he gritted his teeth at that) who was interested in Crete and ships.

"Ella doesn't know one end of a boat from another and she gets seasick on a canal boat."

In the morning I left him tucking into a full English which somehow he had wheedled/charmed me into cooking for him. He even had the gall to ask for my season ticket.

"I wouldn't mind popping down to the Lane. Chelsea tomorrow. Be a pal, have a look for it."

I took great delight in telling him I had given it to Gerald in case he ever managed to take Dad to the Spurs. Not that he ever tried.

I was back at the University by 11 am.

It didn't seem to me at all disloyal to tell Rydal about Joe. He deserved to know that his rival was still on the scene. Gracious as always, Rydal was genuinely pleased he was okay and that I had my friend back. How different friends can be!

Rydal assumed that the Wyatt trail would now be much easier given Joe's involvement. To which I agreed, "Once he's sober." Whether he would go so far as to tell us the details of the possible forged letter was another matter. There might be money in it and this always heightened, if that was possible, Joe's selfish streak. Put it another way, Joe had occasionally a generous streak running through his totally selfish nature.

I was meeting Helen for dinner at seven so after a relatively lazy few hours , despite Osbert's music, I walked down the hill and into town. All the time wondering about Helen – was our relationship going anywhere? One thing was certain I was determined to clear up the book thing and confronted her over the starters.

"No. Not Emili – it isn't even pronounced the same – Emily Sandford, she's a sister on the ward. I don't think you've met her. Her boyfriend is hugely into World War II. He even, get this, drives a jeep. They're forever going to jives and stuff. They dress up in 40's gear and stand on steam railway platforms. She was round and left it by accident. I told you. Why the inquest? Text her if you want. In fact I will." She was getting shirty now.

The reply was almost instant:

'Gosh, your fella jealous or something. It was my book. Len is well into WW2. Off in the jeep soon. Em.'

I felt a fool and was amazed she was still willing to see me. It wasn't jealousy, but she wasn't to know that. Now I could be honest with her about it all. So I gave her virtually the full story. She thought my friend Joe was a heel and that I should chuck him, not give him my flat.

"It is generous, I suppose, but then an address like One Spitalfields Market is better not left empty, he will keep it safe for me."

We were getting closer. She was fascinated by my family

and made me promise to take her down to Marlow.

"Why not? Come and meet Sis and Dad. Though I'm not sure I want my brother-in-law ogling you."

She laughed "I'll wear my shortest skirt."

That alluring prospect once again led to a disappointing drift just when I thought we could get closer. Perhaps if I took her to see the family, things might develop. I certainly wanted them to. So I said we could go down at the weekend and we fixed it for Sunday. I phoned Sonia and she said:

"Bring her to Sunday lunch. And we can have a walk by the river."

Saturday was a day off for catching up – I had plenty of stuff to organise. Not to mention shopping and cleaning. I took a stroll from the block up to the cathedral – there was a service going on – but I wandered about the huge nave – it was monumental if a bit spartan.

I bit the bullet and phoned Guildford police station on my mobile. I got through, unfortunately, to the man himself.

"Well, well, Stephen, lovely to hear from you."

The tone implying it was anything but.

I explained that Joe had been in touch but that I didn't know where he was now. I suggested he was avoiding his wife and that this was par for the course.

"So that about wraps it up" said Williams "should Mr Lief's whereabouts become evident please let us know. I hope you sort the car out to your satisfaction. Cheerio."

And that was it. Wrapped up. Except that it wasn't at all and if it was ever going to be wrapped up properly then it was probably up to Rydal and myself.

I walked the long way back past the Stag and down through the University. As I passed 'Stig' as I affectionately thought of the sparkling silver sculpture now, I noticed that he wasn't alone. Sitting behind him, screened from the road, were his entourage. His female companion and her young – also in shining metal. One small one on its long thin legs, looking like a little silver Bambi

CHAPTER 9

Helen arrived at 303 on Sunday morning as she threatened –
in a tiny skirt. Gerald would blow a fuse! I wasn't really
convinced it was appropriate for Sunday lunch with your
boyfriend's family but hey, I wasn't complaining.

We arrived at 'The Finches' about 1 pm and I did the
introductions. Sonia went all motherly – since my mother was
no longer there – and Dad was pretty hopeless at situations
like that. Gerald at one point found himself between Helen's
short skirt and Isabel's bosoms, she was still there. He looked
like a man who had died and gone to heaven.

The meal itself was exquisite and even the children
managed to sit through it. Isabel took them upstairs afterwards
and we all 'retired to the drawing room for liqueurs' – that
could only happen in Marlow! The drawing room, as Gerald
snottily called it, was a lovely room – the patio doors opened
onto a balcony which overlooked the Thames. It was mild
enough to sit on the balcony and watch the boats – still plenty
plying up and down in late October.

Helen was chatting to Dad about one of his favourite
subjects – the river. And soon he was discussing his career –
as the talk got further back in time we knew where it would
stop. And sure enough, despite Helen's probing, she got no
further than the 1950's.

Dad was very proud that he became a captain of a ship

eventually. And he was happy to talk about his voyages to the South Atlantic (long before the Falklands War) and even his trip round the Horn. He had thrilled us when little about his encounters with huge whales and vast icebergs and now I could see Helen falling under his spell.

Gerald was rapidly falling under the influence too – but of malt whisky and I could see him trying to corner Isabel whenever she came down from amusing the kids. Sonia was smouldering with anger and I thought it best to get out.

So Helen, myself and dad set off for a walk along the river into town. Helen had never been to Marlow and she was delighted with its chocolate-box prettiness. Then Dad took her along to the boatyard where his boat was being prepared for the winter. We clambered on board, ducking down as we went below. Dad put the kettle on – I was hoping he might leave the two of us for a while since it was so cramped and so cosy. But Helen kept asking him questions and I could see she was going to have another go at "where were you in the war?" Later I was on deck but could hear it all – though they were both unaware of this.

"So did you see any action during World War II?" Helen asked.

"I was in the Mediterranean. Based in Alexandria in Egypt. I suppose the most harrowing part was when we had to sail into the Cretan ports of Heraklion, to take off the defeated troops. The Germans had overrun Crete thanks to General Student`s paratroops. It was, they say, the first ever invasion by parachute! We got them all off and saved a lot of lives. We were attacked all the way back to Alex and there were some hairy moments."

"What ship were you on?" Helen asked.

"Funny, I don't recall the name of it." was Dad's vague reply.

I had never heard this before. Why would he tell her and not me? I suppose because she wasn't family and perhaps he thought she was just someone his son was dating. None of my dates had ever amounted to much.

But there were clearly places where he would not go, like the name of the ship. Dad would never forget such a thing, I knew that. He could give the name of every boat he had ever owned and there were plenty! And whatever the nasty moments were on the way back to Alex, he wasn't about to share with anyone either.

Once again, I was puzzled by Helen's interest and how close it seemed to come to Ella and her boyfriend's. Coincidence? How could it be anything else? But to put my mind at rest I would try and find out if there was any link.

The most disturbing thought was of course, if it wasn't coincidence, then what was Helen doing here with me, grilling Dad about Crete?

When we got back to the house, world war had broken out there. There was much screeching in Spanish and broken English. Plenty of broken crockery in the kitchen. Children crying, Sonia crying and Gerald nowhere to be found. Gradually we got some sense out of them – though I think we had all guessed already. Gerald had made a whisky-fuelled grope at Isabel's greatest assets – and got crockery broken over his head for his pains. He had driven himself off to A&E in Maidenhead and out of the storm.

It was left to me, ably assisted by the sensible Helen, to negotiate Isabel's departure. The au pair agency was well used to this sort of scenario and a rather bored young woman said:

"Not Isabel Verricho **again**. It's the size of them, men can't resist. We'll send someone round in a car to collect her – female of course. We'll sort the contract details later. There will be compensation to pay, I'm afraid. I hope the gentleman has a sore head – sounds like he deserves it."

As luck would have it, Gerald drew up in the A. M. covered

in bandages, just as Isabel was leaving in another car. They exchanged frosty stares and that was that. Helen and I couldn't help laughing – even Dad saw the funny side.

When we get back to 303 Helen and I told Rydal all about it – she had dashed across to his room. So once again I failed to get her alone and before long came the usual excuse – an early start the following morning.

Was I being used? And if so, what for? Rydal thought it was paranoia. To which the standard response is:

"Just because I'm paranoid, it doesn't mean they aren't out to get me."

In the morning I decided to see Emily number two. I was wondering how I could find out where a Ward Sister lived. She may well be much older and married – not that Helen was a young student nurse of 18. But in fact, it was easy; when I walked up to the nurses' home you couldn't miss the amazing brilliant green genuine Jeep. Nor the couple, looking like something out of a 1940's film, who were clambering into it. "Who's that?" I said to a passing nurse.

"Oh, that's Emily Sandford, she's a Sister at the hospital, she also fancies herself as Betty Davis. You know: 'Don't let's ask for the moon, we have the stars' and all that crap."

And she snorted with derisory laughter, quite cruelly, I thought. There didn't seem much point in pursuing it, I was relieved – Emily Sandford was clearly the real deal. Ergo, so was Helen. Perhaps it was Emily and boyfriend who persuaded her to grill Dad? Anyway, I wasn't going to think about that anymore.

Rydal and I were heading down to Portsmouth to see Maria. He had rung her and she had said, as you would to a distant acquaintance, that it would be nice to see us both. We might be able to jog her memory – her words. On the way we came off the A3 at Hindhead and I went to my garage – obviously Ella was off on holiday – but I wanted to discuss a replacement for my burned out wreck. Norbert, he of the stickler insurance company, had been on the phone and I had the go-ahead to spend the write-off money.

I popped into the showroom, they knew me through Ella.

"She's away on holiday" said Mirabel her colleague "you know Joe's done a runner again, don't you? Well we reckon she may have gone to see him."

If only you knew, I thought.

I explained why I was there and had a good look round their second hand cars. Rydal and I both liked the look of a white three year old 318 with not a lot on the clock. I made a note of it and would hope Ella could get me a big discount like last time. Another reason why I wasn't going to confront her about Crete – well not yet anyway.

Maria was at home with her parents in a pleasant modern semi-detached house. Mr and Mrs Kyriakos were lovely people who clearly doted on Maria and were so thankful she had recovered. The fact that three weeks were a blank in her life mattered nothing to them. They were wary of us probing, scared perhaps they might lose again what they had just got back – their daughter. But hospitality was de rigeur and we were made so welcome. Maria and Rydal chatted about the course and when she could return. He offered to help her with her studies. She was grateful but there was no spark behind her eyes when she talked to Rydal. More worryingly, there was when she talked to me. I felt myself being drawn in to help her fill in those weeks – ironically when I had not been there at all.

I asked her about poetry and quoted the Wyatt poem. When I read:

"Whoso list to hunt…"

I swear there was a flicker of recognition. I explained to her carefully and calmly that someone had written that half-line and put it into my car's documents. I suggested that someone was probably her. I said it was almost certainly her handwriting and gently pointed out there was no one else who could have put it there. I didn't dare go further and mention Joe, Dove-Kemp and her flat being ransacked. We were under orders from the medical staff at the hospital not to. She was still too delicate.

"I know the poem" she said "it has always been one of my favourites. I can imagine writing it out – I know it off by heart and have done since school. But I'm afraid, if I did leave it in your car, I have no idea why. I wish I could help you."

At this point those ice blue eyes bored into mine. I felt guilty as Rydal was sitting next to me. But such eyes were hard to avoid or forget. Rydal missed nothing I knew but he had the grace and fortitude to say or show nothing at all. Our journey back up the A3 was much slower and sadder than our journey down. On the way back we discussed Maria's safety. We had no way of knowing what or who she had seen the night of the accident, nor did she. But someone, somewhere might know and want to prevent her ever remembering. Of course, they might just hope she never remembered and leave her alone. But, Rydal, pragmatic as always, pointed out that since we couldn't offer her round the clock protection and obviously the police wouldn't, all we could do was hope she would be okay.

What Rydal said next was fairly reassuring:

"I told her that if she did remember anything about the 'accident' or connected with the Wyatt thing – to tell us first and no-one else and she agreed."

I spent the rest of Monday stocking up on food, clothes and all the other things of normal life that I had neglected. An early night – Osbert had gone to a Halloween party somewhere in the University, a very scary figure, the effect of which was lost when he opened his mouth and said in broad Brummy:

"Oim a weetch doctor!

November dawned grey, cold and very wet. The early morning radio had reports of flooding all over Surrey and Sussex. Frustratingly, Gatwick was closed and so Ella would be returning to a different airport and then via coach. I couldn't find out which one – Heathrow, Luton, Stansted? No one seemed to know. All I got was:

"It's the floods. Everything is disrupted."

It meant that I couldn't spy on Ella's arrival and see if it was with or without boyfriend. Nor could I follow boyfriend, which would have been useful. Attempting to get up to Hascombe to see Ella was probably a waste of time as well.

In fact I felt almost marooned up Stag Hill! I took a chance on the trains getting through and decided to go into London. I had my own research to do and I could check on Joe. He wasn't answering his mobile, naturally, so I would just have to hope he was in.

I was in a reading room at the British Warships Museum by lunchtime having seen not a drop of water on the ground once I crossed the Wey (admittedly a raging torrent) in Guildford on my way down to the station.

I thought it would be a simple task to put a name to a ship. Johnson is a very common name, but Trevor isn't. Only it was in the 1940's. I got nowhere. One of the staff told me it was impossible with just a name since the records were nowhere near 100% accurate. The only hope was the name of a ship – which was just what I didn't have and couldn't find.

I was scrolling through microfiches of naval reports about the evacuation of Crete – it was all fairly dull. I switched to the internet and used the Warships Museum's own site. I was looking for a list of ships involved in the evacuation. There didn't seem to be one. So I tried a different tack – was there a list of all ships in World War II in the Mediterranean? Not even that. In despair I asked at the desk. A kind old lady – or so she seemed – said that what I wanted didn't exist. All I could do was trawl through a list of ships involved in action in World War II from 1942 onwards. She said that's all she could suggest.

But then, with a twinkle in her eye and in a very stagey conspiratorial whisper, she said "Follow me."

And she opened a security door and led me down several corridors and flights of stairs to a dusty basement. Another security door and into a room full of shelves floor to ceiling.

"Not exactly Google is it?" she giggled. She clambered up some steps and brought down a huge volume. It was so heavy she dropped it and the noise was magnified in that room.

She put her finger on her lips "Shhhh!" and giggled.

It was then I got a waft of alcohol. And I knew I was in the basement of the British Warships Museum with a tipsy employee!

But the volume was a revelation. I spent a long time poring over it because it contained details of all ships based in the eastern Mediterranean during the War. There was even a list of the crews of HMS Warspite, HMS Marlow, HMS Guildford – No. I was drifting off from tiredness brought on by all those names!

I walked in a daze up to Spitalfields and let myself into the flat. All was quiet; Joe would always have the TV or radio on. The place was a bit of a mess – no surprise there. When I opened the bedroom door it was the shoes I saw first – my shoes. He would be wearing … But they were impossibly in mid-air. Disturbed by the draught of the door, his legs swung around and I looked up into his hanging face.

I suppose you always wonder how you will react to a sudden and terrifying shock. I froze – for what seemed like an eternity I just stared at my friend's body. The idea that I must do something came to me slowly but when I knew I must stop him hanging by grabbing his legs I couldn't translate the thought into action.

Some other primal instinct came to my rescue and I lurched forward and held his legs taking his weight. It was no use; he was cold, pale and rigid. Eventually I let go, and as he swung horribly, I rushed out of the room and dialled 999 on the hall phone. Back into that room I couldn't go. When the emergency services arrived, I was shivering and shaking and making no sense.

Chapter 10

There was a note – I had read it but couldn't recall a word. It would surface again later. Forensics took it away. As I sat sipping tea made by a friendly woman police constable clearly detailed to look after me, the police and men in white overalls busied themselves in the bedroom. A plain clothes officer – a detective inspector I assumed – was organising things. He talked to me briefly, just getting a few details of myself and Joe. I would be taken to a police station later to make a state-ment. He reckoned that it was a classic example of suicide which the note seemed to confirm. He didn't expect forensics to turn up anything suspicious. But he did intend to phone Guildford and speak to Detective Inspector Williams and to contact Ella, providing she was home yet from Crete.

At the local police station an hour later I told them exactly what I had found when I went into the flat. I also gave them details of Joe's disappearance and his research and a full account of what he had told me when he first contacted me. Any details I had left out would no doubt be supplied by Williams.

Someone had rung my sister and a police car would take me down to Marlow – they didn't think I should be alone – "suffering from shock probably" and the flat keys would be returned to me in a day or two.

I sat in the back of the police car as it sped out to the West on the A40. The lights of London were comforting. They helped me to blot out what I had seen. When we reached Marlow I was in a state of collapse. Sonia put me to bed, Dad was bewildered and Gerald was nowhere to be seen. I drifted off with the help of some pills of Sonia's and dreamed terrible dreams of hanging figures. In the early morning light, I stared out at the misty river and wept for my lost friend and swore that I would discover what had happened to him. The details of the note were now clear in my mind:

'I can't take the guilt any more. I was responsible for the accident which nearly killed Maria. I was scared and I abandoned her. I have betrayed my wife so many times that she has now found someone else. I can't see a way back. I don't want one.'

There was more. But that was enough for me – it was all in Joe's distinct handwriting and all a pack of lies. The Joe I knew never felt a moment's guilt, was far too selfish and self-centred to think such noble thoughts and was the last person to take his own life. The police might be fooled by it, but I wasn't, not for an instant.

But most significant of all, if it was lies and it was, whoever penned the note knew that Ella had a lover and yet to my knowledge Joe and I were the only ones who knew!

Later that morning, I heard a voice in the hall I thought and hoped I would never hear again. That same terrible monotone conveying disbelief of everything I said. Sonia called out:

"Stephen, Inspector Williams is here to see you."

We used the drawing room. The river through the balcony doors looked cold and grey, 'The Finches' at its most un-inviting. Strange how I wished that Williams could see it in the summer when it was so elegant and sophisticated, watching boats drifting past from the balcony. And the town and bridge at night full of lights and laughter.

But laughter was in short supply now. Williams began:

"There will be an inquest of course. My colleague, the Detective Inspector you saw at the flat, is pretty sure it's a clear case of suicide. The note gives convincing reasons. He thinks the Coroner will agree and the whole thing will be wrapped up next Monday. That's when it's fixed for up in London. The funeral can take place soon after, the same week I imagine, in Hascombe at the local church. Mrs Lief wants that. I've seen her – she arrived back from Crete to this terrible news. She's bearing up. She asked after you. I said you'd be in touch soon. I also told her about the coincidence of you being in Crete at the same time as she was."

I didn't like the last thing he said one bit. There was something in his tone – it wasn't the usual deadpan at all and much more menacing.

On he went, inexorably, like the tide coming in.

"Now Detective Inspector Rowse, that's his name by the way, needs a bit of Rowsing if you ask me" he laughed at his own joke "is not the brightest button in the box. But, to be fair, he didn't have the advantage of my previous knowledge of the case. When you phoned me to tell me Mr Lief had been in touch I noted the relief in your voice when I said that was that. And all the time you knew **exactly where he was**! In your flat. No one else knew did they?"

"Not as far as I know."

This wasn't true of course, Rydal and Helen knew but I saw no point in involving them. Mistake!

"There's also a slight problem with the note," Williams began again "I've had it looked at by a handwriting expert on the advice of Mrs Lief, who I showed it to. She says that superficially it looks like her husband's handwriting but there are one or two other things about it that are different. When I asked what these were she was unable to pin them down but she said it reminded her of someone else's handwriting."

His eyebrows rose, quizzically, and it dawned on me that he was suggesting, astonishingly, that the handwriting was like mine! It's true, both Joe and I and Ella have remarked on several occasions, how similar our handwriting was.

"You can't seriously be implying…"

He cut me short. "Not at all. I'm just passing on a remark of Mrs Lief's for what it's worth. But, Stephen, put yourself in my place – here I have a suicide – in **your** flat, of a man who had an accident, or might have had, in **your** car. **You** visit Crete at the exact same time as his wife, and by the way, Mrs Lief informed us of your previous history as lovers. And the suicide note has a look of **your** handwriting about it. If I also tell you that forensics are not happy with the idea that Mr Lief could actually have killed himself that way, without assistance, and you see my problem."

I felt icy cold and yet I was sweating. The implication in his words was clear. It dawned on me I wasn't the only one who thought that Joe's suicide was suspicious and the note a sham. What had never occurred to me until this moment was that someone might think I was responsible.

"Good God" I said "you can't be seriously be thinking that I had anything to do with Joe's death. He was my best and oldest friend".

"Did I say that?" said Williams "But I think perhaps I will need to speak to you again in a day or two down at the station. When it is clear just exactly who is in charge of this case, myself or Rowse."

When he had gone, I sat in the drawing room staring out at the river, numb and shocked. Slowly the reality of what was happening sank in. But for the delay in appointing Williams in overall charge (which was obviously what he wanted. I think he sensed his big break) I would be down at Guildford police station now being interviewed, possibly even arrested. Another idea was forming slowly in my mind, given what he had said. I could not say he hadn't got a case. Ludicrous though it was, someone looking at the facts dispassionately might agree with him. But how had the 'facts' arranged themselves to suggest my involvement? There was only one answer to that. Someone, very cleverly, had arranged them that way. I was being framed for my own friend's murder. And I had, at the most, several hours to act before Williams came back. What could I do? Who could I confide in? Would I have time to see Ella – would I be able to? I didn't know the answer to any of these questions.

Without formulating a plan as such, I said hurried goodbyes to Sis and Dad, packed a suitcase and drove off. I parked in a lay-by by the river and phoned Rydal. I told him all that Williams had said to me and that I wasn't waiting around for him to come back. Rydal said it was madness to try and evade the police but if I insisted he would say nothing. More than that he said he would try and think of somewhere for me to hide. He advised me to get rid of the car as soon as possible. I was blessed in such a friend, such a rock.

"What about Helen?" he said "Shall I tell her?"

This was tricky. I wanted and needed Helen very much but something, some still small voice, advised caution. The truth was, bitterly, that I didn't entirely trust her – and I didn't know why.

"Not yet" I said "no need to worry her. I'm going to Hascombe now in the car. I think I have time before I ditch it. I'll find some way of contacting you – I can't use the mobile any more. I can't go to the inquest or the funeral which makes me sad. Perhaps **you** could somehow – it's not fair of me to ask I know."

I tore up the roads to Hascombe – so many questions for Ella. If I wasn't prepared to trust Helen, then I certainly wasn't prepared to trust Ella. In fact, I wanted to confront her. But I suspect she realised this because when I got to the gates of her "mansion", which in effect is what it was, there was a police car in the drive. The person I most needed to see was 'in communicado' and I didn't dare phone.

By now, for all I knew, Williams was installed as head of the investigation and might be planning to contact me soon. As if by magic, my phone rang and the caller's number confirmed my worst thoughts. I left the car in Guildford station car park – amused at the idea of not needing a parking ticket for the first time ever. And only a little guilty at the problems I would be causing Norbert Dent back at my insurance company. I got cash from a machine – yes, they would know that eventually – but Guildford Station cash point would be the last trace I'd leave.

It was going dark now and I had nowhere to go. I wasn't leaving the area though, the only way I could find out who 'killed' Joe – I was sure now the 'suicide' was really murder – was to stay and search. I was just about to throw my mobile into the dark waters of the Wey when it rang and Rydal's number appeared. One last call. Thank God I took it. Rydal had been busy, he had found a room on campus that a student was leaving empty for at least a month, not Bolivia this time, but Bali. A much more hedonistic student, obviously. Anyway, Rydal had somehow got a key. The room was in a block but fairly isolated and if I was careful I might be able to stay there unseen. Rydal arranged a signal knock, he **was** good at this sort of thing. After that call the mobile made a satisfying splash in the river. I went into town and bought what was more or less a disguise at the local fancy dress shop and walked up the hill to the University.

As Rydal had promised, the block was out on a limb and the actual room was slightly detached from it anyway. The key was where he said it would be. I let myself into a flat, not a room. It wasn't a student residence but, by the looks of it, an employee's of the University. That's why it was separate and remarkably, the entrance wasn't overlooked at all. I pulled down all the blinds and used the reading lamp. Whether I could live here unnoticed for long I wasn't sure. But it would do for a few days at least. The first knock startled me, I was very jumpy never having been 'on the run' before, the second had me listening carefully and the third after several long agonising seconds meant it was Rydal.

I was so glad to see him. He had several shopping bags and plenty of cash. And he was the voice of reason I needed. Skulking about I began to feel guilty, as if I was to blame for all this. Rydal assured me I wasn't at all. But someone else was. The inquest might yet find suicide but neither of us thought that likely. What we had to decide is what to do next. I was overwhelmed by his friendship and loyalty. He could walk away, even give me up to Williams. But he didn't!

We talked late into the night going through all the possibilities as to why someone would want to frame me for Joe's death. It was clear to both of us that the fake suicide could have easily been made convincing – if not to me then certainly to the police. I was the real target.

So maybe the two accidents were also targeting me. Only I wasn't in my car for the first one, and by luck, escaped the second. Third time lucky! Not quite yet.

"Joe was supposed to be in the car with you – so it looks like he was a target as well" said Rydal "I became a target simply because I happened to be with you at Allington."

"Dove-Kemp was on the verge of success and fame, celebrity status in his world and wealth. Joe was threatening that because he had found something important at Allington and taken it. I was Joe's best friend and when I appeared at Allington Dove-Kemp assumed I knew of it too and quite probably you. Joe was the target of the first accident, I became one later." was my reasoned argument.

What didn't fit into any of this was the Cretan mystery. We racked our brains for a connection but only came up with the obvious one – Ella – who was currently out of reach. We were assuming there was a link, but why should there be?

Sleep on it was what we agreed. Rydal would come back early morning and help formulate a plan of action.

CHAPTER 11

It was a beautiful mild November morning – more like September. Breezy enough for clouds of leaves to blow across the University lake – all this I could see out of my bedroom window but I was fairly confident no one could see me. The three knocks came half an hour later and in came Rydal with breakfast. This young man was something else!

I tried my disguise out on him – big bushy wig, moustache, beard and hat and long rain coat. He burst out laughing.

"You look like a flasher! If I saw you in the park I'd run a mile. Let's tone it down a bit and make it more subtle, shall we?"

And he got to work. I have to say the end result was pretty good – the Flasher had gone (I already had a soft spot for him) to be replaced by the well-respected, very dull looking office worker that no one would really notice at all. Rydal, with a twinkle in his eye, christened me Jim Jarvis and even gave me a potted biography. He was enjoying himself immensely. Jim worked in the University in some dull unspecified office doing dull University stuff. Keep it vague. He came from a dull town in Surrey – take your pick – but Dorking had his vote.

Dullness personified, I tucked into breakfast. But behind all this fooling there was real grief and real fear. This wasn't a game, however much we tried to pretend it was.

Rydal would see Maria again in the hope her memory could be kick-started. He would also let Helen know that I had decided to lie low but give no details. The inquest was set for the following Monday and he would be there on behalf of Maria. Ditto the funeral that might follow. He had his studies to continue at the same time.

I was 'free' to pursue both the Wyatt and the Cretan mysteries though severely hampered by lack of wheels; I would just have to use public transport. Most important of all was to speak to Ella. And that had priority. Williams might already be looking for me but it was unlikely he thought I had 'run' yet and so Ella would not know that either. Nor did I want her to meet Jim – so no disguise.

By mid-morning via Godalming and Hascombe buses – very slow and desperately frustrating, I was once again at the bottom of her drive. No police car on the drive. But Ella herself just getting into her sports car. I got in the other side. Open-mouthed and terrified, she was about to scream when I covered her mouth:

"Don't be frightened. We need to talk. I need your help."

Immediate fear over, she relaxed a little, but not much. Still alarmed and wary she said:

"What do you want?"

"We need to talk, Ella, about Joe's suicide."

"I can't" she replied "I have to be at work this morning to discuss taking more leave. God knows I need it."

"Fine" I replied "we can talk whilst you drive us to Hindhead."

The journey down to the A3 and then along it was a very surreal one.

I began:

"Joe didn't commit suicide; both you and I know that. He wasn't the type. You suggested to Williams that it was me who

93

killed him. And I want to know why!"

Ella gripped the wheel hard. "I was scared. Someone killed Joe in your flat. Williams said you followed me to Crete. He said the note wasn't genuine. I don't think the handwriting was Joe's. Now you're here bursting into my car, forcing me to drive and listen. What am I supposed to think? Yes, I admit it, Williams nearly convinced me. But he didn't. I know you and Joe were best mates. And we had some good times together you and I. So no, I don't believe it."

"It's been made to look like I was to blame. Well I'm not. But you – I saw you in Crete with your new man. I followed you into the museum that day; know what you were looking for. But most important of all, your boyfriend tried to crash my car. My passenger got a good look at him and he matched this photograph."

She glanced at the photo of the two of them together in Crete but never wavered for an instant. "Yes, that's Rick. So why can't I have some fun; Joe had plenty. As for your 'passenger' recognising him in some crash well that's complete nonsense. He must have been mistaken. Why on earth would Rick want to do that – it's crackers."

"And the museum?"

"Oh that" said Ella calmly "Rick is interested in ships, always has been apparently. He just took the opportunity to find out more about World War II and Crete. I tagged along – so what?"

I had to admit my whole argument was a bit threadbare – or sounded it. Ella was always very good at pouring scorn on things. Rydal might have made a mistake – in a sudden terrifying situation. And perhaps I was being paranoid about the ships.

"Look, when Williams contacts you again, can you put him straight about me? I won't be around to defend myself; I'm clearing off before he arrests me."

Ella nodded. As we entered the A3 tunnel we both fell silent

– probably both collecting our thoughts. The tunnel had made the approach to the town very quick and we were nearing the garage in minutes. I would have to decide whether to accept her offer of a lift back when she had sorted her prolonged leave and risk her phoning Williams as soon as she was out of my sight or disappear. I told her I would wait but as soon as she went into her office I left the garage and crossed the road to the hotel opposite where I bought a drink at the bar and sat by the window – if police cars drew up before long I would know for sure it was all an act. But they didn't. She came out to her car then went in again. Salesmen in suits with clipboards stared very professionally at cars. Mechanics crisscrossed the forecourt, the garage's name and location emblazoned on their overalls. Nothing seemed out of the ordinary. But I still didn't trust her – so slipped out, after she had left and made my own long and tedious way back to the University via taxi, bus and train. I couldn't even pass Stig and his entourage at the main entrance but crept in via a gap in a hedge and a hole in the fence.

Three knocks late afternoon. Rydal had seen Maria – small things about the University and the course were coming back to her. She even had a hazy memory of a tutor she liked.

"I hadn't the heart to tell her about Joe." said Rydal "She has told her parents that she is still remembering small details, but told no one else except me. Soon her parents may contact the police though. Surrey police have been in touch asking if I have seen you. Williams **is** in charge now and wants to interview you to eliminate you from the enquiry, as the euphemism goes. I spoke to Helen; she was really upset especially about not being able to contact you. She almost begged me to tell her where you were. But I kept up the stonewall defence of 'no idea'. Oh, and on a lighter note, Osbert asked where you were, he wanted to meet up for drinks at the pub and watch the 'Veela sink the Otspoor'!"

I was shattered, this being 'on the run' lark was very wearing. But late that night sleep wouldn't come. I went over and over Ella's words – that was what she would say if she was involved and if she wasn't. Rydal had seemed less certain and admitted he might have been mistaken but he still felt the man in the car and the photo looked the same. I was drifting off and yet I had one ear still listening out for police sirens. When I heard the occasional one in the distance I knew they were coming for me. As they got nearer I panicked, but they all faded at the same point and I realised they were ambulances headed for A&E at the hospital nearby.

"Poor Osbert" I muttered "not much chance of the Villa sinking…"

I was wide awake! That list of ships. It was on the internet. I knew the password to access it. I got it up on the screen and scanned the ships in the Eastern Med in 1941 until I came to the letter 'H'. I knew what I would find. The words came back to me – "I know you'll like the name, right up your street" – Lane more like. White Hart Lane.

HMS HOTSPUR!

By lunchtime I was on the riverbank in Marlow – as Jim Jarvis, I didn't want Sonia, Gerald or any of the family, bar one, to see **me**. Not that I think they would betray me, though Gerald was a loose cannon after the Isabel affair. I wasn't even sure what his status or even residence was at the moment.

Dad's boat was where it always was and I was pretty sure I'd find him there. I went on board having first removed the Jim stuff. He was busy with the engine when I said softly "Dad, it's me." He turned round calmly enough, when you had seen the action he had, I suppose being calm came second nature.

"Stephen. Am I glad to see you. You know the police are looking for you. That detective was at our house this morning. Don't worry, Sonia didn't say anything and she told the children not to. What is it, Stephen? Is it about poor Joe Lief – he committed suicide, didn't he?"

I filled Dad in on what I thought he could take. The bit about me being framed for it made him go pale and he had to sit down. Being calm is all very well but when you are in your nineties...

Of course, he believed my story, he never doubted me for an instant. I gave him a brief resumé of the Wyatt thing and my belief that Joe's death was because of that, as were the accidents . But I also told him that there seemed to be some link between the man causing the accidents and Crete.

Dad began to look increasingly uncomfortable. I think he knew what was coming, especially when I reminisced about how he took me to football matches.

"Your ship in the early 1940's, when you worked below decks as a torpedo operator or whatever, was it HMS Hotspur?" I asked with trepidation.

"Don't go there, Stephen. It's not something I want to remember. They were difficult days. I lost friends. I just don't want to talk..."

I cut him off abruptly. "But don't you see? You have to. I need to know about the evacuation of Crete. I can and will research it. But I'd prefer your version since I know I can believe it."

"We evacuated hundreds from Heraklion and during the voyage to Alex hundreds more joined us. That's all."

I could tell I would get nothing more. When I left the boat I was a very heavy-hearted Jim Jarvis once more.

It took hours to get back to the University – there had been a rail crash at Reading and everything was delayed or cancelled.

97

It was late evening before I crept through the hedge and slipped silently into the flat. There was a message for me from Rydal.

'Am going to Cambridge tomorrow – getting a lift from another student. Maybe Jim should tag along. Meet in Cathedral car park at nine. R'

This suited my purposes perfectly; the time had come to stir up the irascible Professor.

CHAPTER 12

It was a very misty morning – the Cathedral loomed up like a huge mountain – the edges all blurred. Rydal's friend Julie was going to see her boyfriend who was at Cambridge University. I don't think she fancied the drive at all and when we got on to the M25 it became hair-raising. It wasn't just fog Julie didn't like, she didn't seem keen on speed, changing lanes, merging on and off motorways and to be honest, any car, anywhere near her. I was sweating but Rydal had gone white. The gear box was suffering too as she repeatedly crashed the gears. Off the M25 onto the M11 and the fog dropped like a curtain. Julie pulled onto the hard shoulder (or what she thought was the hard shoulder) but it turned out to be the middle lane and cars began to screech around us. I could take no more and told her to swap with me. I drove slowly and carefully until we reached an exit and got off the M11. Mercifully, the fog lifted and green fields appeared and carpets of leaves lined the side of the road. We made it to Cambridge in the end and Julie was very grateful, more or less begging me to drive back. Cynically, I saw my chance and asked her if she used the car much.

"Not unless I have to. Mark usually comes to see me. The car usually sits in the Halls of Residence car park. To be honest, if you want, Rydal told me you hadn't got a car, you're welcome to use it, Jim."

Music to my ears. Not perhaps the 'Jim' but certainly the car! It could compromise my 'disguise' but wheels were so useful.

This time I phoned Professor Dove-Kemp from a call box – when I eventually found one that wasn't vandalised, stinking of urine or phoneless. I got through to his secretary who passed on the message that I wanted to see him about the letter and was in Cambridge. I had an appointment at 2 pm.

At 2 pm I was back in his room again at the top of the tower. I found it hard to concentrate and not start laughing when I remembered how Rydal and I listened to his tutorial from his bathroom!

He was very wary of me. There wasn't exactly steam coming out of his ears, but there was controlled anger there. I saw no point in beating about the bush. Nor did I bother with Jim, I was myself, since he would be more likely to believe my audacious suggestion.

"I have the letter that you are looking for; Maria gave it to me for safe-keeping. I am willing to do a deal but that depends on whether you are willing to pay for it?"

"How much?" came the angry reply.

"Let's say a thousand." I had no real idea of its value to him or to anybody else for that matter. Nor did I care since it was all a bluff anyway. But he appeared to fall for it.

"Very well, then. But I need proof that you have it."

"Certainly" I said coolly, not having any. "I will contact you with the proof and tell you how I want the money."

And it was over. I raced down the stairs and out of that dreadful college. Perhaps he was phoning Williams, though I doubted it.

The bait was laid. The trap (well me, actually, watching my Spitalfields flat) would be set that very evening.

The drive back to Guildford was uneventful but I did get a set of keys to the car with the offer from a more relaxed Julie, having seen her boyfriend, to use it any time virtually.

I told Rydal everything about the Dove-Kemp interview – he whistled and praised my cool and my courage – then I headed off to the station. Several hours later, in the gathering dusk, I was placed in the market where I could see the stairs leading up to my flat. It could be a long night.

And it was, punctuated by bangs, flashes and whizzes in the distance. It was Bonfire Night after all. I think modern trendy Spitalfields felt itself above all that. I was wrong though, about 11 pm, everyone went outside and the sky lit up – the market now had its own display.

It was after midnight when I was about to call it a day or a night that two figures dressed in black slipped up the stairs. I could see them bent in front of my door and then they were gone, inside. I had just got the flat 'back' from the police but couldn't face going inside so for all I knew it was a mess, I'm sure it was when they left empty-handed half an hour later. I had taken a gamble that I would be able to follow them. To my surprise they separated, one got into a car, the other walked on. I followed the walker at a careful distance; there was just the trace of a limp in his rather awkward movement. It was to be a tube journey and via several changes we arrived at Kew. Out of the station and down the road past some shops he stopped and knocked at a smart villa – I suppose it would have been called so in the past – a balding bespectacled figure came to the door, my burglar shook his head. They exchanged a few words and he was off in the direction of the tube station. I didn't retrace my steps to follow him, I had a hunch I had found somebody more important. But it was far too late and possibly dangerous to do anything then.

So I booked into a small hotel round the corner – no doubt used by tourists wanting to spend a day or two at the gardens. In the end I became one of those tourists because the following day was Sunday and since I could think of no pretext to knock on the villa's door, I decided to wait until Monday and hope he left for work.

I spent a desultory day walking the damp Kew streets, littered with last night's rockets, trying desperately to find some vibrant life in what was open (which wasn't much) in the famous gardens. I was back outside his house at seven on Monday; if he had work to go to then I would follow him. I was getting quite good at this, lurking behind lamp posts etc.

We didn't have far to walk. The Public Records Office at Kew was our destination.

I was worried I would lose him because I wouldn't be able to follow without a pass key or what not and members of the public would not be admitted so early. But my luck was in. He went into a building without using any keys or swiping any cards and I could see him put the light on in a window on the ground floor. It was a very dark November morning – dark and dank. The warmth of an office felt very appealing. In I went. The door I wanted proclaimed:

J.E. Easterton Archivist

I knocked and at the sound "enter" I was face to face with J. E. Easterton, balding, bespectacled and it has to be said, beaming with good nature.

I had rehearsed what I was going to say but his sheer niceness threw me totally off-guard. I expected belligerence and was ready for an argument but not this.

"It's about the letter and… last night." I stuttered.

"Ah yes" he said "it was a bit late for the Professor to let me know the original wasn't available unless of course you…"

"No" I said, flying by the seat of my pants "but he just wanted some clarification of your views on it anyway."

"Oh, I see Mr… ah…"

"Jarvis, call me Jim."

"Well, Jim, I can understand, given the sensitivity of the

subject and the Professor's desire to 'cash in on it' shall we say, that he wouldn't want copies flying around, but not to make any seems unduly cautious, even foolish – what would happen if it went missing?"

I said nothing.

"At least I had a brief look at it when he first found it, I suppose, and so I can expand a bit on what I told him on the phone. What about the coffee? We can chat over that. And a sticky bun if there are any left. Let's go down to the canteen, it'll be quiet there this time in the morning."

It was. And none of the sticky buns had gone. For breakfast? Jethro, for that was what the 'J' stood for (I couldn't wait to find out what the 'E' stood for) had four big sticky buns. I had coffee and croissants. It was curious to sit opposite his owlish, if benign gaze, as these pastries disappeared into his mouth with obvious relish.

Buns gone, he began "Well, Jim, I'm pretty sure it was the real McCoy. I did a few secretary hand checks and got the fancy new machine to examine the ink and yes, I do believe it really was a sixteenth century letter, supposedly from Thomas Cromwell to Thomas Wyatt. It was the fashion to make letters like 's' and 'r' in a particular way in the 1530's you know."

Amazing. The astonishing import of the letter, its significance for Tudor and the rest of English history were all lost on this delightful academic. All that mattered to him was the lettering.

"As I understand it the letter proves that Ann Boleyn was the victim of a conspiracy organised by Cromwell involving Wyatt among others and that she was innocent of the charges. So why did you say 'supposedly'?"

"Of course, when I said it's genuine, what I meant, young man, is that it is sixteenth century. It certainly is sixteenth century secretary hand. That doesn't mean the content of the letter is genuine. It's possible the letter dates from the late rather than the early sixteenth century. It could have been written by Cromwell, but it could equally well have been written by another shrewd spymaster to discredit Cromwell. I'm thinking of Elizabeth's ministers – the Cecils.

Their agenda was very much to prove that their mistress' mother was pure as the driven snow and Elizabeth unquestionably the rightful heir to her father. Exposing Cromwell's plot to blacken Ann Boleyn was paramount – a letter such as this would do that superbly."

When I thought about this, really it was common sense. It was how history worked. The next generation doctored the previous generation's writings until they ceased to be a problem. Or, on occasions, rewrote them or even fabricated them. It's exactly what Elizabeth would have done or have ordered to be done. Suddenly the letter, wherever it was, became even more important.

The sticky buns were clearly what were important to Jethro as he went to the counter for another two. When dispatched they seemed to galvanise him. Wound up like a wondrous toy on Christmas morning, he couldn't stop.

"The thing is not **everything** will have been destroyed or altered by William and later Robert Cecil. Think about it, Queen Mary would have been thrilled to have found anything disinheriting her hated half-sister and, for that matter, half-brother Edward. She would have gathered such information to her and kept it safe and secret for future use. Similarly, anything that suggested Ann Boleyn (her mother's hated rival) was innocent would have been kept secret too but for very different reasons! I doubt the Cecils got their hands on that. I imagine there is a stack of correspondence waiting to be unearthed. I even have some ideas as to where it might be found."

Seize the moment. "I would be very interested to know where. More sticky buns?"

The kindly old man seemed to have forgotten the Professor's

existence. He was quite willing to discuss where other evidence might be found. And although my views on the relationships had been turned upside down, it seemed to me very useful, even essential, to find other evidence. It would make Maria less of a target for one thing if presented to Dove-Kemp or alternatively might put that devious historian into our hands.

I got the feeling that poor old Jim Jarvis was destined to spend his brief existence looking at records.

Jethro was warming to his task. He didn't know me from Adam and didn't seem to care. The light of historical research was in his eyes:

"I would start with the places that Mary was secluded in when Ann became Queen. She was moved about a bit, as was her poor mother Queen Catherine. But her main residence was Hartley, Hertfordshire. Henry's palace there has been rebuilt and changed many times since then. Now it's the very modest Hartley House, I believe. You should try the Hitchin Record Office in Hertfordshire, I have a friend there who will help you. And the house itself may still contain some papers though there will be more at The Record Office."

Enough! I would probably be there hours unless I made a move. Jethro had more or less forgotten who I was and why I was there. He gave me the name and number of his friend. Told me to be sure to call in again or ring him if I needed any help. Then wished me a fond farewell.

Back at the University, safely ensconced in my flat I told Rydal about my adventures. He agreed that finding other evidence to support the missing letter would be useful, more than that, it might get Dove-Kemp and his less salubrious friends off our backs. Most important of all, it might mean Maria would be free of them too, since the whereabouts of the letter would be less significant.

Chapter 13

Rydal really had to get some studying done with exams approaching so it was down to me. Desperate though I was to find out about HMS Hotspur, I put Maria first and agreed to the Hartley/Hertfordshire quest.

Then Rydal told me that Maria had arrived back in Guildford. She was moving into her old room, her parents were here to support her. I could tell he was very excited and I felt a twinge of jealousy that I would be unable to see her or support her in any way.

"Tell her Stephen sends his love and best wishes but can't see her at the moment. Bloody Jim Jarvis is to blame! Don't really say that last bit."

If Rydal for once permitted himself a wry smile or a sigh of relief at my plight I would have understood. But no, he genuinely regretted that I couldn't see her.

"And don't forget it's the inquest later today," he reminded me, "I will be in the public gallery and will talk to you about it tonight. Though I expect it will be opened and then adjourned if Williams gets his way."

I winced. "God, I'd forgotten all about it," guilt overwhelming me. Here I was pursuing sixteenth century love letters whilst the inquest on my closest friend's death had gone out of my mind entirely!

I stayed put for the rest of the day, imagining what Rydal,

from the vantage point of the public gallery, was seeing. Who was there? How would they behave? I was thinking particularly of Ella. In fact, I was so deep in thought that it took me several seconds to re-focus on the strange noise. What was that? It was a key turning in the lock and the front door opening. I dashed into the bedroom in a panic. Back from Bali already? Hedonism not what it used to be? Since my things were all over the flat there was little point in hiding so I strode as nonchalantly as I could into the living room to be confronted by a rather large lady in a bright pink uniform holding a mop and bucket.

"You are not here" she said helpfully, in what I took for an Eastern European accent.

"Boily" she tried again.

Was she here to boil the kettle? Check it or something? Had I misunderstood?

"Boily" she repeated, still valiantly clinging to her mop and bucket.

We had reached a kind of impasse. The only thing I could do was agree and let her get on with whatever she had to do. So I nodded and said:

"Boily!"

She cleaned around me – very efficiently. It was worrying that I hadn't had time to don Jim Jarvis so she got the real McCoy, as it were. She didn't seem impressed, 'tut-tutting', well the Eastern European equivalent, at my slovenliness.

After much musing I worked out 'Boily' was 'Bali' and that she thought that the flat was empty because that's where she had been told the occupant was. We had a further conversation in broken English which established that she had to clean it once every two weeks. So I could look forward to her visit on November 14 – I would make sure I was out. The problem was would she make sure her superiors weren't told I was back from Bali and could I reassure her that cleaning once every two weeks was fine by me. A twenty pound note did the trick and I think/hope we got it clear in the end.

Rydal returned from the inquest in the evening. I told him all about the cleaner, which amused him a great deal.

"The inquest was opened and adjourned. Williams was there and had requested that. He also said there were several people he wished to interview, one had disappeared and the police were actively searching for him."

Who could that be? I wondered.

Rydal continued:

"Ella was there, I don't know her but other people in the gallery said it was the deceased's wife. I didn't see anyone else of significance."

He left to do some studying though he was so nervous about Maria's impending return that I doubt he did any. Hartley for me in the morning courtesy of Julie's car.

On the way to Hertfordshire, the M25 yet again, I stopped at the services and when I finally found a phone that worked dialled a number I knew well.

"Hello, old sport, good to hear from you."

"How's the car?"

"Funny you should mention it…"

Jensen gearboxes are not my strong point so I just said 'yes' and 'um' now and again until he had finished. Then he said something very alarming.

"There was an inspector chap here asking about you. I said you were ill. He didn't stay long, seemed rather bored by the old Interceptor, come to think of it."

Bless the car, I thought, I'll never denigrate the Mark III again.

In the circumstances, asking for leave seemed slightly irrelevant, given that Big Vinyl would eventually twig I was on the run. So I said goodbye. Did he ever wonder what the phone call was actually for? Probably not – to him it would be natural for us all to check on the well-being of you know what.

So they really were actually looking for me, though not with any great urgency by the sound of it.

Hartley House was in the centre of the village of Hartleybury. A very pretty place it was too. Jim had never been there before! It wasn't open to the public. The owners were away and the place was locked, shuttered and bolted. Fort Knox looked easier.

But Jim was up for a challenge. Was I developing an alterego with a different personality from my own. I'm pretty sure the Stephen I knew would have shrugged and driven off. But Jim was having none of it. Hartley was a nut to be cracked.

So Jim (myself, of course) went round the back. But it wasn't like going round the back of a semi or detached in suburbia. Hartley may have been a slimmed down version of the pile that Princess Mary knew – and most probably loathed – but it was still formidable in size.

I could get round the back, however, by squeezing through several hedges. There was no one about. There was a big duck pond or perhaps small lake, depending on your point of view and who you wanted to impress (should that be whom?)

I got between the expanse of water and the wall and looked for foot holes to a window quite high up but reachable. I scrabbled up the wall and had a go at the window. Stuck fast. I banged it a bit, but it didn't move at all.

There was another one further along the wall so I tried again. This did move. The catch was rusty and gave way inside and I clambered through the opening. Would I ever get out?

I was in a kind of scullery – not a word I commonly use – but it seemed to fit the vaguely musty Edwardian pantry (there's another word from my childhood) that I was in. I clicked the latch and crept down a darkened corridor, opening doors from time to time on other servants' quarters. I would be unlikely to find anything on this floor. What I needed was a library or study, or even office.

I made my way down a wide staircase. Mustiness everywhere. Much of the furniture was covered in ghostly sheets, or they seemed so in the gloom.

At the foot of the stairs I crossed a marble floor and picked a door at random. The room was full of books from floor to ceiling. This was more like it. There were desks with drawers a-plenty too. So I started opening them. Most were empty but I did find one roll of papers which had the words "I give to Mary" in an italic hand written on it. The other side was less intriguing:

Baked beans
Toilet roll
Washing powder.
Broccoli

Now my historical knowledge is thin but I doubt that in her 'captivity' Mary was cruelly force fed broccoli and baked beans!

None of the other drawers or shelves revealed anything. I could have looked in between all the book leaves I suppose but that would have taken till at least 2020, so I didn't even try. By now my nerve was failing anyway as I was aware of all sorts of noises in the distance. Creaks, muffled footsteps, groans even. My imagination was getting the better of me. Jim's bravado was a distant memory but Stephen's timidity was all too present. I think common sense had prevailed and I was not going to stumble upon some vital clue simply blundering, however quietly, about an unfamiliar house.

So I found the staircase and eventually, by trial and error, my point of entry. Getting out seemed less easy than getting in. It had to be done backwards and as my lower half emerged I heard:

"Ere wot you a doin ther!"

I had no option but to clamber down the wall to meet my accuser, I had visions of a gamekeeper in plus fours, with huge whiskers and a shot-gun. What I found was a young lad with a cheeky grin.

"That's my way in, mate."

I saw my exit strategy at once.

"Now listen here, my young man. I could see that someone had been using this window to get into the house. The land-lord asked me to keep an eye out…"

I made a grab for him. But he was as quick and elusive as I hoped he would be and he scarpered. I did much the same in the other direction.

I had decided that the Hitchin Record Office might be a trifle safer. As it turned out – it was and it wasn't.

So I took the country lanes into Hitchin. Jethro was as good as his word and Ben Bracket, his friend, was happy to help. More than happy – rather more than. Ben took a shine to me. Even with the Jim Jarvis whiskers etc. My father would have said, very politically incorrectly, "Ben batted for the other side."

He was a whizz with records, I fondly recalled the gin-tippling Miss Stope, and he had already looked at what might be useful.

"I think you should spend some time on the Hatfield House material. It's very extensive and no one has read it all. So you will have to be lucky, it's like looking for a needle in a haystack. It will take you all day. There's a nice pub, 'The Duck and Ferret', nearby if you fancy a…"

"No thanks, I'll be hard at it" I said quickly. Having no wish to sample the delights of 'The Duck and Ferret' or any other delight Ben had in mind.

By 3pm I was thinking I'd prefer to be at the pub. I was so bored. The Cecils may have been spymasters but they were very dull ones judging by the records Sir Robert left.

As the light began to fade and people began to leave the Reading Room, I came upon this curious document.

It was a note, memo, whatever the equivalent was in Tudor times, from Robert Cecil to an underling. I got Ben to 'translate' it and de-secretary hand it for me:

'The Lady Mary in that year travelled to Surrey where she was kept very quietly. And thence into Kent where for a time Allyngton was her residence, it being a Wyatt household. On her stay, so my informant knows, she was acquainted with various letters. Two of which concern them that we have interest in. She took away with her one of the letters. Neither letter had come to my father's attention. She returned to Hartley but stayed to hear a secret mass at (here it got very difficult to decipher even for Ben) Bra or Bor where one Says...'

Possibly the most frustrating document I have ever come across. Ben offered to take a copy home and pore over it if I fancied supper. I declined the supper but took a copy.

When I got back and showed it to Rydal, he found it utterly fascinating and set to work on the internet. Several hours later he was ready and began:

"*them that we have interest in*' was the key phrase we both agreed. It could easily mean Wyatt and Ann Boleyn. It could mean somebody else entirely. But letters at Allington taken by Mary – I doubt it.

I reckon 'but stayed' means stopped on her way to Hartley. But given she was travelling from Kent – it could be almost anywhere in or around London.

Mary was more 'prisoner' than guest at Hartley and it wouldn't have been wise to take the letter there. I expect she, her room at least, was regularly searched. She could have given it to someone she trusted. But who could she trust? Clearly the people who organised the secret mass. Wherever that was, the letter was 'kept' there. The problem is where and who with?

It could be in Kent, in London, in Essex or Surrey. But she had spent a lot of time in Hertfordshire – at Hartley but also at Hatfield and Hitchin. I think given it was a secret Catholic mass she would know the place and people very well. My guess is Hertfordshire – not necessarily on the way though – she could make a detour. After all she was probably giving thanks for the 'dynamite' she had found at Allington. The question is what did she do with it?

'*At Bra or Bor where one Says…*' Well I had a look at places in Hertfordshire beginning with Bra or Bor. There aren't any – but there is Bro – Broxbourne. It's only a few miles south of Hartley in the Lea Valley and would have been on her route home. What do they say about it I wonder?"

I could tell Rydal was feeling pleased with himself, he was building up to something, so I played along looking suitably impressed yet puzzled, waiting for the denouement. It wasn't long in coming.

"Well I looked at Broxbourne on the internet – it has a church dating from the fifteenth century, so it would have been there when Mary was at Hartley in the sixteenth. It would ostensibly be Church of England when Mary was 'imprisoned' but who knows the leanings of the vicar or parishioners. But in the church is a tomb to the famous local family and they were called…

Drum roll needed here – so I supplied a sort of fanfare.

"Say"

"Say what?" I said, rather let down.

"No, Say, S-a-y. The tomb is of Sir John Say and his wife. '*Bra or Bor where one Says…*' The Says were bigwigs around there at that time. I'm certain she heard mass at or near St Augustine's Broxbourne. And I bet the letter was left there with someone."

"But it won't still be there" I said, a wee bit dismissively.

"If it was hidden it might be. Maybe Mary never had time or opportunity to use it."

"But if this note of the Cecils is true, then they will have gone looking for it" I replied.

"But did they find it? Who knows? Let's go as soon as possible."

"Look" I reasoned " if it's survived unfound for 500 years, I think it would be dreadful luck if it was found tonight! We'll go in the morning. Unless Julie needs the car."

Wednesday was a waste. Julie was happy to let us have the car providing we took her shopping first in Reading.

"I can't afford the shops in Guildford. Who can?"

On our way to Reading it occurred to me that Julie's general offer of the car for my use was actually a very clever ploy to get herself a personal chauffeur. Not just that, Rydal came too and was entrusted with all her purchases as they wandered round the stores, so she had a sort of personal shopper as well. By the time we got back up Stag Hill it was early afternoon and if we were to beat the onset of evening, we would have to motor.

But Julie wanted to eat and sick of refectory food she fancied a nice pizza and she knew just the place. So, frustratingly, we all sat round a table in Pizza Vicenza in the centre of town, no nearer Hertfordshire than hours ago. She could afford the restaurant prices in Guildford because we were paying them!

We gave it up. Rydal studied. I shopped for supplies and clothes, clothes that my alter ego, Jim Jarvis would approve of. Should I pop into the salon to have my whiskers trimmed – Ah no!

At least we got a better day on the Thursday and with Julie safely tucked up in bed, 'Sloth had undone her', we set off early. Mistake! Grindingly slow progress in the rush hour round the evil M25, followed by a zillion road works in Hertfordshire meant it was midday before we pitched up in front of St Augustine's.

"Still at least we are here" I said as I clicked the latch, only it wouldn't click. Locked! It had never occurred to me that it wouldn't be open. Then I did a most unchristian thing and swore and kicked the door. More seriously, Rydal was reading the notice which told us if we wished to see the interior the key was available at number seven Church Street.

We knocked on the door of the modest semi-detached bungalow and were greeted by fierce, violent and prolonged barking. The door opened to reveal an old toothless man just restraining a young and far from toothless Alsatian.

"Yus?"

"Sorry to trouble you" I said "but have you got the key to the church? We fancied having a look round."

"Enid! Kay!"

I kept one eye on the Alsatian which was showing a great interest in my trouser leg and one eye out for the approach of Enid and or Kay. It was Enid, who had some teeth, since as she came down the hall, she was fitting them in.

Kay turned out to be the 'key' and she was brandishing it. I took it gingerly from Enid and was off down the drive sharpish.

St Augustine's was a beautiful old church by the river. Inside it was grand and inspiring with arches on both sides of the nave all the way to the altar. There were plenty of Say family tombs clustered in the church. The grandest being that of Sir John Say and his wife dated 1474. We looked around for obvious hiding places but there weren't any. The tombs had doubtless been renovated many times down the centuries. The chancel walls and arches looked original though. As we searched, rather forlornly, it was becoming more obvious that Mary, or her retainers, had probably entrusted it to **someone** and that it could be anywhere.

There was loose and crumbling masonry and marble, there was newly renovated spick and span masonry. But there were also untouched areas which had stood the test of time. If the Cecils' men had searched the church, they obviously hadn't explored these and so we poked and prised, hoping the vicar or verger wouldn't come tearing down the aisle shouting "Oi!"

It was Rydal who pressed a rather dull floor tile at the base of the tomb, it slid back and inside a small hollow there was something. It was grey and crumbly with age but it was definitely a written document. Our eyes met in astonishment. The thrill was akin to searchers with metal detectors coming upon a Saxon gold hoard.

Should we take it? Was it stealing? Desecration even? We eased our consciences by telling ourselves it was for a just cause. We almost crept out of the empty church. The key made a loud grating sound as we turned it. The toothless man's dog barked like a police dog at a felon when we returned the key. But we held firm and headed up the road for Hitchin. Ben would be pleased to see me – but needs must!

On the outskirts of Hitchin it was Rydal who put into words what we were both thinking. If we show this to Ben or anyone then it ceases to be our secret and becomes common knowledge. Do we want that? One day perhaps, but not yet. What do we want it for? To help Maria and to deal in some unspecified way with our nemesis – the Professor. Caution told us to turn round, well not just caution, I didn't fancy getting any closer to Ben to be honest.

We turned round and headed for home.

"We'll just have to become experts on Tudor documents." said Rydal.

"You will" I replied "I've got a date with a certain destroyer from the 1940's."

So we took the document to Rydal's room. Before we could even look at it, Rydal had an email from Helen.

'Hi Rydal

Any news of Stephen? Don't worry you can tell me, I won't let on. The very idea of his planning to bump off his best friend is ridiculous.

I'm going down to Marlow again to see his family. Did I tell you I went the other day? They're so worried and his Dad is such a sweetie I enjoy comforting him. Am finding my sea-legs (or is it river-legs?) too, messing about on boats!

Cheers

Helen'

This cheery and fairly tasteless (it has to be said) email concerned me in several ways. I couldn't see Helen myself, and I needed to, but she seemed almost more fond of my family than I was! Also I was stupidly jealous of the fact Gerald might be leering at her and worse in my absence. Curse Jim Jarvis! The very celibate Jim Jarvis. The only female company I had had was the shopping-mad Julie and the incomprehensible cleaning lady!

Slowly Rydal unrolled the parchment, or whatever it was, only it more crumbled than unrolled and bits fell off. We were in danger of destroying what might be a vital Tudor document. What could we do?

"Put it in the fridge" I suggested, for no very clear reason. I had heard that such things should be kept cool.

But Rydal had immense patience and he proceeded very slowly and carefully. Hours later we had at least part of it flat – we couldn't actually read it but perhaps with magnification.

However with luck the greeting and the final signature had survived and were larger and clearer than the rest. Well, relatively so. The letter, it was one, was addressed to someone called Thomas and was signed by someone of the same name. More than that as yet wasn't definite. But it was likely that the letter was written to a Thomas Wyatt, but which one and when? The date was very faint and given that it was secretary hand as well, hard to decipher.

I left Rydal to it. I could tell he couldn't wait to get started. He was going to enlist the help of some history students he knew. It was time that I turned to World War II again.

CHAPTER 14

Money was becoming a problem. Despite Rydal's generosity it was hard to see how I could carry on as Jim Jarvis. My salary was still being paid but straight into my account which I daren't access. I'm sure my flat in Spitalfields was being watched and also my family in Marlow, in case I turned up. Julie's car needed petrol and I could hardly ask Julie to fill it for me. This couldn't go on.

However, the internet was available in the University courtesy of Rydal's student card and the following day I was ensconced in the library/learning centre. It was cold, windy and wet outside. The rain was rattling on the windows. The place was humming with activity, students cramming for exams or just putting in a shift before the Christmas break, which wasn't far off.

Wikiboats, first stop, gave me the bare bones about HMS Hotspur. The destroyer was built in the 1930's and was involved in the Spanish Civil War, albeit in a peaceful capacity. In World War II it participated in the battles at Narvik, Dakar and Cape Matapan. By April/May 1941 it was part of the Med fleet and involved in the evacuations of the defeated British and Australian troops from Crete to Alexandria. I'm sure my father was on board then, given his reaction to my probing. For interest I followed the future of the ship – it was pretty uninspiring – the Far East in 1942 but no real action, then escorting convoys across the Atlantic until the end of the war.

It finished up being sold to the Dominican Republic and renamed 'Trujillo', then 'Duarte', finally being scrapped in 1972.

The detail of the evacuation I got from several sites. Roughly it went like this:

On May 28, 1941 the decision was made to evacuate troops from Heraklion. The troops, who had crossed the island to Heraklion in all sorts of dramatic and romantic ways embarked in the early hours of May 29. The ships were underway by 03.20 hours. Admiral Rawlings was now in overall command. HMS Imperial was struggling at 03.45, the steering having jammed. She narrowly missed colliding with other ships. HMS Hotspur was sent to investigate. The order came to take everyone off HMS Imperial and they all jumped across. Having completed this successfully HMS Hotspur sank HMS Imperial with two torpedoes.

After this drama, the Hotspur, clearly overloaded by the British and the Australian troops from the Imperial, was attacked along with the rest of the fleet by Stuka dive bombers. But she made it into Alexandria – fortunately for me since I wouldn't have been born if Dad hadn't made it.

Now I saw why he might be reluctant to talk about his time on HMS Hotspur. From what we, Sonia and I had gleaned, Dad had actually fired torpedoes. So he literally sank HMS Imperial. Scuttling a ship is not something sailors like to talk about. But it was hardly his fault. I know just obeying orders is not much of a defence but in the end what else could they do, let the stricken ship become a German one!

I would chat to Dad about it and make him see it was nothing to be ashamed of. I was still no nearer seeing why Ella's boyfriend was so interested in this same event. But it didn't seem to be anything to do with Dad, the whole thing was just a bizarre coincidence I decided. But somehow that didn't satisfy me.

There was a bibliography supplied and just to make sure I thought I would take a look at one or two of the books. One in particular, the one I saw at Helen's which came from her World War II mad friend, Emily Sandford, not forgetting Len, he of the immaculate Jeep.

"Warfare at Sea World War II" was not on the shelves at the University. Bus into town and Guildford library produced the same result. As did a trip to Waterstones – it wasn't that old a book but it wasn't easy to find. I could buy it, or rather Rydal could, on Amazon but that would take some time. I wanted to see it now!

Back in Guildford Library, I got the assistant there to check all the local libraries and she found a copy still on the shelves in Hindhead.

I took the bus, I was now of course in full Jim Jarvis regalia. I could browse the cars in the garage and see if Ella was working before collecting the book.

I couldn't see her at her usual desk but Mirabel wasn't there either. I was pretty confident no one could recognise me so I strolled around the showroom admiring the gleaming black, silver and white machines. An open-topped black leather model caught my eye – unfortunately at the same time I caught a salesman's eye and sure enough, over he came.

"Lovely, isn't it, sir? Top speed of 160 and at cruising speed an amazing 40 to the gallon. What are you driving now, if I may ask?"

"No, you mayn't" I thought, but what I said was "a ZX3."

"Ah! Nice car. We could probably give you a good price for that against this beauty. What year?"

I made up a year! "09".

"Ah. Now Ella over there has got one of those" and to my horror he pointed and then waved as Ella and Mirabel came chatting and carrying coffee back to their desks.

He was beckoning her over, no doubt to confirm that the

ZX3 '09 would get a good price. Over she came.

But I wasn't there anymore. I was out of the showroom door and off down the road. Leaving an open-mouthed salesman, a bemused Ella and giggling Mirabel. I don't think she recognised me but I wasn't taking any chances.

Hindhead library was quiet on a Friday afternoon and I soon found what I was looking for on the shelves. Since I didn't have a library card and Rydal's student one wouldn't wash here , I settled down in a corner and turned to the chapter that dealt with the evacuation from Heraklion. All seemed straight-forward. I could find nothing significant at all. Just one sentence puzzled me slightly:

'Dominic Wiessel in his excellent 'Escape! The Story of Crete 1941' suggests the evacuation was a model one, always excepting his tantalising remark about the torpedoing of HMS Imperial.'

As I took the book back to the desk, I asked the assistant if they had Wiessel's book by any chance. She looked on the computer and said it should be on the shelves. I scoured them with no success. When I went back she said that books often go missing and shrugged. I gave it up; it would have to just go on tantalising.

Then an elderly lady grabbed my arm.

"Excuse me, young man, but I overheard you asking about weasels. Library assistants are not like they were in my day – I worked at The Bristol Library you know. I think you will find what you are looking for here."

And she pointed imperiously at the flora and fauna section. It seemed quicker and far less complicated to take a look rather than explain. So I did. She kept her eyes trained on me. So I felt obliged to look more closely. All the while regretting my decision not to tell her it was Wiessel not weasel. But then, there it was, actually in the flora section but nevertheless the book I wanted. Someone had returned it lazily into that section and but for the elderly lady...

She accepted my thanks with pride.

"I haven't lost it you know, after all these years. Once a librarian always a librarian as they say."

I had never heard anyone say that but I refrained from telling her, nor did I show her the book itself. She left smiling serenely, apart from casting a withering look at the assistant.

Wiessel seemed to agree that the operation went off smoothly, almost perfectly. He detailed the delay occasioned by the problems to HMS Imperial and the rescue effected by the Hotspur. I was skim reading I suppose, a bad habit of mine, and as usual nearly missed a significant passage:

'It was thought that HMS Imperial had suffered only a near miss earlier but it turned out that the rudder had been damaged. Its steering became erratic and it narrowly avoided a collision with several warships. Admiral Rawlings decided that with time of the essence HMS Imperial had to be sacrificed. HMS Hotspur was ordered to pull alongside the damaged ship and all personnel, soldiers and crew, transferred across. But it seems there were several Australians below deck much the worse for drink and they had to be left. HMS Hotspur pulled away and torpedoed the Imperial which sank with the Australians still on board.'

Astonished by this I hastily went to a computer desk and got on the internet. On Google I typed in *'Crete, Imperial, Hotspur'* and found a site www.crosswaite.plus.com and once on this read with increasing alarm:

'At around 03.45 the Imperial's steering, evidently damaged the previous day, suddenly failed. Her rudder jammed over

and she swung around, narrowly missing Kimberley, Dido and Orion before disappearing astern flashing "my rudder". Rawlings now stuck where he least wanted to be, was unsure whether to wait to see if the Imperial could be repaired or whether to transfer her troops to the Hotspur which had gone to investigate. The decision was made and everyone capable of jumping did so as the Hotspur drew level. Thus loaded, Hotspur set off, torpedoing the stricken Imperial at 04.45, and unfortunately sending to the bottom several Australians who were too drunk to move."

There followed an account of the attack by Stukas, the loss of several ships and the eventual arrival in Alexandria.

What was I to make of all this? I checked other websites and also the shelves on World War II history, admittedly this was only a small library. No mention at all of the drunken Australians. On the more 'official' Royal Navy websites the scuttling was rarely mentioned but if it was, it quite clearly stated that the crew were transferred (a euphemism for 'jumped') from the Imperial to the Hotspur, implying everyone escaped.

What was the truth? Where did Wiessel and Crosswaite get their information from, was one just using information got from the other? Wiessel was the likeliest source, but where did he get his information from? Why was there no mention of it on the other sites? That wasn't hard to fathom – if you'll pardon the pun!

Is this why Dad was so reluctant to discuss Crete and his time on the Hotspur? Was he working in the torpedo bay then, in the early hours of May 29? Did he fire the torpedo? Who knew what, when that torpedo was fired?

Perhaps he felt guilt. If so my heart went out to him. Had he been carrying guilt around with him since 1941? That was a dreadful thought. As long as no one brought the subject up, perhaps he was safe from its pangs. Of course, rationally, he should not feel guilty at all , he was following orders if he did fire and how could he know that there were men still on board.

The more I thought about it, the more unlikely the whole incident seemed. The Royal Navy, an institution I had grown up to admire and respect, especially as my Dad was in it, would never perpetrate such an atrocity. Dare one call it war crime? No. Wiessel and Crosswaite had their facts wrong or were simply quoting malicious rumour (German inspired?) as if it were fact.

But an uneasy feeling was slowly gaining ground and at the back of my mind something was nagging. What was it? Something I'd noticed in passing which chimed with my new 'knowledge' if that's what it was. It wouldn't come to the surface, not yet anyway.

It was another tortuous journey on public transport from Hindhead to Guildford. When I got back to my haven Rydal was waiting with good news. Williams had contacted him to say that forensic results suggested that Joe's hanging was suicide after all. Rydal said:

"Williams sounded crest-fallen as if his 'baby project' was in ruins. I imagine his superiors more or less told him, in the light of forensics, to drop the whole thing. He said I had to pass the message on, though I protested I'd not seen you, that you were no longer a suspect in the eyes of the Surrey constabulary and could come out of hiding. It wasn't a trick because I phoned my Dad who has some contacts at Scotland Yard and they confirmed much of what I thought. I'd still steer clear of Williams, mind, if I were you , he didn't sound so convinced."

So Jim Jarvis was no more! In elation I threw off his things "Off, off you lendings!" I didn't exactly do a naked jig, but almost. And that was the scene the cleaning lady walked in on, a bemused student applauding a near naked dancing older man! Fortunately, **near** naked!

All she said was:

"Bloody student! All the same!" and beat a hasty retreat.

Of course, euphoria was short lived. What was there to celebrate? Joe was still dead. I, for one, had this in common with poor Williams (was I feeling sorry for my nemesis?) I sensed Joe's death was not suicide, forensics or not. And I had, possibly, a father with a guilty secret.

Nevertheless, it was still a relief to head back to 303, where my legitimacy as a resident was albeit not much greater. Later that evening, after a few drinks at the Union Bar, in a sort of semi-drunken ritualistic ceremony, Rydal and I consigned Jim's false whiskers and his clothes to the lake. The strains of "Pack up all my cares and woe, here I go singing low, bye bye Jarvis" could be heard wafting over the campus. One could imagine even Stig and his brood would prick up their ears, used as they were to drunken student revelry.

Why was it always in the early hours, often after drink, that things at the back of my mind drifted to the front? As I lay there with dawn breaking I heard again the tones of Ella's boyfriend in that hotel lobby in Crete and the accent, so elusive then, spoke clearly to me now of bush and outback. Australia! Benjy's origins had never been in doubt because his accent was so strong and now his mysterious arrival on Crete began to make some sort of sense.

There wasn't much research I could do at the weekend. I had more or less exhausted the internet, finding nothing else of note. It was hardly going to have the details of Australians on board HMS Imperial in May 1942 on its way from Heraklion to Alexandria as part of an evacuation. Would they be on any list? All sorts of stragglers attached themselves to vessels briefly just to get out, I imagine. Perhaps they were crew? Unlikely given their drinking, but possible.

I thought the weekend of my new found freedom was ideal for visiting. And I had plenty of people to visit: Dad, Helen and Ella to name but three. But there was another person I had forgotten , well not forgotten, more put to the back of my mind for the time being. And she visited me.

It was about ten in the morning when there was a knock on the door and I opened it to a vision of loveliness. Maria. Not as I remember her, pale and unconscious, the ice-maiden, nor the recuperating girl of Portsmouth but the young healthy and astonishingly beautiful student. I gawped I suppose. Maria smiled, clearly used to this and said:

"Hi, Stephen, how are you? I thought I would just say hello, Rydal said you were back and no longer under suspicion. Can I come in?"

Stupidly, I had left her standing at the door, so confused and overwhelmed as I was.

She was dressed simply in blue jeans, trainers and a blue American University sweater – University of Boise – how on earth do you pronounce that? "Oh, I see you went to Bwas, Boyce, Boees!" Rydal told me later that it was the even more unlikely 'Boysie'.

She startled me by her desire to know whether she should go to Joe's funeral or not. Apparently, the new inquest had confirmed suicide, Williams having thrown in the towel, and Joe was being cremated on Monday, the day after tomorrow.

"I don't know what to do? Everyone tells me I was close to him, very close. But to me he's a stranger. I am sorry for him and his family but I don't grieve. I'm very unhappy because I feel so guilty but I don't grieve."

And she began to cry. So I put my arm round her. Beast that I was! And comforted her because she couldn't cry for my best friend, who I should be crying for, not cuddling the girl he was in love with. What strange situations life puts us in. I was also aware that if Rydal were to suddenly walk in then I would have betrayed two friends at once. Not to mention Helen. Three! And yet I knew I wanted to hold her not just to comfort her.

"I don't think you should go to the funeral," I found myself saying, "it would upset Ella very much and the family. They would hate you and you don't deserve it. I have to go but I'm expecting hostility – the fact that I was suspected for a while will make that inevitable. But you can and should stay away."

"It's what I thought" she sobbed "thanks for your advice. I knew you would help. I'd like to stay but I promised to help Rydal with this letter he's translating. You know, the one you found. It's all very intriguing."

When she left, the room seemed dull and flat, empty of her beauty. And I felt the same. This wouldn't do, I had a girl-friend, albeit one I didn't completely trust. And it was high time I went to see her.

Helen was working, one of her friends told me, so I went up to the ward at the hospital. Something I wasn't supposed to do. She gave me a beaming smile and a hug, what a morning. First a goddess cries on my shoulder, then a sexy nurse hugs me! What next!

Next was a sudden realisation as we chatted about my resumption of normal service and our similar resumption that there was in Helen's enthusiastic responses to my questions about my family, she had recently seen much more of them than I had , the faintest, tiniest, almost but not quite non-existent trace of an Australian accent. My face betrayed nothing, but alarm spread through my mind. Was I imagining Australian accents because of some sort of new found guilt about HMS Imperial and my father?

Helen's behaviour began to acquire a pattern in retrospect. The fact was I couldn't trust her at all but had to keep her sweet if only to find out what, if anything, was going on. So I agreed to take her down to Marlow with me as soon as. We found an empty room and shared a long passionate embrace, once again I was being offered something which at a later date would probably be withdrawn. But I was wise to this by now.

I rang Sonia and invited myself and Helen for Sunday

dinner, explaining that I was now not part of any police investigation and that I could do with some family time, given the ordeal that I was going to have to face on Monday.

Sonia was full of praise for Helen. "What a girl, stick with her Stephen, she's been an absolute trooper whilst you went missing. Always down here, comforting Dad especially and spending a lot of time with him to try and stop him worrying."

"Really?" I thought.

The rest of the day was lazy. I drank a few beers with Osbert and we watched the match on TV. Villa beat the Arsenal 3-0, so we were both happy. Osbert was off to celebrate with the University of Surrey Aston Villa Supporters Club – otherwise known as Osbert and friend.

Rydal and Maria were together in his room poring over the letter – was I jealous? I left them to it.

I went for a walk off campus. Nodding to the stag and family, a quick look in the cathedral, it was full and very solemn things were being intoned solemnly, and off into the hills. If only, actually the sprawl beside the roaring noise of the A3. But I spent the time thinking, 'figuring' as the Americans might say, and searching for a pattern in all the mess.

Since Rydal and Maria were tackling Wyatt, I would concentrate on HMS Imperial. That meant talking to Dad about it, without Helen, but also watching Helen when the subject could be raised between the three of us. That was Sunday's task. Monday there was a funeral to get through. After that Ella might need consolation and I might be able to spot lover boy. The following days would be searching for any information on and verification of the drunken Australian allegation. Who knew where that might lead? "I've never been to Oz" I said to myself jokingly!

My ramblings had taken me down towards the railway station. Lost in thought, I hadn't intended to arrive there, or had I? Since I had ceased to be Jim Jarvis, using Julie's car had become awkward to say the least and she was cooling on the arrangement too, not enough willingness to shop I expect. Anyway, she had got it back. It was ridiculous, I know, but I thought I might just as well take a peek in the car park. I knew I would find an empty space, a burnt out shell, a monstrosity on bricks or something worse, perhaps a million parking tickets blotting out the windscreen.

I imagined the phone call to Norbert Dent. How sticky he would be about what fate had befallen one of his firm's courtesy cars.

I was stopped short in my reverie by the sight of the car, exactly where I had left it. And none the worse for wear. I still had the keys in my pocket. At the very least I expected a flat battery. Not even that. It hummed to life beautifully. I had a set of my own wheels again.

As far as I was concerned it was up to Williams or Norbert to let me know when I no longer had use of it. Like a boy-racer, I shot up the hill, tooting the horn and laughing. I gave Stig a few toots as I careered round the corner into the campus and nearly into a camper van coming the other way. The driver gave me 'the Surrey snarl' as we had come to call the ungracious driving habits of that county but that was all.

CHAPTER 15

It was a bright sunny, if cold, morning in Marlow as Dad, Helen and I walked by the river. Crews were rowing past, the famous bridge was choked with cars and people, the town looked its best. But I suspect none of us was interested. I think Dad knew what was looming. We were on the High Street, Helen had popped into a shop and I seized my chance.

"You know when you took part in the evacuation from Heraklion, Dad?" I said pointedly.

"I told you not to mention that again." was his guarded reply.

I ignored it. I had to know.

"What happened to HMS Imperial?"

He went very still and silent. I thought he wasn't going to answer.

"We scuttled it on Rawlings' orders" he said quietly "it's not something I'm proud of, but it had to be done, the ship was damaged and would have fallen into enemy hands. So as soon as everyone was off, the order came and we fired."

"Whose 'we' exactly?"

"Myself on one torpedo and Johnny Jackson on the other. Always two if possible, so no one knows who sank the ship."

"And everyone was off" I was relentless but had to be quick. I could see Helen paying for her card (a friend's birthday). "Everyone?"

"Yes, that's what we were told."

"What about", heart in mouth, "the Australians below too drunk to move?"

"Oh, that old chestnut. We were assured by the top brass that was a propaganda idea put out by the Jerries. An attempt to drive a wedge between the Allies; it happened all the time in the war" he said, a mite too defensively for my liking.

As Helen negotiated the traffic, I asked Dad:

"Honestly, Dad, do you believe the 'top brass'? Because I read about these drunken soldiers in a reputable history book."

Angrily (I rarely saw him angry, such a mild-mannered man) he replied "What are you trying to say Stephen, that I torpedoed a ship with our soldiers still on board? Nonsense – the Navy would never do that! I'll find my own way back" and he turned on his heel and walked away.

Was I satisfied? Satisfied that Dad believed them then and now – almost. What he didn't know and what pained me, was that I was asking for his benefit.

Helen crossed the road to me, puzzled by Dad's sudden departure.

"I said something about the war in the Med which upset him."

Helen started momentarily, I saw surprise register on her face but very quickly, though not quite quickly enough, she resumed her composure:

"What did you say?"

"Oh, it's nothing important. I'll tell you later. Let's enjoy the morning without old grumpy" and I laughed it off.

Her sparkling conversation and obvious come-on made me feel even more wary. What was she doing? We wandered back along the river and on a quiet stretch of path she kissed me on the lips.

"Don't you think, it's time, Stephen?" She said avidly.

"Look what I've got" and she dangled the key to Dad's cabin on the boat in front of me, just as we reached it.

On board, we locked the door and made use of the tiny bed. It was strange, our first love-making. Passionate but with a feeling of something held back or rather that there was another reason for this, other than passion that made it a little hollow. I was doing this to show I had nothing to suspect of her. She was doing it for much the same reason. The outcome was the opposite of what was intended.

As we strolled back along the bank to 'The Finches' in time for lunch, in the cold sunshine, my fears I knew were far from groundless.

Lunch was a glum affair. Dad was silent and brooding, Helen was too cheery to be genuine, the kids were fractious, Gerald subdued still since the Isabel affair and Sonia knackered after cooking dinner all morning that nobody seemed to have the stomach for. We fled early and I dropped Helen off at the hospital with a kiss and an invitation from her to come round soon for more of the same.

I gave Rydal's room a wide berth, not wanting to queer his pitch with Maria, though really of course wanting to do exactly that. I felt a heel having been with Helen on the boat only a few hours earlier but I consoled myself with the thought that her heart was certainly not engaged either.

I spent a fruitless time on the internet searching for a sailor called Johnny Jackson who was on board HMS Hotspur on that fateful morning in May 1941. Dad wasn't going to tell me any more about the incident. The Navy denied all knowledge of the Australians. I could contact the authors but I think they had told me all they knew in their books and blogs.

I had a list of personnel (well some of them) from HMS Hotspur but not restricted to 1941 never mind May. That would be a needle in a haystack. But then so was the second torpedo man!

And then late in the night, with the accompaniment of Osbert's mood music, I stumbled upon a site that gave me this. It was a reply to a general question about destroyers and their capabilities.

'Yes. Destroyers did have two torpedo 'chutes' as you call them. And it sometimes meant no one knew who fired the torpedo that sunk the ship. My grandad was one. That's how I know!'

And this was from Gilbert R Jackson, dated fairly recently.

So I got in on the act and asked the redoubtable Gilbert if his grandfather was ever on HMS Hotspur. Talk about a long shot.

Within minutes, and that's the wonder of the Web, came a reply:

'Yes Sir! My grandad was John Jackson and he served on HMS Hotspur from 1939 to 1945 – he claimed to have sunk several Nazi ships during his time. I know this because he left a detailed war diary – I never actually knew him, he died before I was born.'

Bingo! Not perhaps regarding the last sad statement but Bingo! nevertheless.

We struck up quite a conversation and by two in the morning I had an invite to go and see the diary. The trouble was it was in Cheshire, and Gilbert was going way for several months. He wouldn't or couldn't fax me a copy. So I had to be in Cheshire, Bramhall to be precise, by the following afternoon. That meant leaving immediately after Joe's funeral in the morning and racing up north.

I got a couple of hours sleep and donned my best and only suit and tie for something I never thought I would attend. I went by train into London. The church was near Waterloo, so a brisk walk and I was there for ten. Just. The church was packed, I was at the back but could see Ella down at the front and the Liefs across the aisle from her. There was no love lost between them. The Liefs had always objected to Queen Eleanor as they called her and resented her largesse – she was very rich and had been pretty generous but expected a lot in return. I was more interested in who was with Ella, but there were only her folks. No mysterious boyfriend. Nor could I see him anywhere in the church.

The vicar gave the usual bland if sincere sermon, clearly not having any real idea who Joe was and being careful to skate round the awkwardness of suicide. I was lost in sadness by the end – thinking of when I found him and how his murder was being erased from history. I vowed not to let that happen.

Afterwards I spent time with the Liefs, remembering the good times and said a few words to Ella who was particularly acerbic.

"Didn't think you'd dare show your face here. After all it's only a week ago the police were looking for you. I, for one, am still not totally convinced…"

She stopped short, as a Lief uncle drifted over to offer condolences.

I didn't go to the buffet lunch at the pub across the road. I hung around outside hoping to see 'boyfriend' but failed to. I cursed the fact I had to leave so soon. But I had a train to catch. Taxi to Euston and Intercity to Manchester. In under two hours I was on Stockport station waiting for a train to Bramhall. Ten minutes later I was walking the plush tree lined suburb in search of Carshalton Close.

Number 17 was a long low bungalow owing something to ante-bellum mansions in its style, boasting veranda and pillars. Gilbert himself opened the door.

"Ah, Mr Johnson, good to meet you" his vigorous hand-shake nearly broke my wrist. "In here, we'll leave the good Doris to her packing." I got a brief glimpse of the good Doris, a harassed lady surrounded by bags and suitcases.

Gilbert took out a leather bound diary from his desk drawer, holding it like a piece of fragile china and opened it at the relevant page – May 28/29 1941. I began to read:

'Trev Johnson and me were on duty that night. I'd been asleep all day, so had Trev. We'd heard that Imperial was a gonner, drifting into other boats. Then we heard that Rolly Rawlings had said sink her. Me and Trev went up on deck. It was black but the lights were all on as we got alongside and blow me, they all jumped. There were some wounded and they were having to jump too. Poor sods. One or two were sort of thrown into the arms of mates of mine. It was all a bit crazy. Someone shouted across 'hang on, wait, there's men below.' A captain came up on deck on the Imperial and said 'they're bloody drunk, I can't shift em.' I heard shouts of 'help them' – it was all confused. I saw more men come across and I thought it was them, they were Aussies and a bit the worse for drink. Then we went below and Bang! Trev and I went back up and watched the poor old Imp disappear into the Med.

About an hour later when we came off duty, we met an Aussie corporal who, still drunk, swore at us, called us 'murdering bastards' and took a swipe at me. It was Trev who separated us.'

"Strong stuff, eh" said Gilbert "but there's more".

He then turned to May 31st.

'Had a good chat with that Aussie corporal, sober now, but still angry. He didn't blame me or Trev. He said that some of his mates had been drinking since they left Heraklion and had passed out or were in a bad way. He shouted for help but everyone was dashing up on deck so as not to miss Hotspur. In the end he had no choice, he said a quick prayer and ran. He only just made it. 'I lost good mates' he said 'Jack Erdington, Dean Smith, Joe Lescott and Ben Summers all from Melbourne, like me' and he wept and wept. I made a point of remembering the names. It was the least I could do. I feel bad but I swear to God I thought they were off. Some of the officers knew though, I reckon. Trev never spoke much to

me after that and in Alex we got separated and ended up on different ships. Sometimes I wonder if he knew more than he was saying.'

And that was it. According to Gilbert there was nothing more relevant. He said I was welcome to read the whole diary whilst he went on packing. I was grateful and decided there and then to do just that, I would find a hotel for the night. Gilbert and Doris were leaving at nine so I skimmed the diary. Gilbert was right, that was it. He photocopied the relevant pages for me. We shook hands and I wished him Bon Voyage. They were flying at eleven to New York – "as long as Doris takes her calm-me-down pills." She was looking a bit twitchy as I left. I took a taxi to Stockport and got a room at the Britannia Hotel which the taxi driver recommended. The next morning I re-read the diary and puzzled over it as we hurtled back down England to Euston. When I finally got back to Guildford I knew the names off by heart – it was like a sad litany:

'Jack Erdington, Dean Smith, Joe Lescott and Ben Summers all from Melbourne'.

I knocked on Rydal's door. I wasn't going to just burst in in case Maria had stayed the night. He opened the door and it was clear Maria hadn`t stayed. Rydal looked pretty downcast:

"She wouldn't stay" he said "to be honest she only stayed to help me with the letter. Her heart's not in it, what we had has vanished. I suppose it wasn't much anyway, Mr Lief was more her style even then. Now it's you."

Said without a hint of bitterness or jealousy. Just stated as a fact. I tried to brush it off as nothing, but my head was pounding. Rydal explained that she had made no secret of her feelings for me and he had to listen to all that. No wonder he looked downcast.

But at the mention of the letter he perked up. "I'm doing

well and I promise you it's amazing. I don't understand it all, I'm not a historian. Just wait until it's complete and then I'll go through it all."

I shared my news with him about the Australians.

"Well" he said "it looks like we're both busy on separate tracks at the moment. Let's give ourselves a few days then have a big pow-wow."

It was calmly said but I could read between the lines. Rydal wanted a few days to 'get over' Maria and all I could do was agree.

So I spent the rest of the day on the internet. The Department of Justice in Melbourne, Victoria was where copies of the births, marriages and death certificates were held for that city and that state. There were indexes and the actual certificates could be ordered online for a fee, naturally. I also found the telephone directory for the city of Melbourne. Records of servicemen who died in World War II were on a different site – but that was fairly easy to access too.

I started with the service records – not surprisingly there were no records of death in 1941 for any of the names. If it happened, and I trusted Johnny Jackson on this, then it didn't happen officially. It may be that the Australians just didn't know and were never told. But what about the families? Sons and husbands who went to war and never came back. What was the explanation?

That was found soon enough. There was a website devoted to Australian soldiers missing in action, presumed dead. And they were all on it. Jack Erdington, Dean Smith, Joe Lescott and Ben Summers. The relatives had been informed in all cases. And that was it. No mention of the ship. They weren't part of the crew, they were part of an Australian company which was fighting alongside the British in Crete and I suppose the relatives believed they never made it off the island. From what I could gather from the various accounts, it was a sudden chaotic withdrawal, with confused messages to soldiers to get to Heraklion whichever way they could. Lots of soldiers never made it and if they were found then there were details of when and where on Crete. But not everyone was accounted for by any means.

But would the relatives be satisfied by this? Might they have heard rumours? Perhaps the Australians who did return, even the one who spoke to Johnny Jackson, made a point of going to see the relatives to tell them the truth. Maybe a fuss was made but probably they got nowhere. The Navy was very good at closing ranks. Cover-ups were a British wartime speciality.

But I would have a bloody good try at tracking the families down. So I started with Jack Erdington.

CHAPTER 16

The Melbourne phone book had only three Erdingtons listed. There could well be some ex-directory, but what could I do about those? It was the dead of night in Melbourne and phone calls would be horrendously expensive. I needed email addresses – but how could I get these?

P Erdington	5 Woolabong Road, Torquay
J J Erdington	The Cliffs, Melbourne 16
S Erdington	Zimarra Drive, Toowonga, Melbourne

I used Google to explore all three and got lucky with P Erdington who had a computer business in Melbourne and a contact number for Torquay. His email was supplied. If only he was in Devon, I thought. I fancied a trip down to Torbay, scene of many a dull holiday!

What to put in the email? I was unusual having a dad who was in the War. In most cases it would be grandads surely. It's just my dad was quite old when I was born. Should I ask about grandads or just relatives? In the end I settled for this:

'Hi there,

I'm English and I am at the University of Surrey in Guildford, near London. I am researching the evacuation of Crete in WW2 and am trying to find the descendants of a Jack

Erdington who I believe was on HMS Imperial at some point.
I found your email address online. I hope you don't mind me
contacting you.
  Stephen Johnson'

With a click of the mouse it winged its way across the world
and arrived on a computer in Melbourne. I would have to wait
until P Erdington got to work and looked at his emails. Unless,
of course, they were re-routed to his home. And he was up all
night looking at them!

But no. By the time I went to bed there was nothing. When
I woke, still nothing. Who knows, perhaps P Erdington
dismissed me as a nutter, maybe he was on holiday on the
Barrier Reef or Ayers Rock or wherever.

But just after breakfast I got a reply. Predictable really…

'Hi Stephen
  Thank you for the old email, Pom. (Just a joke!)
  Not my relative. We only came out from England in 1976,
from Torquay would you believe! The wife insisted (or should
I say Sheila!) we move to Torquay in Victoria.
  But I tell you what, I'll do some scouting around for you,
see if I can root out any Erdingtons in Melbourne. They could
be my relatives, since some of my family did come from Oz.
  Be in touch.
  Bruce (joke!!) Phil really!'

What began as a thoroughly disappointing email had
improved startlingly by the end. I decided not to contact the
other Erdingtons but to wait on Phil's detective work.

In time if he was interested he could help me with the other
names. I gave Dean Smith a miss, having briefly seen that
Smith was as common in Melbourne as it was in Guildford!
There was only one Lescott in the phone book and using
Google on Godfrey J Lescott (who lived in the delightfully

named Ferntree Gully area) produced another stroke of luck. Godfrey J had a bookshop, lived in it for all I could tell and supplied an email address. It was evening in Melbourne and worth a shot. So I sent the same email with the names changed.

An hour later I hit the jackpot!

'Dear Mr Johnson (bless him – it was like a letter)

Thank you for your enquiry. I am usually asked about books, sometimes ones about family history, invariably relating to Great Britain. But this is the first time I have been asked about my grandfather Joseph.

My father told me that his father, Joseph Lescott, was on Crete in World War Two and was thought to have died there but his body was never found. However, in 1946 my grand-mother, Hetty Lescott, received a letter from a Corporal Parnaby saying that Joseph had died when HMS Imperial was sunk en route from Heraklion to Alexandria. He was certain of this because he was on board too but survived and he had seen and spoken to Joseph.

We researched this further and discovered that HMS Imperial was scuttled by HMS Hotspur because it was badly damaged and so that it would not fall into enemy hands. Most of the crew and soldiers on board escaped by jumping onto HMS Hotspur. But at least four Australians, including Joseph, couldn't. We never told my grandmother that it was because they were drunk!

Naturally we raised the whole thing with the authorities but met with a stone wall and a deafening silence. We could never prove anything and all efforts to trace Corporal Parnaby's descendants proved fruitless. So we gave it up.

Do you have new information? If so I would be very interested to hear from you.

Regards

Godfrey Lescott'

This was fascinating, essentially confirming Johnny Jackson's diary.

That seemed to be the end of the Google trail for the time being. Ben Summers was a complete dead end, nothing in the phone book or on the internet. So I replied to Godfrey – thanking him and assuring him that should I have any new information I would email him at once. I would just have to wait and hope Phil Erdington could help.

And just as I was about to switch off the computer this pinged through the ether and changed the rest of my day.

'Dear Mr Johnson,

Sorry to trouble you. Rather slipshod of me but I forgot something you perhaps should know. During the course of our researches, we came across a family in Melbourne called Jones who seemed to be exploring the same thing. They (there were several of them, I don't recall their names) said that their grandfather was called Summers and that he had possibly drowned off Crete when a ship was sunk by its own allies. They were very confused, not what you would call reliable witnesses.

However, and here is where it is particularly relevant to you, they said that Mr Summers' eldest grandson was living in London. They also claimed that he was occasionally researching there. Their attitude towards him was rather dismissive. I felt they were somewhat disorganised so I can't imagine what this member of the Summers clan was like.

This all happened over five years ago now so the trail might be cold. But, fortunately, I retained the name and address of said grandson. And I supply it here:

B Summers
8 Thorley Walk
Stratford
London

Something of a poet and musician I believe. A pity he was not
a Bard of Avon. If I recall, I think his name was Benjamin.
Regards
Godfrey J Lescott'

Something of a musician! I could hear his strumming coming round the corner even now. I knew that I hadn't seen the last of him.

My mind was already calculating how long it would take me to get to Stratford. Living in Spitalfields, I knew exactly how to get there.

In the end it took what seemed like no time at all. The trains were all on time. Everything synchronised. Maybe it was because of the coming Olympic games that East London had finally got its act together. The stadium was already there and it looked pristine, if a little smaller than I imagined. There were huge shopping malls being built – it wasn't Stratford as I knew it. But I liked it, the air was full of promise and even expectation.

But then so was I. At last, I felt I was getting close to the truth. I was expecting a lot from Benjamin.

Except he didn't live there anymore. Nobody did. Thorley Walk had gone to make way for 2012. It was due to go anyway and not soon enough, the old cynic on the corner told me. He also told me that everyone had been re-housed, in some cases in much better accommodation and still nearby. I asked him where the local pub was – it seemed the best way to start looking for Benjamin. My first plan had been to check out any buskers in the fancy new stations being erected but the sleek new lines didn't have the right acoustics one forlorn tramp told me when I asked where the buskers had all gone.

The local 'boozer' was the Duke of York and I had the landlord mostly to myself – the recession was biting hard in East London. The landlord was jowly with a big nose and a gravelly voice, he would have been right at home behind the bar in the Winchester Club. I knew about such things because Big Vinyl was also a fan of 'Minder'.

The minute I mentioned an ageing hippy with a guitar, his face lit up.

"Benjy, you mean, he used to sing here from time to time. Not much good to be honest, don't tell him that! Not seen him for a while but I know someone who'll know where he is and she's in the back. Joy!"

I wasn't sure whether he was thrilled she was in the back or that was her name. But from the kitchen came the epitome of what health and safety was invented for. She had a half-made sandwich in her hand, a fag with a ridiculously long ash (how do they do that?) in her mouth and the grubbiest apron I have ever seen.

"Wotcha darlin'."

It was Chas and Dave time again.

"This young man is asking about Benjy. Do you know where he is now?"

She looked me up and down. The ash dropped onto the sandwich as she laughed then coughed. When her hacking cough stopped minutes later she said:

"He's gone into town. He works part time in a club in Soho. The London Kit Kat, Wardour Street. Buy him a drink and give him a kiss from me. Tell him I'm still here in the Duke if he ever fancies a cuddle."

More laughter, more coughing, more ash!

I thought of stopping off at the flat in the market but I didn't want to miss Benjamin so I stayed on the Central Line to Holborn and then took the Piccadilly Line to the Circus. I knew what sort of club to expect. And though the Master of Ceremonies would not say 'Wilkommen, Bienvenue, Welcome' and Sally Bowles would not be singing, the atmosphere would be similar.

The place was deserted. Not even a faintly tipsy, yet some-what sullen and mysterious dancer. Just the sound of rag-time on a piano in a back room. And when I popped my head round the door, there he was!

He could have said 'Of all the gin joints... etc.' but then he wouldn't remember me. And I could tell from his quizzical expression he didn't.

"I'm Stephen Johnson. You must be Benjamin Summers. Joy said you'd be here. She sends her love."

"Hi, mate, what can I do for you? If you want a job there aren't any. The boss isn't here anyway. I'm just the music man."

There was no point in beating about the bush.

"I got your name from Godfrey Lescott in Melbourne. He met some of your family when he was researching what happened to his grandfather and yours during the War in Crete."

There it was all out. No bush left to beat.

Benjy's mouth dropped open. It took him a while to gather his thoughts.

"Wow!" he said "that was a surprise and no mistake. I was in Crete not so long ago, on the trail. Decided to give it up, though. Now in you come and off we go again. Was your grandad on that blasted ship too?"

"Not exactly" I replied "but I have an interest."

I told him who I was and that my dad was on the Hotspur and that I had heard rumours of what had happened. I left it as vague as I could.

He offered, very genially, to take me to the pub across the road and tell me all he knew. He didn't want to talk in the club because 'walls have ears'.

Settled with a whisky and chaser, not the first of the day I suspected, he began his story. I was, as you can imagine, an avid and increasingly astonished listener.

"Well, Steve" I love the instant familiarity of Australians.

"I've been over here a few years now. Came to watch the cricket, would you believe? Quite liked London, it was the music that really got to me. Can't live without it. Sure, there's opportunity in Melbourne but not like here. You can live by music here, all over the place. I had no real ties back home. So I just stayed.

The family understood. I've always been a rolling stone. Even in Oz, I would disappear and then contact them from Perth or Hobart or even Alice once. My sister asked if I could do a spot of researching the old Summers' family obsession. So now and again I had a go – but I'm not much good at that sort of thing. I guess you know what it's all about.

My grandad Ben – I was named after him – went down on the Imperial off Crete in '41. Together with some other Aussies. Drunk down below and torpedoed by the Brits. Officially, it didn't happen.

It's never been my obsession, Steve. Let it go, I think, what can you do about it now? But a few weeks ago I got a call from another Aussie in London. Don't know how he traced me but he said he was interested in the Imperial, bit like you Stevie?"

And he looked at me, but I kept my counsel. So on he went.

"Anyway, he said he had a lead. A man on Crete who knew all about it. His father or grandfather, I forget which, was on the ship too. And he had information to sell. Would I like to come along?"

Well I fancied some sun, I like London but not the weather. So I agreed. I met Rick at Heraklion Airport and went with him and his girlfriend to see this guy. It was all a bit cloak and dagger. We drove for miles to a small resort, Elounda, where they filmed that TV series 'Who Pays the Ferryman' and then we went on a boat and this grizzled old Greek fisherman told us what his father had told him about HMS Imperial.

The guy's father was one of the crew. He was one of the last to jump ship, literally they had to jump across. Before that he was ordered to check there was no one else on board. He went below and he heard a lot of shouting and cursing. He went towards it. There were four men, he said, Australians he thought. They were staggering about. There seemed to be a fight of some sort, or certainly an argument. He couldn't speak English but he tried to persuade them to go up on deck but they couldn't understand him. Then an English officer came down and ordered them on deck as the ship was going to sink. They ignored the officer, called him some names and started drinking again. The officer produced a revolver and ordered them to climb the stairs. But it was hopeless, they were too drunk. In fact one of them was more or less unconscious. The officer could do no more and left. The guy's father followed him. He wasn't allowed to be present when the officer spoke to the Captain. But later the officer found him on board HMS Hotspur and told him not to say anything about the drunken men. Ordered him. Then they watched as the Imperial was torpedoed and sank.

When the fishermen had told us this and Rick had given him wads of notes, he brought us back to shore. Rick was very, very angry. I was more sad. So sad I got myself some dope and tried to forget.

The next day Rick asked me if I wanted to help him. He scared me, I think he was mad. My folks are a bit obsessive but Rick was something else. His girlfriend didn't seem that bothered though. Rick said he had found a lot about HMS Hotspur and its crew – most were long dead. He was tracking down the ones that were still alive. But also, and this is a bit chilling, even the ones that were dead, if they were responsible, had kids and grand-kids! By then I really wanted out of it. I could tell my sister back home about the fisherman and his story but I wouldn't mention Rick.

Then it got really worrying. Rick said it was time for revenge. Said that was now his life's work and would I join him in it. 'Pay back the bastards' he said. 'The ones who gave the orders right down to the ones who carried them out.' I didn't want any part of that. I said I'd think about it and scooted out of Elounda fast. Trouble is, he knows I know about his plans. So I don't like being surprised. You're not from him, I guess. I sense you're okay, Stevie boy."

As he got more in his cups, he became a lot less cautious. I could easily have been from Rick. He had no proof I wasn't. He was very vulnerable. What he had told me had me worried for Dad.

I walked him back to the club, he was a bit unsteady. When I left, I heard the blues, not rag-time anymore, on the piano.

On my way back to Surrey, I texted Sonia and told her to look after Dad, he was precious. What more could I do? I needed to find Rick but Ella wouldn't tell me anything. I was determined to make a start in the morning but I was overtaken by events, as usual.

CHAPTER 17

I woke on Thursday morning with a bad hangover. Osbert had invited me to another of his parties when I got back the previous night. Like the other one, they spread far and wide throughout the campus. At one point I remembered sitting by the lake with some girl and talking Tudor history, about which I know little and quoting Wyatt's poetry. Not sure what happened next, but I think Rydal came to rescue me and put me to bed and Maria may have given me a goodnight kiss – I do hope so!

I also recall Rydal saying:

"We've finished the letter and it's amazing. Come round in the morning and we'll go through it. You won't be disappointed."

Nor would I if Maria would be there! So a quick shower and breakfast and by nine I was banging on his door. My banging head dulled by paracetamol. He opened the door bright and cheery as ever – did he ever drink?

He made me coffee – even his coffee was first class – and then showed me the version that he and Maria had produced, all in modern English, an accurate 'translation' he assured me. Just as he began reading, Maria arrived and it was all I could do to concentrate. Her very presence was now disturbing me so much.

Rydal read:

'To the Right Honourable Sir Thomas Wyatt, Knight
My dear Sir Thomas,

(This was modern? Rydal assured me it was as near as he could get).

Thank you for your letter which I received very safely from the courier. I am returning this with the same, he has been well fed and stayed the night. Rest assured he can be trusted to ensure that the letter does not fall into the wrong hands. And that only myself and one other besides you are privy to its contents.'

What a lot of words, saying very little. Rydal gestured me to be patient and carried on. Maria was laughing at the scene – what a gorgeous, gorgeous smile she had, but back to Rydal…

'Heartfelt thanks from the King to you for your desire to help in this matter. It is certain that the present Queen is guilty of the most heinous crimes including adultery with several persons. However, your agreement to allow rumours to circulate unopposed about your visit with the Queen to Calais will help and add substance to the accusations. These may even extend to the legitimacy of the Lady Elizabeth.

Fear not, loyal Sir Thomas, if the said rumours lead to a period of dwelling in the Tower, which will, I assure you, be made very comfortable to you. Your release will be certain and the gratitude of the King I can promise will be much. False rumours are nothing and the Wyatt family will prosper much under the present King and his legitimate heirs.

Your esteemed and humble servant
Thomas Cromwell'

"Wow!" I said immediately "Dynamite then and a different kind of dynamite now. That's if it's genuine!"

"Depends what you mean by genuine" said Rydal cryptically "It's a real letter from Henry VIII's Chief Minister, Thomas Cromwell to Thomas Wyatt, sent in 1536. We know 'cos we found it and it's certain that Mary Tudor hid it or one of her people did. But as to whether it tells the truth, that's another matter. Cromwell was notorious for being devious. As to whether the sentiments expressed by Cromwell and those attributed to Wyatt and also to the King are genuine, who knows? It was an age of spying and double-crossing.

I did some research. Thomas Wyatt was arrested and taken to the Tower along with several others accused of adultery with Queen Ann, all trumped up charges with no substance according to most historians, the others were all tortured and executed in horrible ways. It's thought Wyatt actually saw the execution of Ann from his window in the Tower. But Wyatt was released with no stain on his character, which is what the letter suggests. Also the Wyatt family prospered at Allington as a result of Henry's generosity. So I think Wyatt probably did agree to betray his former lover though maybe he had no choice, the rumours would have been circulated anyway and he might have shared the fate of the others – so is betrayal the right word? They key word is 'unopposed', Wyatt agreed not to defend himself or disprove the rumours for the time being to help the King. Cromwell could have circulated the rumours anyway but presumably Wyatt could easily have **disproved** them – which suggests they were untrue or, at least, that he had a very strong 'alibi' as it were."

"And" I added "it doesn't mean that he didn't have it off with Ann in Calais anyway. He could have been playing a double game. In fact, the truth is virtually impossible to know."

We paused in thought for a while.

"So where does this leave us now? And what do we do with this letter?" I asked.

Maria who had been listening attentively said "The first thing to do is to photocopy the original several times. And then store them in safe and different places. The original should be lodged with a solicitor."

She was right. In a way we should have done this by now. She offered to take the letter and copy it there and then on her printer which had a copying facility.

Whilst she was gone, Rydal and I agreed that to seriously damage Dove-Kemp's claims and also to make us all safe from his ruthlessness we should put the letter in the public domain as soon as possible. Some respected institution like the British Museum seemed the obvious place. And we needed a solicitor, like Maria said.

"No more narrow squeaks on country roads" I said "and no more fancy lectures hinting at historical bombshells."

We felt quite pleased with ourselves. At least one problem was about to be sorted. Maria didn't return immediately so we went down to the University refectory for a meal. After that I thought it was high time I saw Helen again on the assumption that 'keep your friends close but your enemies closer' was a wise idea. I didn't care to explore my other selfish motives. But if Helen was willing, why not?

But Helen was working; a note on her door informed me. So I strolled down into the town to clear my head. It was bright, if cold, the Wey was dappled in the sunlight, I had a coffee in the theatre overlooking the river then mooched around the very expensive shops. My phone rang as I was gazing at a fabulously expensive shirt in some glitzy Italian clothes shop, it was Rydal:

"Is Maria with you?"

"No" I replied "I thought by now she'd be with you."

"Well, no. I haven't seen her since she went to copy the letter. But I did check with her room-mate who has been in all day and she never arrived to copy anything. We checked the printer – no record. And now I can't find her anywhere and her phone is off."

Rydal was being a bit melodramatic, I thought. "Don't worry, she'll be okay. The amnesia doesn't affect her physically to any extent. She won't have collapsed or anything."

When I got back, Rydal was in a state, so was her room-mate Debbie. It wasn't like her to go missing with her phone off. Given what happened to her, she still felt quite vulnerable. As darkness fell, we became very anxious and rang the parents and the police. Rydal and I charged round campus asking all her friends if they had seen her. No-one had.

Maria had vanished into thin air. And, so had the letter!

With darkness came fear. We had contacted her family as soon as but they had not seen her. They were to be traumatised again it seemed. They were on their way up the A3. Surrey police were also searching for her; the duty sergeant told us there were cameras everywhere these days. She would soon turn up. The police hinted at a possible boyfriend in the background somewhere.

But we knew different. Rydal and I were sure that this was all to do with the letter. Thomas Wyatt haunted us still. In a way poor Maria was a victim again of Tudor machinations. We told the police about the letter and as before, received uncomprehending stares. Nothing happened because of Tudor secrets these days; we were simply not taken seriously. That's not to say that they didn't think her previous accident and her present disappearance weren't connected. The main line of thinking was more extreme amnesia had set in, which could happen, and that she was wandering somewhere lost.

It was only a matter of time before a patrol or a CCTV spotted her.

When her family arrived, the police in the guise of a pimply spotted youth called DC Parkin, reassured them along these lines. Thankfully at the moment Williams was on leave, somewhere in the Caribbean, according to Parkin.

There was little more we could do that night, so after a hopeless and fairly desultory final search around the campus, we went to bed. But not before we had agreed to go to Cambridge in the morning and finally confront Dove-Kemp ourselves. No more skulking behind toilet doors, running from castles or setting subtle traps, this time we would face him. And we would try, if possible, to record surreptitiously any conversation we might have. That way perhaps the police might take us more seriously.

Having checked emails to find nothing from Australia as yet, we headed off early to beat the traffic. Astonishingly, the M25 was jammed solid at 6.30 am! We crawled around clockwise towards the M11. That junction was a mess. Through various side roads we rejoined the M11 further up and eventually crawled into Cambridge itself late morning. The weather had turned icy and the wind bit into us as we made for the College.

This time we called in at the Porter's Lodge only to discover that Dove-Kemp was at a conference in London all day. Undeterred we took the train and an hour later were heading for the conference venue: Dante's Hotel on Russell Street, not far from the British Museum.

The lobby of the hotel announced that the Tudor symposium was underway in the Grand Ballroom and so we crept in at the back. No sign of the illustrious professor so we crept out again. One of the boards in the foyer stated:

Ann Boleyn Seminar
Professor Dove-Kemp
4 pm The Green Room

We had half an hour to wait. Rydal went up to the desk and

began his usual charm offensive on the girl there. Then he asked:

"I'm here for the seminar at four. I was rather hoping to have a quiet word with my old Professor, he taught me at Cambridge. Is he staying here? I don't suppose you know where he is now?"

Bless her. She was easily reeled in – he was so plausible and persuasive. We were going up in the lift, heading for Room 370 when I congratulated him on his ability to wheedle information out of people.

"Wheedle's my second name." he laughed.

"Oh really, Wheedle Tarn I suppose, high above Ullswater!"

We were on the third floor outside 370. Heart-in-mouth time. What would we do if a) he turned violent, b) refused to talk to us, c) denied all knowledge, or d) highly unlikely, pointed to Maria tied up under the bed!

We knocked.

And again.

And again.

Well perhaps he was in the loo or having a quick fag in the lounge. Gone for a stroll? So we tried the door – it swung open. Unusual.

It was a typical middle-market London hotel room. Beige walls, hung with pictures of flowers and wild life, beech furniture, grey carpet, with a rather untypical body lying on it oozing blood from the head.

The window was wide open and as Rydal knelt beside the Professor, there was no doubt that's who it was, I looked out. There was a ledge running beneath the window leading to the wide flat roof, there was a figure all in black moving awkwardly along the ledge and as I watched, it jumped onto the flat roof. I clambered out onto the ledge. 'Don't look down' I told myself as I looked down. Instant dizziness. Somehow I tottered along the ledge and for reasons I'm still not sure about, jumped across to the roof. I was in pursuit of the dark figure. Why? What would I do if I found it? Wrestle it to the ground? No. I don't think so. I was working on instinct and adrenalin. I had also left Rydal in Room 370 with the corpse of a Cambridge professor due at a seminar down below at any moment.

I raced along the roof, finding an open door, I went through it and clattered down hundreds of stairs to a grey service corridor full of pipes. I hurtled along it and came out at the car park just in time to see a car career down a ramp and speed away. It was far too dark by now to have any idea of the colour or make of car, let alone the registration. And the driver was just a blur.

I heard someone rushing down the stairs and prayed it was Rydal. As he came through the door, he said "Run!"

We belted down the ramp; fortunately the car park seemed empty. But whether someone in one of the hundreds of rooms above us saw two young men escaping fast, I don't know.

In minutes we were in a coffee shop by the Museum.

"He was dead" Rydal said "I checked his pulse – nothing. Massive wound to the neck severed an artery. Quite professional I should think. No knife I could see. I didn't wait long but legged it after you. That ledge was a bit scary" breathlessly it all came pouring out in a frantic whisper.

"I just saw a figure and ran after it" I said, apologetically. "I didn't mean to leave you there."

"It's probably the best thing we could do, get out fast. Someone would have seen us on the hotel stairs or in the lift. The trouble is the receptionist got a pretty good look at me and she gave me his room number." Rydal was shaking as he said this, a result of shock and of the realisation that he was probably the prime suspect in a murder.

As we tried to relax with our coffees, we discussed the dire situation. Who, apart from the receptionist, saw us go into the lift – no-one. Nevertheless the receptionist, so lately the target of Rydal's charm, was now his likely nemesis.

Would she be able to describe him? Yes, emphatically. Would he be easily found as a result of that description? No, fairly emphatically.

"You're reasonably nondescript." I said.

"Gee thanks!" he replied ironically. "But more seriously, I like the sound of that word, nondescript. It's what I want to be. What do we do?"

"We could adopt a high risk strategy "I said "stroll back into the hotel right past her and sit down in the seminar room."

"No. What are we doing drinking coffee? We need to get back to Cambridge and the car." Rydal said "Though Cambridge is a rather scary destination, given what's happened."

I glanced at my watch, almost four. Chances were they would give him ten minutes or so and when he didn't appear at the seminar, fairly soon after, someone would go up to his room and find him. No seminar today, or any other day.

As yet, we hadn't even begun to speculate why it had happened or who the figure on the roof was.

As we left, the streets were beginning to fill with commuters and soon the rush hour would be upon us. We went into a clothes shop and bought Rydal a scarf and hat and dark glasses. So, on the train back to Cambridge, he would bear no resemblance to the person described by the receptionist, when she came to describe him that is. As to the coffee place, it was very busy, and who notices anyone drinking coffee? Let's hope anyway.

The journey to Cambridge was uneventful, the drive to Surrey post-rush hour was blissfully serene and we were on campus by nine. Nerves less jangled. But sleep seeming unlikely for a long time, we tried to piece together the events, the reason for them and most of all how, if at all, it helped us locate poor Maria.

We got nowhere at all in coming up with a reason for what we had found in that hotel bedroom. For us Professor Dove-Kemp was the main orchestrator of our deliberate 'accidents'. Why was he dead? Who would want him dead? Aside from us, Rydal pointed out, a little callously. Did this mean we were safer or more in danger than ever? Did it mean that Maria's disappearance was not necessarily down to Dove-Kemp at all but, chilling thought, to whoever killed him? And if they were so ruthless then what chance did Maria stand? Was the figure I followed escaping over the roof a hired killer or our real enemy? And what was their motivation – the letter or letters? One could get tired of saying or thinking none of it made any sense, but it didn't make it any less true.

There was also the extra worry that we were at the scene, Rydal was known to be at the scene and for all we knew a thousand eyes or CCTV cameras had seen us at the scene. We might perhaps expect our old friends Mid Surrey CID to come knocking in the morning.

CHAPTER 18

But morning came, streaks of pale grey in the east and a bitter Siberian wind but no knocking on the door. I hurried down to the Union to get the morning papers – there were plenty of stories about the death of a famous Cambridge historian on the brink of some exciting new information about the Tudor period. The police had no obvious leads and no suspects had emerged. It looked like the receptionist may not have mentioned Rydal – yet!

One thing was sure we had to try and find the Professor's killer so that the crime would not eventually be laid at our door. We had precious little to go on but at least we knew about the letters and took them seriously as motives, unlike Mid Surrey CID.

We had a paper trail of sorts in that I had followed one of the persons who had burgled my flat (in vain) and they had taken me to Kew and Jethro Easterton. My stomach felt slightly queasy at the thought of more sticky buns but the delightful archivist might just be able to point me in the direction of the burglar – I had a momentary image of those two figures moving silently into my flat whilst fireworks whizzed and popped around Spitalfields. One was the same height and moved in a similar way to the figure in black scrambling and jumping over the hotel roof!

There was no time to lose and though it was Saturday and

unlikely that Jethro would work, I went to the Record Office on the off-chance.

All the offices were locked. So I walked round to his house and knocked on the door. No answer. Please don't let him be away, where do archivists go on holiday in November? Where does anyone go on holiday in November? Just then I felt a warm nuzzling on my calf and turned to find the most enormous dog I had ever seen. Struggling to control him on the end of the lead (who was taking who for a walk?) was Jethro Easterton.

"Hello there young man" he puffed "sorry about Angus, he's a bit frisky after the park. Just let me sort him out and you can come in for a bun."

"After much scrabbling and scraping at the door and thereafter furniture, the redoubtable Angus was handed over to Mrs Easterton – a tiny roly-poly lady who beamed at me as she said in broad Scots,

"Ach, noo stappit Angoos, there's a good wee laddie."

Since Angus showed no signs of 'stapping it' she dragged him off. Later she returned with tea and coffee for Jethro and me.

"Ach" she said "we're almost oot a sticky buns."

This great tragedy seemed to disturb the pair of them and I began to despair of my visit. At least Angus was out of the way, no doubt tucking into a plateful of you know what in the kitchen.

Finally, I got to ask Jethro about his midnight visitor and his links with the Professor. The police hadn't called as yet, though he was expecting them. I was quick to point out that whatever the motive for the murder it was almost certainly not connected to the letter. He seemed relieved at that. He knew the man who came that night. I didn't mention the burglary for fear of alarming him all over again and also because I didn't want the police to know yet. He was a part time assistant at the Thomas Cromwell Archive in Richmond, called Hugo Lats, but apparently he had been off sick for some time. Jethro had no idea where he lived but would try and find out on Monday morning by contacting someone he knew at the Archive.

He also told me that Ben Brackett had phoned him after my visit, asking for the phone number of 'that nice young man'. He winked as he said:

"I thought it best not to encourage him, so said nothing."

When I got back to the University there was still no news of Maria. Rydal had left me a note.

'Gone down to Portsmouth to be with Maria's parents. They are distraught. I'm not much help but they like to talk about her. Check your emails!'

But before I had time, my sister called. She said she just wanted a chat. But she was checking I was alright, I could sense sisterly devotion. Also she wanted to tell me that Dad was worrying her.

"He's been a bit down recently, and I can't get to the bottom of it. He asks about you a lot and I think maybe you two know something I don't. Be a good brother and let me in on the secret, mainly so I can help him. Bless him, he is in his nineties."

What could I do? I couldn't tell her. So I flannelled:

"There's nothing going on between us, Sis. Not that I know of anyway. You know Dad, it'll be something about his boat. If it's not the bilge it's the boom or whatever."

She laughed and I swiftly changed the subject.

"How are Gerald and the kids?"

Not a good idea. Sonia spent the next half hour moaning about the latest au pair the agency had sent. This one had, if it were possible, bigger bosoms than Isabel and a bigger bottom. Gerald was well and truly in the doghouse though he couldn't be blamed for who they sent, but he could be blamed for looking at her. Apparently, she spoke virtually no English, did virtually no work and just ranted about Gibraltar being Spanish!

I said I would go down for lunch on the following day and try and help with Dad. I was being made to feel guilty, of course, because Sonia did all the looking after. She wouldn't be so pleased that I was coming down to see him if she knew what I was really up to!

So late Saturday evening I booted up the computer to have a dekko at my emails and this was waiting for me:

'Hi there Steve,

How's the weather over there? Raining I guess. We're sweltering here in Oz. Bush fires all over the country. Soon be Christmas on the beach. To be honest could never get used to singing carols about snow when it's thirty degrees.

I checked out a few Erdingtons and came across a woman in Adelaide who was a descendant of a Jack Erdington who died on Crete. I gave her your email address. Hope that's OK.

Off tracking wombats tomorrow (ha ha).

Try and send a decent cricket team over next time.

Phil!'

The excitement created by this was short lived because my next message clicked up straight away – from a Judith Stones in Adelaide, South Australia.

'Hello,

I was given your email address by a Phil Erdington of Torquay in Victoria, he said you were looking for descendants of a Jack Erdington who died during the evacuation of Crete in 1941. That was my grandfather.

I hope you are a patient man because I now need to tell you some complicated family history but you will soon see why.

My grandmother was told that her husband (my grandfather) died during the evacuation of Crete in May 1941. He was actually missing in action, presumed dead. No body was ever found. My grandmother Moira visited Crete in 1946 and laid a wreath at the Memorial in Heraklion. My grandfather never saw his son, Samuel, who was born in 1940, though at least he knew he had a son.

Samuel was my dad. My mum told me that everyone accepted the story until one day a letter came from a Corporal Parnaby saying that my grandfather actually died on HMS Imperial. Worse than that, he and three other Aussies who were drinking below decks died when the damaged HMS Imperial was scuttled by HMS Hotspur somewhere between Crete and Egypt.

My mum said that Dad was never the same again. He tried to find out the truth but couldn't. Corporal Parnaby died soon after he wrote to us. The Australian Government and the Justice Department in Victoria couldn't help, they had both been told that there were no casualties when the ship was scuttled.

By this time, myself and my older brother and sister (the twins), were old enough to know what was going on. We loved Dad dearly, we were a close family. But the bond between the twins and him was special. I was jealous at times of course, even Mum was. We watched his decline; it was a combination of shame, guilt and anger at being robbed of a father. He drank a lot.

On 7 November 1994 he fell into the sea off the Point, a notoriously dangerous place, and drowned. It wasn't an accident because he left a suicide note in the hotel where he was staying. He couldn't take it anymore and said he wanted to die, like his father.

You can imagine the effect on the family. My mum and I suffered but the twins, they were 18 at the time, just starting their lives, both successful students at Victoria University, had what can only be described as breakdowns. We had two distressed 18 year olds to deal with.

Over the years, they made some sort of recovery but could never let Dad go. Neither could settle into lasting relationships. They never married and didn't seem to want a family. They had each other in a way. Leah was very much under Richard's spell. At times I felt she would have liked a steady relationship but he could always manage to spoil it for her somehow. He was obsessed with the past and forced her to be.

They began researching the events that led to Grandad's death and both decided the only way to do that properly was in Europe. They left for England in 2000, we heard from them at first but then nothing.

To say we were worried is an understatement. We contacted the police in London and Surrey, the county we had their last address for. It's been over ten years now. I thought of coming to England to look myself or even hiring a private detective but it would be like looking for needles in a haystack. Now you have given us some hope.

I notice your address is Surrey too. Perhaps you have some information. Please, please email us at the earliest opportunity.
Judith Stones'

It was late so I went to bed but turned restlessly most of the night, wondering what to do.

Sunday morning was cold and wet but I had to be in Marlow by lunch time, I had promised Sonia. Rydal was still away comforting Maria's parents. I badly wanted to see Helen and thought of inviting her down to Marlow with me – but that wouldn't be fair. I texted her before I left and suggested we meet that evening. She replied immediately, for once she wasn't working and invited me round for a meal and whatever else I fancied. My emotions were all over the place and to be honest, I wasn't sure what I wanted from Helen. Apart from one thing, I wanted to know if Helen was her real name.

By lunchtime the rain was lashing down. The Thames was choppy like the sea; even twee Marlow looked wild and dangerous. There were trees down too I was informed by a policeman who stopped me in the town centre to tell me the road was closed to 'The Finches'. By now the wind was ferocious; I parked miles away and staggered into the gale. I arrived soaking and battered.

When I rang the bell the door was opened by what appeared to be an enormous pair of bosoms but on second glance turned out to be an enormous pair of bosoms attached to a very, sulky, very arrogant Spanish au pair.

"You want something?"

I tried to explain who I was and why I was so wet and wild looking but she was having none of it and promptly closed the door. Nonplussed I stood there, dripping, until Sonia rescued me, opening the door and apologising for Carmen.

"She doesn't speak much English. She's not used to our ways yet."

Once inside I soon realised that things were, if anything, worse than when Isabel flourished. Gerald was ogling Carmen, Sonia was angry and jealous, the kids were noisy, since Carmen took no notice of them, let alone looked after them and Dad looked thoroughly miserable. Dinner was agony, Carmen had cooked it. It was I'm sure a wonderful paella but the fish eyes and fish heads and tails didn't go down too well on a Sunday lunch time in Buckinghamshire. Gerald nearly choked on a bone.

Dad and I escaped upstairs, it was impossible to go out, but there was no relief there since the one thing I wanted to mention, I couldn't. So we had a very stilted, for us, conversation about his boat.

I made my excuses to the family and fled but not before I saw Gerald put his hand on Carmen's ample behind in the back kitchen. She screeched and gave him a stinging slap. I couldn't help laughing. Why did Sis keep agreeing to have these monstrous Iberian Amazons? And why did they keep sending them in the first place?

It took me three hours to drive back. There were trees down everywhere – 'hurricane? What hurricane?' – I don't recall the weatherman predicting the mayhem I encountered on that dreadful journey. Rydal was unable to get back he emailed, so he was spending another night in Portsmouth. Clearly there was no news of Maria – her poor family must be in agony. I felt very sad, I was going to see Helen but I would much rather go to see Maria.

Helen had gone to a lot of trouble. Her room was more like a boudoir. As night fell, she lit romantic candles and poured glass after glass of red wine. I was careful not to drink that much, her potted plants received most of it. She was in a slinky black outfit and when dinner was over, it was obvious there was something else on the menu. When she went to 'have a shower' said with the implication that I was welcome to join her, I rapidly examined the contents of every drawer in the room. Just as I heard the shower stop I found it – her passport – it wasn't the hoped-for shiny magenta coloured one but a very different looking one. I fumbled with it as she came into the room and dropped it half-opened under a chair.

She was wearing a dressing gown as she held me and we began to kiss, slowly circling to the mood music that had been playing for some time. My intention was to steer her to the bedroom, but we ended up on the rug. I could see the passport under the chair and manoeuvred us so that it was hidden from her. The stress and the drink had taken its toll and she was very disappointed. She sat up, tears in her eyes, making the usual comments expected in that situation: "it didn't matter" though it certainly did to her! With her back to me I made a grab for the passport and pushed it under a cushion. Not a wise choice as the sofa became the scene of Helen's next attempt to seduce me. Admitting defeat in the end, she rolled off and went to the bathroom. I had seconds, no fumbling now, but steely resolve. I opened the document. A younger darker version of Helen peered at me from an Australian passport in the name of Leah Erdington. The shock, even though I knew it was a possibility, was palpable. I stuffed it back whence it came and was all smiles and apologies when she came back.

She hid her true feelings well whilst commiserating with me and laughing, blamed herself for choosing too good a wine. Our talk was desultory, she wanted me to go, I wanted to go yet neither of us could find a way of achieving what we wanted and so the long night wore on. More alcohol, more angst but no further forward. Music, TV, films – nothing was of any use. The mood was strange and wrong.

It was well gone midnight when I left. Much of the time I had been only half listening to her, my mind was far more concerned with what she was hiding not what she was saying. What did she want of me, why this sexual charade, the visits to my family at Marlow, and the chats with my dad? Before we met she must have targeted me as the son of a former sailor on HMS Hotspur, there could be no other explanation. But how much did she know of my dad's involvement? And what was her intention? And where was her brother? I already had my suspicions of who he was, of course.

I wasn't sure what to do next, but the situation seemed urgent. Helen was working for a few days but had suggested Marlow at the weekend. I calculated I had some time, but not long, to find her twin. And I knew where to look – it was time to see Ella again.

CHAPTER 19

Rydal was back. I had heard someone coming into the block late and since he didn't have a booming Brummy accent and wasn't singing about Villa (who had won that day) I knew it wasn't Osbert. I guessed it was Rydal but I left him alone.

He was round early in the morning with nothing to report. His sadness was plain to see, his fear that Maria was suffering or worse was already dead, was plain to see too. I tried, falteringly, to reassure him but couldn't of course. The pair of us had no idea where she was. But we did have one name, Hugo Lats, courtesy of Jethro Easterton and when I got a call from him we had an address too.

"Last seen" Jethro spluttered through mouthfuls of guess what "at 17 Cheney Road, Kingston."

Before long we were heading into the horrendous traffic yet again, this time the M3 at its worst. Cheney road was not posh Kingston but decidedly down-at-heel Kingston. It was a fairly rundown council estate. Number seventeen looked deserted and was. We banged on the door, went round the back and banged on that. Nothing. So we asked the neighbours. A very greasy, shifty young lad at number fifteen said he'd never heard of a Hugo Lats and had never seen who lived at number seventeen (next door! Is it true what they say about the South of England?) but nosey Mrs Parker at number twenty one was a very different story. She had seen Mr Lats (nice looking young man, worked in Kew) leave about a week ago. She had 'by chance' overheard him saying to the taxi driver that he was going up north and wanted a lift to Euston Station. "Could've got the tube easy" she added "but no, he thought he was somebody".

Anyway more ear-wigging 'by chance' discovered he was going to stay with his brother in Blackburn. I vowed never to criticise busybody neighbours again.

It was all so simple, Georgi Lats wasn't even ex-directory. The phone book gave his address and we were heading north to Preston on the Glasgow train from Euston by midday. Change of trains had us in Blackburn Boulevard (rather grand name for a bus/train interchange) by late afternoon. We stood outside the Lats' residence ten minutes later. Wondering what on earth to do!

Half an hour later we were standing across the road, in the dark and chill, debating whether to give it up for the evening and find a cheap hotel, when a man came out hurriedly followed by another in a string vest shouting "Hugo, for God's sake, Hugo, stay here, it'll be okay."

Bingo! Or rather Hugo! We followed him easily; he had no idea who we were surely. I would have known him by his peculiar gait; it brought to mind the robbery at my flat and the figure escaping across the hotel roof.

We found ourselves back at the train station and didn't even need a ticket, our returns to Euston would suffice since he got the train to Preston and then to London.

It would be ridiculously ironic and wasteful if we ended up back at Cheney Road! Keeping track of Hugo on the train (pardon the pun), wasn't easy – so far he hadn't spotted us, I felt, as we followed his change of trains but sooner or later...

He was edgy, restless, constantly on the phone. We never dared get near enough to hear his conversations. He was often at the bar or in the loo! He was a worried man.

At Euston, if he got a taxi, we were in trouble. It's all very well in the movies hailing a taxi immediately and saying 'follow that cab' but I doubted it would be quite like that on a taxi rank outside Euston on a wet, cold, late November night. But, bless him, finances were more strained, he took the Northern Line to Morden. We were in the next carriage and thankfully at the end of the line there were only a handful of people on the platform.

Even so we nearly lost him as an elderly lady with a million bags deposited on the escalator steps fell in trying to collect them all. I was tangled up in it but Rydal vaulted the lot and stayed in pursuit, I hoped.

Having helped said elderly lady and smiled through her "Fanks luv, fanks a lot" and then her recent life history, I got a call from Rydal who was outside a house just down the road.

One can tire of standing in the cold outside unfamiliar houses in unfamiliar surroundings but both of us sensed we had to stay. If Lats came out, we had a plan ready. Rydal would follow, I would stay. And that's what we did when he emerged. I felt sorry for Rydal, I knew he was thinking that Maria could be in that house. I hoped he wouldn't be heading north again!

All was quiet. The house, a modest 1950's semi in a perfectly ordinary leafy avenue was in darkness. Lats had locked the door, suggesting it was empty. I slipped round the side and tried the door and all the windows at the back – locked. I've never broken a pane of glass before, but taking heart from the movies again (why was life becoming so cinematographic?) I wrapped my scarf round a half brick and had a go. Thud! Nothing broke. Harder. Thuddd! Nothing. So I threw it. Smash, crash, shatter! The noise was deafening, lights went on in all the houses around about and a dog barked nearby. But no one came. So I undid the latch and scrambled in. The nearby dog, now became rather more than nearby. In

171

fact it had my trousers in its teeth and was snarling. It sounded big and brutal! At least tugging at me (thankfully not chewing yet) it couldn't bark. It was dragging me round the room, I could just make out lounge furniture in the gloom and a TV, as we passed it in our bizarre dance. I picked up a heavy marble object and for the second time in a minute I threw a missile. It let go and howled, I shot out of the room and closed the door. Now I was holding the handle as it repeatedly hurled itself against the door, the dreadful barking was back. We seemed stuck in some awful impasse but gradually the barking subsided, its strength failed and the blow it received took its toll.

The house was dark and quiet. I risked the light switch. The hall was illuminated. No other sound. Or was there? I could hear a sort of muffled shout. I raced upstairs into the room where the sound was. She was on the bed, bound, gagged and terrified. But alive. Maria! She wept as I helped out her out of her bonds and she cried on my shoulder, deep sobs shaking her frame.

I should have taken her to the nearest police station or even more sensibly phoned 999. But I did neither because she wouldn't let me. She was so traumatised she wouldn't let go of me and all she could say was "Stephen! Stephen!" Over and over.

So I phoned Rydal and told him that she was safe but virtually unable to move. He had lost Lats in a maze of unlit streets. He spoke to Maria on the phone and gradually got a response – she agreed to his suggestion that ringing 999 was by far the wisest option. And that's what I did. It was about fifteen minutes but felt like five hours before police and ambulance arrived together. In that time, mercifully, Lats didn't return and the dog didn't wake up.

I went in the ambulance with Maria, who wouldn't let go of me, and spoke to the police at the hospital. They would now be looking for Lats, but my guess was he would have returned to see police cars outside the house and vanished. Cheney road in Kingston would be deserted too no doubt.

I got a bed at the hospital, well a big chair at Maria's bedside and slumbered as she slept, sedated. Rydal got the car and met us there in the morning. More formalities with the police and she was free to go. Her parents had arrived from Portsmouth and took her home, reluctantly she let me go but only after several kisses, which thankfully Rydal and her parents didn't see. She was still too confused to tell us what had happened. And there was no letter in her possession. We hadn't the heart to question her about it yet. We guessed that Lats had it or had passed it on to a third party already.

Back in Surrey an old 'friend' was waiting for me at 303. "Good to see you again, Stephen" he said, as always conveying the exact opposite. Lugubrious was a word invented just to describe him.

"Hello, Detective Inspector" I said.

"Chief Inspector now, my lad. I've been promoted and I'm now in charge of the whole enquiry."

So Williams was back in my life. Wonderful.

He was there to question me about the discovery of Maria and somehow he managed to suggest my behaviour was at best foolhardy, at worst suspicious. I just stopped myself from pointing out that I had found Maria, not the police.

He also informed me that a certain Georgi Lats had been detained in Blackburn. "Wherever that is" he chuckled. I remembered even Marlow was second rate because it wasn't in Surrey! Georgi had denied all knowledge of Maria and had no idea where his brother was; not having seen him for weeks. There at least we knew he was lying!

Before he left the illustrious CHIEF Inspector reminded me that if I knew anything else about the murder of Joe Lief and the abduction of Maria, I should let him know. He clearly was not in charge of the murder of Professor Dove-Kemp and obstinately refused to join the cases, despite the obvious links. Or what he now called "that Thomas White tomfoolery".

Rydal and I both wanted to be in Portsmouth and, although we could not admit this to one another, for the same reason. Ostensibly, I gave us both the excuse of trying to cure Maria's stubborn amnesia. So we took to the A3, south this time. As we went into the tunnel, I was tempted to stop at the garage. Well aware that my intention of seeing Ella had been overtaken by events, it would have to wait.

Maria was resting but her parents were very pleased to see us, they knew we cared. If only they knew how much. When she came down she was pale and drawn after her ordeal, she was also confused to see us both. This stopped her expressing any strong feelings at all. In this curiously antiseptic sort of setting, I suggested that we should try and help her to remember once again. She agreed. She felt that her recent trauma had unlocked some of her memories and things were hazy now rather than buried.

I began: "Do you remember being with Joe on that evening?"

"Not really" she replied "I've been told I was, so it's hard to separate what I now know from what I remember. I know I was with someone and we decided to split up and I had something I was supposed to hide, I've been told it was a letter written to Sir Thomas Wyatt. I don't know where I hid it at all."

"What about the accident itself?"

"Well, again, I've been **told** a lot about it so I'm a bit puzzled about what exactly I remember. I know I was driving. I think I can remember a dark road, very dark."

"By the Arboretum" Rydal said.

"Yes, I believe so. There was a man I'm sure in the other car. I'm sure it was a man but I can't see his face at all."

"Can you see anything else about him?" I asked "was he

tall, small, dark, fair, was he wearing anything distinctive?"

Rydal added "a logo of some sort, maybe, on his shirt or sweater".

He was thinking about our 'accident' and hoping to link the two. Then we got a surprise.

"Yes" Maria said, her eyes lighting up. "Yes, I do remember, I'm sure I remember an orange shirt and a logo. Or at least some name. No idea what though" and she looked crestfallen.

It was my turn again. "What about the Wyatt line? The one I found in the car documents."

She quoted it. " '*Whoso list to hunt I know where is an hind*' you mean. I know it's a Wyatt line, the opening of the poem. Joe was desperate to find something new about Wyatt and then he found the letter, gave it to me (I don't remember all this, you told me) and then I hid it – but where? And I don't know why I would jot down the line. I must have been trying to… It's my handwriting so I must have been…"

She began to cry. Tears of frustration. Tears of trauma. This was a vulnerable young woman who so much had happened to. We instinctively backed off. But as we did so I couldn't resist one last question.

"The poem is a clue. It may be you were just trying to tell someone, whoever, that the Wyatt letter was important. That it was the reason for the 'accident'? Or could it be that the poem is a clue to…"

"It is" she said quietly, but deliberately "It is, I know it is. I jotted it down, I remember because it was so much the secret of and the clue to everything. Oh Stephen, It's in the poem I know it is."

I felt for my friend when she said that. I glanced at him, not a flicker, just pure love in his expression for this beautiful, fragile girl."

"Let's go through every line then" Rydal said unwavering "and explore every word."

So we did. In the next hour we picked Wyatt's famous poem to bits, in a way it had never been examined before. And in a way it was never meant to be!

> *'Whoso list to hunt, I know where is an hind,*
> *But as for me, helas, I may no more,*
> *The vain travail hath wearied me so sore,*
> *I am of them that farthest come behind.*
> *Yet may I by no means my wearied mind*
> *Draw from the deer, but as she fleeth afore*
> *Fainting I follow. I leave off therefore,*
> *Since in a net I seek to hold the wind.*
> *Who list her hunt (I put him out of doubt)*
> *As well as I may spend his time in vain.*
> *And graven with diamonds in letters plain*
> *There is written her fair neck round about:*
> *Noli me tangere, for Ceasar's I am,*
> *And wild for to hold, though I seem tame.'*

Heavy with history and passion, this poem held special clues for us here and now in 2011. What the three of us did was isolate all the words that might be significant. It was amazing just how many ordinary, simple, little grammatical words Wyatt constructed a great poem out of. We came up with this list:

list (2)	net	plain
hunt (2)	seek	neck
hind	wind	Caesar's
helas?	doubt	tame
travail	vain	'Noli me tangere'
deer	graven	
fleeth	diamonds	
fainting	letters	

So we had about 21 words to go at. Some were more unusual than others and more likely to be clues. We spent a lot of time on 'diamonds', perhaps because we were tuned in to crime. 'Caesar's' too would suggest a person or place of importance to Maria. 'helas' being so odd a version of 'alas' was another. But we got nowhere. Maria frowned and puzzled and cried but we drew a blank.

So we looked at whole ideas. Such as hunting or engraved with diamonds. Still nothing.

After a couple of hours we gave it up as she was getting so distressed. But she still felt it was valuable and wanted to continue, so we asked her parents if she could come back with us to the University. Being around us might help. They agreed to let her go up for a few hours.

The drive to Guildford was uneventful except that at one point Rydal said "that car behind us." I looked round and saw a blue Ford Focus.

"I saw one just like it, Maria, across the road from where you live."

Maria was unfazed "Yes, there is one often there, but it's a different shade of blue I think."

So we dismissed it from our minds.

As we pulled into the University campus, I couldn't resist yelling to Stig out of the window. Rydal was used to my rather facile behaviour but Maria was really baffled. Rydal launched into an over-elaborate explanation which killed the joke stone dead of course.

"It's a stag you see, very similar to Stig... and Stig..." and so on.

"But what about the other figures around it?" she said "what are they called?"

Thereby missing the point, I thought, with what turned out to be huge irony.

"Well they're Stiglets I suppose" said Rydal "and the mother, the hind, is…"

He got no further. We stopped. It was a 'how could we be so stupid?' moment.

But on Maria's face there was more than that. There was recognition, understanding and delight. Delight at a memory lost then recalled.

"It's there" she said quietly "that's where I hid it. I can remember it all now. That night when I left Joe and drove up here, I was struggling. He had told me to hide the letter somewhere safe and I was in a panic. I couldn't think of anywhere. When I got to my room and saw someone had got there before me, I knew I had to find somewhere no one would ever think of but that I would always remember." She laughed at this. "Which I didn't until now! I put the letter into a plastic container, walked out here in the darkness, waited till there were no cars on the drive – it took a while – and crept up to the statues. The Stag was too big and somehow too noticeable. But the other creatures were often not seen and then I recalled the line of the Wyatt poem:

'*Whoso list to hunt, I know where is an hind.*'

It seemed so appropriate and if anything happened to me, then Joe might work it out and look there. So I pushed it underneath the seated mother-figure of the group. And I hope it's still there."

We waited till darkness, impatient and on edge. Late at night there were fewer cars around so we wouldn't be spotted, like the proverbial rabbits in the headlights. We climbed up the bank ducked behind the massive stag and Maria felt underneath the hind and smiled as she pulled out a plastic box.

All three of us were excited, we had found the letter. As we turned to go, a strong light flashed from a powerful torch and we saw the gun. Levelled at us. We couldn't see the person holding it, their face was in darkness. But the hand not holding the gun was extended for the plastic box. Maria hesitated. There was a sickeningly loud report and a bullet flew off a stone at her feet. The intention was clear.

"Give it to him" I said to her.

She put the box in the outstretched hand. The light went out and I had the sense of a dark shape moving away down the bank, moving in a way I recognised, even in shadow. Hugo Lats! He had both letters at last.

We stood there, perplexed. Also frightened to move. If we did would he fire again? Maria was shaking and sobbing. Rydal tried his best to comfort her. The image of the stag loomed above us, no longer a joke, almost threatening.

We waited at least fifteen minutes before we dared to climb down the bank and walked sombrely back to the block. We agreed that although the police had to be informed, there was little chance of finding Lats – by now he would be on the A3, possibly even the M25 and had a thousand places to go! Presumably, his was the blue Ford Focus that had been following us from Portsmouth. He would ditch that fairly soon, if he had not already done so.

Back in the relative safety of 303 we phoned Maria's parents and assured them she was okay. They wanted us to drive back down but we managed to persuade them that she was too tired. Imagine if we had said "and besides she's been shot at!"

She slept much of the following morning and we spent much of the afternoon trying to come to terms with what had happened. It was evening before we set off back.

CHAPTER 20

On the way back to Portsmouth we were still talking about Wyatt. I had mentioned the seemingly separate Cretan conundrum but that meant nothing to Maria. Since we were passing, I asked the pair of them if they minded just stopping off at the garage. I could see Ella; they could get a meal at the hotel across the road. So I pulled off at the Hindhead turning. And still I didn't see it!

We pulled into the car park; most people were leaving as it was six. Ella wasn't there – a colleague said she had already left. Rydal and Maria had come into the reception with me. A few latecomers were just getting the inevitable bad news about expensive services. One elderly lady was kicking off and demanding to see the manager, the mechanic, anyone who had been the slightest bit involved in assessing her brakes. The manager came out, flustered and cross at being still at work so late, then a mechanic came out as we were leaving. Out in the car park Maria stopped and said quite haltingly, " the garage… the mechanic… that orange shirt…" Rydal shouted at the same time "the logo". I knew it well. It was '*Orangery Hindhead*'. I couldn't believe how stupid and blind I had been.

'*Whoso list to hunt I know where is an hind*' – I certainly did, we did, in the name Hindhead!

The man who had 'staged' the accidents was, had to be, a mechanic or workman at this garage! And since Ella worked here too – the coincidence was too much!

In the hotel across the road we debated what to do. Maria hadn't recognised the actual mechanic we saw. The others by now would be long gone. I'd noticed that the other staff didn't wear the same shirt or logo. It was the garage mechanics we needed to see.

We would have to wait until the following day. We drove back to Portsmouth, excited but trying to keep calm. Maria told us at last what she now fully remembered.

"As I was driving up to Hascombe, a car coming the other way swerved into me. There was a sickening crunch of metal. I must have passed out. When I came to, he was cursing and shouting so violently, I pretended I was still unconscious. That's when I saw the logo.

He began to sprinkle something on the car – I could smell petrol. He was going to set fire to the car!

I was too scared to move. I was going to die, but I was desperate someone would know the truth. Then, I don't know why, the opening of the Wyatt poem came into my head. Strange how the imagination works. I had hidden the letter under the hind and my assailant was from Hindhead. Somehow I had time to scribble down the first few words of the poem and push it into the car's document wallet.

I remember a whoosh of flame and that's all. How I got out and ended up on the roadside is a blank."

"Brilliant" I said "what a mind to link the two things in one word!"

"Worthy of Hamlet" said Rydal and he was lost in admiration for the love of his life.

Her parents let Rydal and I sleep on the lounge sofas and we passed a restless night.

By 9am we were, yet again, zooming up the A3, along with the whole of Hampshire it seemed as the jams were long.

There had been an accident in the tunnel northbound so we were an hour crawling towards the Hindhead exit. But we got there.

We had a plan. Maria and Rydal needed to be where the actual cars were being fixed or serviced. Of course, there was always the fear that the man we wanted was off that day, on holiday or worse still had left the company. I would go and see Ella in case he came to talk to her. How they would slip behind the scenes was up to Rydal.

Ella was there on reception. She was surprised and not very pleased to see me.

"Oh, it's you... What do you want Stephen?"

"I thought we might have a chat about things."

"Well, I can't, as you can see. Go and get some coffee over there, I have a break in about ten minutes."

So I sat sipping coffee as Ella dealt with a variety of visitors and several men in orange logo t-shirts went to and fro.

I saw Maria and Rydal in the forecourt out of the corner of my eye. There was a mechanic under the bonnet of a big white car, presumably they had seen no one in the works itself and were just checking. I strolled out. Maria gave a cry as the man emerged from under the bonnet, the person I saw I had last seen in Crete. An enormous spanner came flying towards me and caught me on the side of the head, only a glancing blow. The man dashed out of the forecourt and along the road towards some trees. Ella had come out and was shrieking, Maria looked faint and Rydal hesitated. I ran, groggy from the blow, and some way behind. The orange shirt was just visible – I ran through a National Trust car park – the sign told me we were heading for 'The Devil's Punchbowl' and soon I was galloping down a track between trees heading into a deep valley – could we really be in the centre of Hindhead?

He knew where he was going, I didn't. Also if he realised it was only me pursuing him and not several people, as he suspected, he might have stopped and faced me. But he didn't – yet. The tracks began to diverge and I had no idea which one he had taken. I guessed. Luckily a flash of orange in the distance told me I guessed correctly.

I wasn't gaining on him though. In fact he was outrunning me. Should I stop? Call the police for help? It's hard to make any decisions as you are hurtling pell-mell through dense woodland. Inexorably down into the Punchbowl, pursuing a devil quite possibly.

I came to a clearing with a stream at the bottom of the hill. I was dreading this. There were so many tracks! I opted for the only one that crossed the steam but as the path climbed there was no sign, no tracks on the path and no noise. I had lost him. Or so I thought. At what point did the hunter become the hunted? I had this strong sensation he was nearby, watching me and yet, not hiding. There was a loud crashing and roaring and I leapt to one side as a huge red rock rolled past me and smashed into the bank.

Smaller rocks whizzed past my head, one struck me a glancing blow on my shoulder. I dived for cover. But he was obviously high above me and could probably see me. I heard the boom and had seconds to avoid a monstrous boulder as it tore a path through the undergrowth and careered into the stream.

Then I heard a truly dreadful sound, a high-pitched scream followed by more crashing in the trees and then deadly silence.

I lay still for minutes, listening and waiting. Nothing. I felt in my pocket but in all the chaos I had lost my mobile.

Eventually, I moved forward and crept back down to the stream. Spread-eagled on the track was a crumpled shape, high above was an out-jutting rock, the figure had fallen hundreds of feet. That was the reason for the scream. There was a lot of blood. I didn't look too closely but enough to see he was dead, his orange shirt now more red than orange, the logo nearly obscured in his own blood. I felt no pulse at all.

Next to him was his astonishingly unbroken iPhone – grisly thought it was, I looked at his most recent text.

'Leah,

Johnson has found me. I will take care of him. You do what has to be done. Now.
Rick'

I went cold. Richard Erdington was lying dead and broken in front of me. But Leah Erdington was going to do 'what has to be done'. I think I knew what that was.

I used his iPhone to call the emergency services. I was in no fit state to string together a coherent statement. The understanding person on the other end of the line tried to help – she understood someone had fallen – but was fairly confused as to where. As to sending police to Marlow to stop 'what has to be done', she was pretty sceptical. She kept me on the phone so long, presumably to try and get my position. One way or another she worked out that there had been a fatal accident at The Devil's Punchbowl and not, as she first thought from my garbled account, that a drunk had somehow fallen into a punchbowl!

By now I was coming to my senses and realised that if and when police and medics got here it would take a long time to locate me and the body. All this would hopelessly delay any chance of stopping Helen/Leah from doing 'what has to be done'.

I had to stop it. I phoned Rydal, he wasn't answering for whatever reason. I phoned Helen, no answer. Was she on her way? I reasoned if I waited any longer I might meet police and then all would be lost. I pocketed his phone but left Richard Erdington to the Devil.

Halfway back up the track I heard voices. "This way Roger" said a very posh voice. "Oh blimey Caris" said Roger presumably "bit of a sticky wicket, what?"

These two sounded like they had been imbibing from a punchbowl! I hid as they stumbled past. What would they think when they found the 'sticky wicket' at the bottom of the hill.

Once into the car park I was very circumspect, keeping to the edges. As I neared the garage, blue flashing lights and sirens told me I had just made it in time. I slipped past on the other side of the road. Roger and Caris could do all the explaining!

When I lost my phone, my wallet had gone too. I had no money for a taxi or for public transport even. I resorted to that old standby of student days and began thumbing a lift. Not very sensible but I got lucky, this blue Bentley stopped and the driver was going to Stratford-on-Avon to see 'Macbeth' at the Royal Shakespeare theatre and was going virtually past Marlow.

I had to put up with the quips and witticisms such as "Marlow, Bucks not Kit ha ha" but it was a small price to pay for a direct fast drive to my sister's.

He dropped me in the centre of Marlow and with a cheery "When shall we two meet again, in thunder, etc, etc." he was gone. I'd hoped he would take me to the door but to be fair he had actually come out of his way and it wasn't far. I ran as fast as I could. 'The Finches' was quiet, it was mid-afternoon and I guessed that the school run was underway. I hammered on the door – no answer. Dad was out too. And I could guess where he would be. I ran down to the river and headed for Marlow Lock. He moored his boat virtually next to it. It wasn't there.

He didn't normally sail much in the winter but it was a bright, not too chilly afternoon. Which way? Probably not through the lock, so I set off on the path upriver. There were precious few boats moving, most were moored and their owners, mostly grizzled pensioners, were getting started on protecting them for the winter with lots of tarpaulins being heaved hither and thither. I attracted little attention – another Thames-side jogger, though not actually in running gear.

I was beginning to think it was a pointless exercise, I must have been running for over half an hour; would I have to run all the way to Henley? Then I saw Dad's boat, out on the river. I waved and shouted; Dad was steering, oblivious.

"Dad, it's Stephen, Dad, I need to talk to you."

A face peered out of the cabin at me. At one time that face would have delighted me but now it was the last one I hoped to see – Leah/Helen. She disappeared into the cabin but re-emerged soon enough, holding something, it was glinting in the weak watery sunshine. Dad was still at the tiller blissfully unawares. I shouted and shouted, but it was no use, his hearing was poor and the engine noise drowned out my voice.

Leah was at the bow. Dad was sitting astern steering. I was still running along the bank to keep up. I didn't know what to do. Nor it appeared did she. She was hesitating, I could tell. But she didn't alert Dad of my presence. I calculated I had very little time. Swimming was hopeless, the boat wasn't moving that quickly but I would never get to it. I could only watch and hope.

I yelled:

"Leah, I know it's you. Please Leah don't do anything foolish."

But my words were wasted, she knew from her brother's text what she must do. She was just screwing up the courage.

The only thing in my favour was that because Dad had taken me so many times out on the river, I knew that stretch of the Thames well, especially Marlow to Henley. The first place they would need to slow and stop was Hurley Lock but that was some way off yet. But at one part of the river Dad always pulled in close to the Berkshire side where I was running. He said it helped you a lot there if you were going upstream. And that was very near; in fact I could see Dad shifting the tiller slightly as he always did at this point. Sometimes he got very close to the bank – I had jumped it before now.

Sure enough the boat was moving across to that point. Leah could see it too now and it made up her mind for her. She began to move along the port side ledge of the boat, hidden from myself and Dad. Going below would have been the natural thing to do but then I realised Dad would have seen and heard her coming up the steps. Now I knew what she had in mind.

He was steering gradually into the bank, she was inching carefully round the side, I was running pell-mell and suddenly we reached the critical moment all together. I hit the path at full pelt and took off, Dad swung the boat in and Leah appeared, knife raised but crucially hesitated for a split second. I was in mid-air, feet first, doing a kind of karate kick, I caught Leah in her side as she stabbed at Dad – the knife slashed his arm, she groaned and fell over the portside almost as the boat crashed into the bank on the starboard. My momentum took me after her into the river.

I went down to the riverbed but was experienced enough to know what to do – I had fallen (and jumped) off enough times. I kicked furiously to prevent the reeds trapping me and came up arms first – sure enough I felt the boat – I was underneath but it was easy enough to swim away from it. Less easy to get back into it.

I could hear shouting and see the looming mass of another boat – a large white cruiser was bearing down on me. Fortunately, they had seen me, in fact it turned out even more fortunately they had seen everything including the knife attack. They hauled me up onto their boat and someone jumped across to Dad. I could see he was holding his arm and there were red stains on his sleeve. The skipper of the 'rescue' boat was already phoning. I lay exhausted and shivering on deck, Dad was in a kind of daze, of Leah there was no sign.

About fifteen minutes later the bank was full of paramedics and police. It was afterwards in The Royal Berkshire hospital in Reading that I described the bizarre events. I was badly bruised from colliding with the boat but no bones broken. Dad was being treated for shock and a superficial flesh wound – but since he was in his nineties he was told he wouldn't be going home for a while. Sonia had arrived and was in a state of shock herself when she realised it wasn't just a simple boating accident.

Police divers were searching the river for Leah.

The police constable who took my statement constantly raised his eyebrows with incredulity. I could tell he thought I was rambling due to a blow on the head or whatever.

One thing he did say which filled me with foreboding was:

"We've contacted Guildford and Chief Inspector Williams is on his way."

His first words on arrival were not "How are you, Stephen?" but "Royal Berkshire!" I was well aware of his distaste for all things not Surrey, even Buckinghamshire wasn't popular as I recalled. It got worse, "Australians you say!"

Deliciously, I thought of his having to visit Melbourne and Adelaide – what would he make of that! But he was compelled to take me seriously. At last I had witnesses. Not only the people on the cruiser, but there were witnesses on the bank too that I hadn't seen. One man on the opposite bank had filmed it all! Another had binoculars trained on the boat and could even describe the knife, still not found, in some detail.

In that hospital room in Reading I told Williams everything. He already knew about the body in the Devil's Punchbowl. But the Australian connection was all new. Hugo Lats and the Professor's murder were not his case but he now had to take these on board as opposed to dismissing Wyatt out of hand.

The search of the river had found nothing but divers would

resume it in the morning – looking for a body and/or a knife. Police had gone to see Ella but found the house deserted. Georgi Lats in Blackburn had heard nothing from his brother.

"But we are pursuing all these leads, vigorously" Williams assured me. "Is there anything else you would like to get off your chest?"

Only he could use that phrase, still somehow implying that I was to blame.

Rydal and Maria arrived soon after Williams had taken his slow leave. I wanted to leave with them but the police had suggested I was safer guarded here until Leah Erdington was accounted for. Also Dad was staying here and he felt safer with me close by.

I could tell Rydal and Maria were relieved too. I was pleased the pair of them were getting plenty of time alone together. Maria was beautiful and had cared for me, but the whole Helen/Leah business had somehow taken away all my emotions. I felt numb and in need of friendship, yes, but not love.

CHAPTER 21

For the next few days, nothing much changed. I relaxed in hospital, Dad slowly got back to his old self. My friends visited every day. Osbert popped in because Villa were playing in Reading in the evening. Big Vinyl gave me a call, mostly about Jensens, but he did find time to ask if I was okay. Some flowers and cake arrived from the Eastertons. Even Julie drove down!

But of the various investigations I now found myself the astonished centre of, no news at all. The search of the river had been abandoned, the diving team could find no body down there, let alone a knife, the reeds were so thick and impenetrable. Ella had vanished without trace as had Hugo Lats. It had all stalled just as it seemed it would all become clear.

It is easy to become institutionalised. I wasn't looking forward to going to Sonia's to recuperate but Dad was terrified of leaving hospital. He was now fully aware of the Erdington twins' vendetta against our family. His sense of guilt about the original 'war crime' as he, himself, described it was now compounded by the danger his action had put his whole family in. In vain I told him that he was following orders and could not have known about the drunken Australians on board. So in the end the medics thought it best to leave him in The Royal Berkshire a little while longer complete with police guard. Whilst I went back to the bosom of Sonia's family. Or rather bosoms, since Carmen was still in residence.

The weather had turned very wintry. On the first of December, right on cue, the snow came down in bucketfuls. Carmen stared in delight "I never see before." It became much harder to get to Reading to see Dad. But, fortunately, the doctors let him come home; I think The Royal Berskhire was filling up nicely with flu victims and broken bones. We brought Dad home on the Friday, he was more or less his old self again. Unlike his boat which was undergoing extensive repairs.

I had little to do. I still couldn't go back to work; Big Vinyl had been very understanding when the police and the medics had said I wasn't ready. Rydal and Maria were both studying hard for exams – something they had not done for months. Sonia fussed over me, fattening me up with roast dinners. Gerald was his old self again too, eyeing up Carmen at every opportunity. The kids rampaged round the house when not at school. Slowly, I began to think we were all safe. Foolishly!

I pondered most of all now on Ella's disappearance. She held the key to everything still. She had gone because Erdington was dead and his vendetta exposed. His engineering of the car crashes (both) was presumably aimed at me. He thought Joe and I would be in the car on that night near Hascombe not Maria – it was my car, after all. It was likely that he was involved in faking Joe's suicide and this meant Ella was heavily implicated in that too. Poor woman, I could almost feel sorry for her. But where would she go? I knew her so well and I thought if I put my brain to it I could second guess her.

So as I watched the snow building up outside, I racked my brains. She had pots of money and several houses abroad but would she have risked leaving the country? Customs might spot her. No, she wasn't far away. I remembered a cottage we went to once when we had our brief romance. It was just possible she had forgotten I had been there too with her. It belonged to her aunt who was old and bedridden and Ella had the run of it. She kept it quiet, a sort of hideaway, I'm not even sure Joe knew about it. I could picture it. What I couldn't do was picture where it was! It was in the hills somewhere. The Surrey hills? Probably not. The Chilterns, maybe, but not the Marlow/Henley end – further north.

When the snow melted I would have a drive round the Chiltern hills and see what I could find. But the snow showed no intention of melting and hung around for days as I kicked my heels inside. Sonia had a whole shelf of Robert Goddard novels and I set myself the task of reading them all. They kept me entertained and made me realise how much my life had turned into one, with me as the archetypal central figure. What I marvelled most at was the numerous twists and turns the plots made. Were there any twists left in my story?

As Christmas approached and students started to leave Guildford for the holidays, I drove down to wish Maria a Happy Christmas. If anyone deserved a happy time it was Maria. I was surprised and pleased to find that Rydal was going with her to Portsmouth for the holidays so they could spend Christmas together. Rydal was like a child suddenly and unexpectedly let loose in a sweet shop. He couldn't stop grinning. Maria took me to one side at one point and whispered:

"I hope you don't mind Stephen. I do have feelings for you, you know that. But Rydal has been so kind, so loyal, so always there and that's what I need right now."

I was glad she told me this, though a little concerned that her affection for Rydal was more like gratitude and opting for security. But I wasn't about to spoil things by hinting at that.

My feelings for Maria? So strong once, they had faded un-accountably. More than anything it was the drama on the riverbank that convinced me Rydal and Maria belonged together, because I still had to look over my shoulder and Dad's, at least until Leah was found. And then... I wasn't sure and it would be unfair of me to start anything with Maria. I wondered if her words were more of a challenge. Giving me the opportunity to declare an interest, turn my best friend into my rival, even 'fight' for her. If so, she was sadly disappointed – I didn't rise to the challenge at all.

When I got back to Marlow the family were all out visiting some cousin in Oxford for an 18th birthday. But they had left Carmen behind. 'Behind' being the operative word today as she had squashed herself into the tightest dress possible. As I let myself in, she appeared in the hallway, smiling provocatively. Clearly she had been at the sherry or wine or whatever beverage Gerald had got in for Christmas. Basically she came at me, bosoms heaving, eyes flashing and grabbed me round the waist.

"O Steven at last, we alone together. You have waited well. But you cannot resist I feel."

I could and did. I managed to get out of her embrace and legged it up the stairs. Wrong choice! Tipsy Carmen took it as an indication we should move to the bedroom. I managed it to the bathroom and bolted the door.

"O Steven, you want Carmen I know. I show you hot Spanish love."

My protestations that, lovely girl though she was, I was spoken for (as if) served to inflame her ardour. She began to beat on the door. As the wine took hold (she was drinking more out there?) she began to talk wildly in Spanish. And as it eventually dawned that I wasn't returning her passion, she became angry and aggressive.

"You British men! All the same. You lead women on. But can't do anything. You have no passion. Pah! Gibraltar ours!

Malvinas ours." She was becoming very confused both politically and geographically.

Just then I heard the door open and I heard Sonia shouting:

"Carmen, what on earth are you doing on the landing with no clothes on? Is that a bottle? Gerald get into the lounge. Stop ogling and phone the agency."

After much struggling and grappling (in which poor Gerald was not involved) Carmen was persuaded downstairs. I was freed in time to see the agency rep arrive to take her away. The rep was most apologetic as Sonia complained about Latinas and bosoms ending with:

"And I want you to send a man next time from somewhere chilly – Iceland or Norway."

The following day – the man from Iceland or Iceman as I had come to think of him had not yet arrived – we were all pressed into helping Sonia, who had found a new rich vein of assertiveness, with child care, washing, cleaning, even cooking. Mercifully, I was rescued from this by a surprise phone call. There was a downside to the call, it was an invitation from Ben Brackett to visit the Record Office in Hitchin. But it was about a request regarding some 'translation' of two sixteenth century letters. This was intriguing enough to make me brave Ben's company, missing the new regime at 'The Finches' was an added bonus.

More tangled traffic. Why didn't I live out in the French countryside where roads were straight and empty? But no, here I was skirting the outskirts of London on the M25, except my painfully slow progress could never be deemed 'skirting'.

Ben was busy with a customer in the reading room. She was a very winsome young woman who brought out the bitchiness in Ben.

"Well, I'm sorry but as you can see, I just haven't got the time to start trawling through records looking for your family – what was it again? Curlew?"

"Purlew, it's an unusual name, couldn't you…?"

"I'm rushed off my feet."

At this the three of us, there was no one else at all in the Reading room, looked around at the empty desks and work-stations.

"Sorry, ah Stephen…"

And with the wave of his hand he dismissed all the ancient Purlews as well as the present one in front of him.

Ben took me into the 'back office'. I entered warily, took a seat nearest the door, crossed my legs (whatever for?) and tried to look as 'hetero' as I could. Ostensibly Ben had got me here to tell me about the request for the 'translation' of early Modern English as well as the deciphering of secretary hand.

"I remember Jethro said that I should be on the lookout for this. And that you would be interested. The gentleman said he would call in with the letters. I spoke to Jethro on the phone about it. Jethro said it sounded like Lats – whatever that means – and that I should call you, so I did. Oooo! It's almost closing time for lunch. How about we repair to my local hostelry and I tell you more."

There was no escape. As we sat on a cosy (too cosy) sofa in front of a roaring (synthetic) log fire, Ben told me that he had arranged to see the man that very afternoon at two. I explained as much to Ben as I thought wise, leaving him in no doubt that the letters were stolen from me. I neglected to point out that was not strictly accurate. Certainly, as regards the first letter. But Ben didn't seem very interested in that aspect of it at all, he was very ready to believe everything I said. The reason for that was all too obvious as he put his hand on my knee.

Tricky! I had to see his visitor, needed his expertise so daren't offend him but at the same time, had to avoid leading him on in any way. Fortunately, at this moment a gaggle of girls came over and plonked themselves down on the sofas opposite. They were a bit the worse for drink, informed us they were off to the races and described us in slurred tones as "a couple of likely lads".

Ben fled, but to his chagrin I stayed and began to chat them all up outrageously. At about a quarter to two they tottered off to the coach which was taking them to Towcester race course. I ignored all their pleas to join them and headed for the Record Office.

It was as if we had had a lover's tiff. Ben was distant and sniffy and it took all my charm to bring him back onside. The plan was I was to hide in the back office with the door slightly ajar so that I could see if it was Lats or not – I was pretty sure I could recognise him. If I closed the door Ben would know it wasn't, if I left the door open then Ben would make some excuse to take the letters into the back office where I could look at them and decide what to do.

Sure enough at two a bespectacled bearded man arrived with the letters. He didn't look remotely like Lats but it was that distinctive movement that gave him away. Hugo Lats heavily disguised. I left the door open. About fifteen minutes later Ben came into the office and started to open and close drawers, winking at me as he did so. He placed both letters in my hand, one I recognised immediately as the Broxbourne document.

What should I do? Photocopy them? The time this would take and the sound of the machine would surely make Lats suspicious. Ben whispered that Lats had already said no photocopying. There wasn't time to phone the police. Disappearing with the letters was hardly fair on Ben. So as Ben went back into the reading room I did what all comedy sketch writers would be proud of, I shouted 'Fire!' and smashed the glass of the alarm. There was a tremendously loud ringing sound, people appeared from all directions in panic. Ben played up splendidly. A burly chap bundled the protesting Lats out into the car park. In seconds I created chaos in the front and back offices, overturning chairs, emptying drawers and scattering paper, pulling books off shelves. I even tipped a shelf over. I was having fun in a way. Then I ran clutching the letters the back way out of the building. I waited till the panic was over and they all trooped back inside before I got to my car and drove off. I think I had done enough to convince everyone the fire alarm was a diversionary tactic created by thieves. That Ben would not be in any way suspected. And Lats certainly wasn't going to hang around waiting for the police to bemoan his stolen letters. I would thank Ben, from a distance later, for his part in it all. I turned the car towards the M25, eventually joined the M4 and headed for Kew. Though Rydal was a gifted amateur at these sorts of documents, I needed a professional I could trust. And stopping at a handy patisserie I arrived early evening armed with a wonderful array of cakes and buns at the Easterton abode.

But Jethro was on a conference somewhere. It was Mrs Easterton who answered the door and informed me.

"Ach, he's gone to Perrrth, ma hoom toun, but a cudna goo cos of the wee laddie."

"Well, yes, young children…"

"Nooo" she chuckled "not bairns, Angoos!"

At the sound of his name the huge animal came bounding into the room and (why do all dogs do this to me?) started nuzzling into my crotch, ignoring his mistress' cries of:

"Stappit Angoos!"

Eventually, settled on the sofa with a cup of tea, Angus shut in the back room, I learned that Jethro had gone to a conference in Perth, Scotland, thank God not Western Australia, and would be back in a few days. His wife promised to give him the letters and some instructions that I

197

jotted down. Basically, I wanted a 'translation' plus authentication. I had Rydal's version of one but it wouldn't do any harm to have a professional's. The other was naturally the more important since I knew nothing of its contents. I had sneaked a peek but it was more like hieroglyphics than English. I cursed secretary hand yet again.

When I got back to Guildford the place was empty. Nearly all the students, except the sad ones who nobody wanted or had nowhere to go, had left. It was like a ghost town or rather ghost campus. I wandered disconsolately around, nodding to the occasional student I recognised. I even spotted the dreaded cleaning lady in the distance!

CHAPTER 22

The following day was clear, bright and cold, crisp and refreshing in a way. I decided to go for a drive round the Chilterns and see if I could remember anything about that cottage.

I left the M25 and drove up the A413 into deepest Metroland. Ella had explained to me that some of the towns in this area had been built around the Metropolitan line of the Underground as it spread out from London in the nineteenth century. I skirted Amersham and wandered about the country roads up and down single track lanes. 'Great this' and 'Little that' villages. Impossibly pretty and dripping with money. I felt I was in the right area; they looked like film sets. And then I recalled they looked like that because they were. Ella had told me that the village had been used in Midsomer Murders a few times. I laughed, cracking the usual joke about nobody being left in Midsomer, all murdered in various intriguing ways. All I had to do was ask, which I did at the next pub on the road. The landlady was certain it must be Little Eyshott and gave me directions.

As I turned off the main road it was like driving into the past seeing the spectacular manor house, used in an episode of Midsomer, with the breathtaking landscaped garden and moat. I parked and went into the church – yes, there they were, the faded red and cream wall paintings. St Christopher a huge giant carrying a diminutive Saviour. Ella and I had attended a wedding here once, whose it was I couldn't think. As I left the church, I knew where to go. And there it was, the rain from a recent shower sparkling in the cold sun on the windows and eaves. Parclose Cottage. I didn't get too near but stayed partly hidden by a holly hedge. There was a car in the drive. I didn't recognise it, but it had the look of a hire car because there were documents attached to the windscreen.

I retraced my steps down the main street as far as the Red Lion. I got a room there for the night and put my plan into action. I guessed there would be few guests in December and asked for a room overlooking the main road. Because that might give me a glimpse of Parclose Cottage. In fact I had a splendid view of it enhanced by my binoculars.

The light faded quickly as it does in December. But I was up early with the sun and settled down to watch. At nine o'clock the front door opened and a woman wrapped up against the cold came out. She had scarf, woolly hat and sunglasses for the glare. Either this woman hated the cold or she didn't want to show her face. I tracked her down the lane to the main road, past the church, past the Red Lion and into the local shop. She emerged five minutes later wrapping her scarf around her face as she did so, but not quite quickly enough. Ella Lief as I live and breathe! I slapped my thigh and did a fairly ludicrous jig. I was right, she was here; she had forgotten I was with her here once. That was a blow to my ego, our, albeit brief romance, all forgotten. But my euphoria wouldn't be quelled that easily.

The question was what to do next? Tell the police and let them surprise her? A car pulls up outside, she looks quizzically out of the window, sees the police car, heads for the back door – where I would be waiting? No – too much like an episode of Midsomer. Besides I had a few questions to ask Ella myself – just a few! – before Williams and co. got to her.

So, buttoned up against the cold, it was by now below freezing I reckoned, I strode out of the Red Lion and past the church, up the lane, heart beating. I opened the little wicket gate and rapped the knocker. There was a longish pause. I knew there was a passage between the next cottage and I darted down there, in time to see Ella hurriedly leaving by the back garden. I was too quick for her and linked arms with her as she turned down a little lane which led to the church.

"What do you want?" She said in a surly voice.

"Stupid question" I replied "well, certainly not what I got last time we were here."

She gasped – realisation dawned. She had forgotten.

"Let's go into the church shall we?" I said "we should be alone there. We have a lot to talk about."

I half dragged her down the path. The huge door clanked shut and left us in the gloom. The lights illuminated the glory of the Saxon nave and St Christopher. I pushed her into a pew and sat down beside her.

"Right, before I ring the police on my mobile, let's talk. And who knows, perhaps I can spare you the ignominy and humiliation to come."

She glanced at me at this and shrugged. "In what way? You mean you might not tell them I'm here. They'll find me anyway. It's as good as over."

"Depends what and how much you tell me. I think everything might be a good idea."

So she began, prompted by the occasional question from me.

"You don't know what it's like having a husband who's a shit. Student after student he tried to seduce. He got lucky now and then. You knew! You knew what he was like. Humiliating me and living off my money. I deserved better. **You** would have been better!

Anyway in the end I met someone myself. At the Hindhead car dealers as you know. Rick was fun and he was handsome.

I soon found out we had something in common – you! I know now that at first anyway he only courted me to get close to you. I accepted that was part of my attraction to him. I didn't mind, he started as a diversion but eventually became a need. Now he's dead I don't really care about anything. Yes, I'm hiding here but I suppose I knew I'd be found in the end.

What I didn't realise initially was the nature of his vendetta or desire for revenge. It was all-consuming I began to realise. He would do anything, even use his sister. Don't look surprised, I knew about Leah or Helen if you prefer. She wasn't as committed, I don't think, but she was under his spell, her twin. They were spookily close at times. He even told her when and where she could see her boyfriend. Surprised again, Stephen! You weren't the only man in her life, she was fond of you I think, but she had the hots for someone else. I never knew who, though believe me I tried to find out.

Then a plan came to me. I wanted rid of Joe so I could marry Richard but I didn't want my ex-husband helping himself to half my wealth – nor did Richard. He wanted rid of you and your father because of the ship sinking in World War II. Kill two birds with one stone? I knew that on that night, the night of the lecture, you would be in your car together. Richard was a skilled mechanic. He had made sure Joe's car was out of action, I knew he would ask to borrow yours – he always used you! Richard said he would arrange an accident, a fatal one. But he came to the house wild-eyed later that night to say there was only a girl in the car I had told him to follow and everything had gone wrong. Poor Richard he tried again on some narrow road in Kent to get you but made a mess of it."

I interrupted her "So those two 'fake' accidents were nothing to do with the Wyatt letters at all? Maria was…"

"Just 'collateral damage' I believe the phrase is. I knew precious little about Joe's Wyatt obsessions and cared even less. His young sexy student obsession was what I wanted to put a stop to. So I was quite glad when she got what she deserved.

It was my idea to make Joe's death look like suicide initially but more subtly suggest your guilt. Sorry Stephen, it was nothing personal, Richard wouldn't really be mine till his crazy thirst for revenge was satisfied. You weren't the only victim of it – I was too and so was Leah. Leah came one night having been with you and almost begged Richard to stop it all – but he wouldn't. He more or less ordered her to continue – she was so weak when faced with him. It was pitiful. To be honest, I despised her. Now she's probably at the bottom of the Thames, so I am told, where she belongs!

I have no regrets about Joe. Only that I married him in the first place. Framing you didn't work, obviously, so I still didn't have Richard to myself. Then you turned up at Hindhead, always a risk. He couldn't ever play it cool, he overreacted and ran. I cried for days after his death – it was the worst time of my life. Now I'm just numb. I came here because I didn't know where else to go or what else to do.Does that answer your questions? It will have to. Do you believe in God? Look at Christopher carrying Christ, a burden…"

I turned my head to contemplate the great and moving spectacle stretching above us in the semi-darkness. When I turned back to Ella there was a tiny silver pistol in her mouth. Then a terrible noise. I remember thinking whether all the blood spattered over St Christopher's garments would ever come off the wall.

The days that followed were bleak indeed. They seemed like a dream. Williams, back in my life forever now, quizzed me over and over about what Ella said. I told him the truth, not all of it verifiable. He was angry and suspicious because I had tracked her down rather than told the police where she might be. I just let him rant and met his suspicions stonily. I knew he was worried about his reputation and that gave me some satisfaction.

Even Williams couldn't deny that the jigsaw pieces were slotting into place. When I asked him about the search for Leah, he shrugged. I was allowed a private viewing of the film footage taken by the man on the river bank. I'm not sure I was legally supposed to view it but Williams hoped I might see something they had missed about Leah.

It was weird to relive those moments by the Thames, especially to see myself. It was like an out-of-body experience. The zoom was so amazing, expressions were visible. Mine frantic, Dad's disbelieving. I watched Leah especially and knowing her gestures reasonably well, I saw something that no one else noticed. Her expression just before I hurtled into her was caught by the camera because she had twisted round to face the far bank. I wasn't sure but I thought I detected something very interesting and quite at odds with the expected, perhaps not. I would mull over it for days later until I finally thought I understood what it was.

When the new term began in January Rydal and Maria came back to the University. No longer in 303 but still 'recuperating' at my sister's, I saw them occasionally and observed all the effects of growing love between them. No one could be more pleased than I was. We contacted Jethro Easterton to see what he had come up with only to learn from a work colleague that he was cruising the Caribbean and not contactable. We laughed:

"Perhaps he sold the letters and fled to the West Indies."

Not Jethro. His colleague had contacted him and astonishingly I got a call from the Gloriana off Nevis. The line wasn't clear, or Jethro had a particularly sticky bun in his mouth, but he assured me on his return in early February all would be revealed and that it was worth waiting for!

The police investigation into Professor Dove-Kemp's murder had stalled since Lats had vanished. He was the prime suspect, inevitably.

So once again, I found myself with time on my hands.

There was something else that I had to do though. I'd had an idea, so I made a few phone calls which led to a few forms to be filled in. Then I got some information from Australia via email and I was nearly ready. There was one more thing I needed or, rather, person. So one rainy evening I turned up at the 'London Kit Kat Club'. It was early and the place was nearly deserted. I had a drink at the bar, exorbitant prices! Then waited as it slowly filled up with people. Most of them looked like they had just come in to get out of the rain. They were a bit down-at-heel and mostly male. There was an MC, though he didn't look a bit like Joel Grey. It was going to be some sort of 'Britain's Got Talent' affair. The MC informed us that we could perform to CDs or the pianist. He pointed to a dark corner and there was Benjy waving.

What followed, piano playing apart, was dire in the extreme. But at the interval I got to chat to the pianist. I told him all that had happened. He was aghast, said he knew Rick was a bad lot, and hugged me tight, saying he was glad I was safe. Then I broached my idea. He was all for it. Said he would contact his folks and get some details. I said I would be in touch when it was all set up.

And I was, several days later. And several days after that, a spruced up Benjy (minus guitar) and a rather nervous Stephen, I have to admit, presented themselves at the Admiralty.

My idea, well I felt it was more duty, was to try and get to the truth for the sake of the Summers and Lescotts of this world. I was well aware that I was treading where others had gone before, albeit in Australia, and had failed. I just felt I owed it to them to try. Was it guilt? Not on my father's behalf, when he and Johnny Jackson did what they did, they had been told everyone was off the Imperial. Was it guilt on behalf of the British Navy? Possibly. I couldn't have gone alone – after all it wasn't really my cause. But it was Benjy's and he wouldn't have been able to do it on his own, as he freely admitted. Together we were more formidable – well, perhaps less weak.

Intimidating doesn't begin to describe the building, the secretaries, the various ante-rooms we were ushered into and then seemingly abandoned in. Stern admirals glared down at us from the walls, and no less stern officials gave us the once-over as they passed. Benjy, spruced up remember, got especially withering looks. Finally, after what seemed like hours, but was only about twenty minutes, we were called into a room, dark, dimly lit, lofty-ceilinged, with more admirals looking down on us, to be confronted by a man in uniform with a lot of gold and stripes.

He introduced himself in very clipped tones as Graham – my mind skipped back to Allington and Ballantyne – was Graham his first name, hence we were a bit more pally, or his second in which case we weren't? He didn't include any naval title as it were. So what was all the gold braid for?

"Perhaps you could go into a bit more detail about your complaint? Put some flesh on the bones, Hah?"

Well, it wasn't a complaint, my submission had plenty of flesh on its bones and what was the 'Hah' sound all about? Also he was focussing entirely on me as if Benjy wasn't there. Nevertheless, I kept calm and began the story putting in as much detail as I could, naturally leaving out the revenge motif.

"So, to sum up" he said, lip curling "your evidence is merely a passage in a book and a reference on a website. We don't always take Internet sites very seriously here. We have only your word about this mysterious Greek fisherman who seemed, quite frankly, to be telling you a cock and bull story for money. There is, as you will appreciate, nothing in the archive nor in any official reports of the incident. The general opinion, which I subscribe to, is that it was a rumour put about by the enemy to lower the morale of our allies in particular. I'm sorry you have had a wasted journey. Please accept my condolences for your loss. But many men were lost in action and no one knows what happened to them. It is natural to cling to any bit of flotsam."

And with that final tasteless metaphor, his speech, for that's what it was, came to an end. He shuffled his papers and made as if to go. Benjy got up too, but my dander (wherever that mysterious organ resides) was well and truly up!

"Look mate, second, third or captain's mate, I don't care, saying there is no official record of it, therefore it didn't happen is nonsense. Of course, during wartime the Navy is not going to state that it torpedoed a ship with its own men still on board. As to saying there is no evidence – have you investigated it at all? What about corporal Parnaby? You could contact his descendants. Just because someone is a fisherman and Greek, doesn't mean he isn't telling the truth. Saying the Internet isn't to be taken seriously is like dismissing the invention of the aeroplane as of little value. There are real families here, with real grievances who feel they have not had a fair hearing or any hearing. I demand you take them seriously."

Steam may have been coming out of my ears by now. I had surprised myself. But I suppose calm under fire was what it is all about. He gave me an icy stare and said:

"The meeting is concluded. I have stated the official position. Good day to you."

I muttered darkly about the War Crime Tribunals, European Court of Human Rights, the U.N. but we had no choice but to leave.

Now I could see why other better men had failed in the past. Out on the street, breathing fresh air at last, I apologised to Benjy.

"No worries: loved the 'mate' thing. Let's get a drink."

The following morning I was in the house alone when the phone rang.

"Hello, old sport." Big Vinyl!

"The police tell me you've been involved in rather a lot of violent goings-on. Well it might surprise you to know, so have I. Some blighter stole the wing mirrors off my Interceptor! I chased him down the avenue and..."

About one hour later he got round to the reason for the call, to tell me that my job was still open. Bless him. He even said if I felt a bit low I could go round to his place and watch a few movies. I knew what he meant. I had no desire to see 'Department S' ever again. I had been there once before! And then the coup de grace:

"And you can have a go behind the wheel of the dark blue '73 if you like."

To Big Vinyl the apotheosis of motoring was behind the wheel of the dark blue 1973 Jensen Interceptor Mark Three. Providing you were wearing a white suit, leather gloves and sporting a Fu-Manchu moustache à la Jason King. It was weirder than dressing up in a bordello – I imagine!

What I told my boss was that I was thinking of taking a holiday and that perhaps after that I would 'tread the old vinyl' as it were. It was true. I needed a holiday. I could take a leaf out of Jethro's book and head for the Caribbean, away from the driving rain and sleet of January in Buckinghamshire. Or I could try Crete again, perhaps take Dad on a sort of cathartic voyage. But in his nineties I think it would be asking too much, physically and emotionally. And anyway I knew where I really wanted to go.

CHAPTER 23

As we flew in over the city every back garden really did have a pool, no doubt with a barbie beside it. The Opera House really was an astonishing multi-layered meringue dazzling in the hot sunshine. Oz beckoned. I had arranged to spend a few days in Sydney, a few in Melbourne and then my quest would take me to Adelaide in South Australia.

Sydney was delightful. I spent some hot days wandering the harbour, marvelling close up at The Opera House. I did the beaches and had a go at surfing on Bondi. I knew I was distancing everything and unwinding but not forgetting. I would have to go back and face various inquests and court rooms. Williams had only allowed me this trip on my GP's insistence 'for my shattered nerves'. I had to report to the police in Sydney, later in Melbourne and once again in Adelaide.

Melbourne was cooler and greener, Victoria more English than brash New South Wales. I felt more at home, safer if less excited. Melbourne was like an English city ought to be; safe, relaxing, green, classy but lively. Benjy had given me his sister's phone number and I rang her only to get a message:

'Sorry we won't be home for a few weeks. We're all off to Brisbane to see Jeff's brother. Then we'll probably go on up to Cairns and the Reef. Leave a message and number and

we'll get in touch when we get back.'

I did what was asked. So now I had two visits to make, not three. The first was to a bookshop.

The shelves were full of famous works of literature: Austen, Hardy, Laurence, Waugh. It was like being in Surrey University library, the English section. The poetry shelves were well stocked too. I had a look at Australian, American, New Zealand and even Chinese literature (in translation) before the owner, all kitted out in white linen with a panama hat, came over to introduce himself. Of course, he needed no introduction to me; I had 'spoken' to him on the net.

"Godfrey J Lescott at your service" he bowed with old world (or was it new world) charm.

"Stephen Johnson at yours."

He was taken aback momentarily by the accent and then light dawned and a huge smile spread over his face. He insisted on closing early (there was no one else in the shop) and taking me into his home above the shop.

I told him my story as he listened in amazement. It was the confirmation of what Parnaby had told the family that pleased him most. He was dismayed but not surprised that I had got nowhere with the Admiralty. His experience had been much the same with the Australian armed forces. He was glad that he had been able to help me find Benjy and I promised to give him Godfrey's regards.

"All these sad and scarred families" was his lament. He insisted I stay with him for a few days before I headed off to Adelaide. He fancied a trip down the coast to Torquay and offered to drive me there to look up Phil Erdington.

We spent the next day (Godfrey had closed the shop for his holidays, a notice informed everyone) walking Ferntree Gully National Park – it did what it said on the tin – nothing but fern trees everywhere. Godfrey was so enthusiastic about showing me that I hadn't the heart to say "once you've seen

210

one fern tree…"

Torquay was a revelation. It wasn't a mirror image of the genteel English Riviera resort at all. It was wild. There were young surfers everywhere. There was a lot of flesh on display and plenty of raucous, if good humoured drinking. But it was the waves that drew everyone – huge spectacular rollers. The daring young men clung to the side of them as they careered into the shore and the impressed girls screamed in delight. Devon it wasn't! I wondered whether Mrs Erdington would have come if she'd known.

Woolabong Road was just off the shore. When Phil (for it was he) answered the door he got the shock of his life – someone who until now had been a disembodied email had materialised in front of him. His welcome was warm as the West Country, his accent still detectable. We were outside by the pool, helping ourselves to his barbie in seconds. The whole family were round – scores of Erdingtons, none of them relatives of the doomed Jack. But how they made us welcome, even Godfrey, who looked much more the English gent off to Lords to see the cricket than Phil.

I told my story yet again and explained my determination to follow it through to the end by looking up Judith Stones in Adelaide. Phil and Godfrey between them did some researching and came up with an address. My destination was a tiny village called Uraidla in the Adelaide hills to the south of the city. And several days later, having made my goodbyes amid promises to visit when they were next in the UK, Godfrey and Phil waved me off from Melbourne Airport.

What I hadn't told them was my real reason for going to Adelaide and it wasn't immediately to see the Stones family. In fact, that was the last thing I wanted to do – literally the last. When I arrived in Adelaide, impossibly elegant and conservative for Oz, I was in Little Eyshott mode. Under cover. I booked into a city centre hotel and reconnoitred Uraidla. It was cooler up in the Adelaide hills and there were vines everywhere. Wine country. Uraidla was a wine town and I felt sure the Stones were wine folk of some sort. I found a small motel out of town, hired a nondescript car and began watching.

The trouble was Uraidla was so small, soon everyone was watching me watching them. Which wasn't quite what I planned. Nor was I as lucky as in Little Eyshott. A week of 'snooping' around brought nothing. I was ready to give up, feeling rather foolish, when out of the blue there she was walking into Paris Hill Winery. I followed at a discreet distance. She went into the wine shop and was deep in conversation with the woman behind the counter. The information on the door of the shop had already informed me the proprietor was Judith Stones. And the proprietor was not simply chatting to a customer there to buy wine, she was talking quite naturally to her sister!

I waited till their conversation ended and my quarry turned to go. I darted back to the exit and watched as she came out of the winery onto the road. I watched her go down the hill until she came to a car park. I hadn't come all this way to miss her now and raced down the hill. Fortunately, she must have forgotten something because she hadn't left but was looking in the boot. When she closed it she stared open mouthed at the stranger standing in front of her car, only he wasn't a stranger! She had dyed her hair, was wearing glasses and had done a lot to change her appearance but I had recognised her at once.

"Stephen!"

She didn't try and drive off or run, just stood there. She knew it was all over. Only it wasn't.

"Can we talk, Helen, or I suppose I have to call you Leah now?"

"I'm Mary where I live now. I only come here occasionally to see Judy. I presume the police will be here shortly."

"I haven't told them and I may not. Can we talk somewhere?"

There was a coffee bar close by and we went there. I began:
"I watched a film someone took of the incident on the boat.
If I really believed you would have killed my father I would
have the police with me now. But watching the video I saw
something surprising. I think you were dropping the knife and
diving from the boat seconds before I hit you. Your expression
and your movements were familiar enough for me to
recognise that. That led me to believe you had made a decision
not to harm Dad but to swim for it."

"All Australians are good swimmers" she replied coolly "I
can swim underwater for a long time; I reached a part of the
bank screened by undergrowth. No one saw me clamber out.
Astonishingly, I got away. Until now – what will you do with
me Stephen?"

"I know what I saw, at the last minute you couldn't do it, kill
an old man in cold blood. You chose not to. Yes my lunge was
dramatic but it wouldn't have saved him. In a sense you chose
to. If you'll explain it all to me, there may be no need to
inform anyone that I ever found you."

So Helen/Leah or whoever she was now took me back to
her small house in Oakbank about half an hour's drive, and
told me everything. This is her story:

"Richard was my twin as you know" immediately there was
a sense of deep emotion held in as she spoke of her dead
brother "he was the elder by a few minutes. To me he was
always my older brother, my guide, for many years of my life
he was my life. I did what he did, followed where he led. We
thought and felt the same – at least until very recently. I would
never doubt him or not do what he suggested. Judy always
thought and still thinks that he dominated me. It isn't as
simple as that with twins.

We adored Dad and we saw him struggle with the truth that

came in the letter from Parnaby. He aged, went smaller some-how, couldn't cope with the shame of drunkenness and the sadness of his father's needless, treacherous death. He hated the British and cursed everyone involved. When he committed suicide he passed his hatred of the British Navy on to us. Richard became obsessed and I followed Richard's lead as always. We made a pact; Judy was horrified when she found out later and jealous because she felt left out. Lucky Judy.

Our pact was to find if anyone we regarded as responsible was still alive and punish them. Richard's idea of guilt was fairly vague. He just wanted to hurt someone who had had any part in the scuttling. He researched day and night on the Internet. And he found your family. Your father was involved in the actual mechanics of firing the torpedoes. We could find no record of his death. And we found out he had children – you and Sonia. It was you that Richard targeted. He reckoned – it sounds terrible now – that to kill you would make your father suffer more.

So, chilling though it sounds, we came to England ostensibly to live and work, a new beginning for the pair of us, but really to kill you."

She began to sob and soon the tears were flowing at the enormity of what she was saying and what they had planned to do. I held her, well aware of the bizarre irony of the situation, I was consoling someone for the guilt they felt at having tried to kill me! I can't explain it but I felt more for Leah at that moment than I ever had for Helen.

"Richard wanted to get close to you but indirectly. He knew about Joe and Ella, don't ask me how. He was a mechanic; Ella worked at the garage in Hindhead. He got a job there and courted her. But what he discovered was that Ella had a hatred of her husband as strong as his was for you. They planned to kill you both. By now Richard and Ella were lovers. I think it was from this moment I started to lose faith in what we were doing. Perhaps I was jealous. I didn't like Ella. I heard about her suicide – I didn't shed a tear.

The plan was to stage an accident. Ella knew you would both be in the car that night. But, as you know, it all went horribly wrong. Richard tried again but failed – you told me about that incident. I had been told by Richard to befriend you. I'm a trained nurse. I got a job at Guildford, The Royal Surrey and by an amazing coincidence Maria was a patient on the ward and you came to visit. Richard was thrilled and told me to make a play for you. I was happy to, because the truth is, I liked you; when we made love, it wasn't all pretend, you know. I just couldn't break free from his spell. I know I made mistakes and you became suspicious – I wonder now if these mistakes really were mistakes or more 'Freudian slips'. Perhaps my subconscious was trying to warn you.

Anyway, Richard was now committed to Ella's agenda and this led to Joe's death. I was angry with my twin brother – I raged at him questioning what the point was of that crime. For the first time I felt free to question him. By now the focus of Richard's revenge had shifted to your Dad. He thought that you would be charged with Joe's murder – I never bought that part of the strategy – sensibly as it proved in the end. My task was to get closer to your family, so I spent a lot of time supposedly comforting your father about your disappearance. That was a difficult role not made any easier by your stupid brother-in-law who couldn't keep his hands to himself. If it wasn't me, it was the au pair.

You were right when you said I decided at the very last second not to go through with it. When I saw you on the bank I panicked, I felt I owed it to Richard, it was his last wish that I kill your father. So I crawled along the boat trying to force myself to do it. In those moments I saw everything clearly for the first time, perhaps Richard had to die for me to escape from his iron will. The desire for revenge was just destroying lives. If you live for revenge you don't move on in life – if you can't forgive 'you destroy the bridge which you have to cross' as they say.

I dropped the knife just as you hit me and not because you did. I dived off the boat and swam underwater – it wasn't easy, the current was strong and the reeds were thick. But I was lucky. I had always planned to escape anyway so I had clothes, money and my passport hidden ready at your sister's. There was no one in, I had had a key made. In an hour I was at Heathrow, my flight was booked. I was in mid-air before the divers even went into the Thames to look for me. I don't know who the detective was in charge of things but thankfully, he was a buffoon. Until now no one has even thought to visit Australia." I smiled at the thought of the buffoon, the perfect epithet for Williams. But mostly I held her as the tears flowed and she asked forgiveness, which I was more than willing to give.

We spent the next few days dealing with our situation. Her guilt seemed fierce and to be honest the appalling actions of the British Navy in Crete made me feel some residual guilt too. Slowly, walking in the cool of the Adelaide hills, drinking its beautiful wine we rekindled our old desire, lit by a strange new flame. Before I left for England (I had a date with the buffoon) we were real lovers and I made a promise, which delighted her, to say nothing at all about finding her – to let everyone believe she was drowned in the Thames – and I made a pledge to return.

CHAPTER 24

We were all gathered at Kew for a private reading of the 'translation' of the letter that had caused so much trouble – in more ways than one. Rydal and Maria were now a very happy item and I could meet Maria without any regrets, there was someone waiting for me on the other side of the world, and it was my secret.

When I had got back to the UK, I had met Williams and told him that my holiday in Australia had yielded nothing. He shrugged, suggesting: "Bloody waste of time. I would never have let you go in the first place. Judges too soft!" He had no doubt Leah was at the bottom of the Thames somewhere – long might he go on believing that.

In fact Williams, to his immense frustration, was very short of people to investigate. Ella was dead, Richard Erdington was dead, Leah was dead (he thought) and Lats had vanished without trace, but believed to be beyond reach in Eastern Europe somewhere, according to his brother. So I was his only target. But I was palpably innocent. No wonder he looked and sounded so put out. But, despite him, his bosses quickly put everything to bed, inquests were completed and the various murders, suicides and thefts were filed away until such time as the Thames gave up Leah's body or an Eastern European police force produced Lats.

Jethro, fresh from his cruise, invited myself, Rydal and

Maria to his home for a private rendition of his modern version of the letter. He pointed out that it was legally the property of the Allington Castle estate to whom it was to be returned. He also suggested that the letter we had found was the property of the Church of England which was prepared to loan it to Allington so that the two could be displayed side by side in some future exhibition or whatever. We agreed, we had little choice but to hand it over.

So there we were, in the sitting room at Kew with platefuls of buns and 'Angoos' safely out of the way.

Jethro began: "First of all I must commend young Rydal here on his modern version of the letter found at Broxbourne. I couldn't have done a better job myself."

I didn't have to glance at my friend, I knew he would be blushing.

"Now to the letter hidden at Stag Hill. It was a difficult task because it was in a bad state of repair, not sure why. The language was particularly tortuous and unusual. The hand it was written in at times almost (but not quite) indecipherable. Sections of it were even encoded. But, fortunately, we have several keys to Thomas Cromwell's codes and cracked it. Incidentally the use of codes, known only to Cromwell, proves the letter was written by him and not fabricated by the Cecils later to discredit him."

His eyes twinkled at the thought of the hours he had spent on it. Here was a man in love with his job.

Although he had a written version, he wasn't to be denied. So we sat back and listened:

"April second 1536.
To the Right Honourable Sir Thomas Wyatt
Sir Thomas. We need your help in a matter. It has lately come to be known that the Queen, and this is dangerous to report abroad, has played her husband false. We have sworn testimony of this from divers people. We have hopes that the

matter will come to trial at a certain date but it would help all parties, especially one whom we know well, if others were found to acknowledge the truth of this matter.

We know that at one time you and Mistress Boleyn were close acquaintances at court. We are also to know that this acquaintance was renewed at Calais when Mistress Boleyn was Queen. We know nothing untoward about this. We ask that you remain silent if your name is given as one of the accused, whoever they shall be. It may be perhaps that you remain within the Tower a certain time.

Believe, Sir Thomas, your release is certain when this matter is resolved. And that the gratitude of myself and moreso of one other will be great. If you feel you cannot help us in this matter, I am instructed to say to you that your closeness to the Queen may also be shown by a testimony of one Sir Richard Coyninge who will swear that in December he saw yourself and the Queen alone in her bed chamber and naked. I am certain you will recollect that the Lady Elisabeth was born in the September after. This information will remain solely in my possession and the Right Honourable Sir Richard will say none of this unless asked by me or one other.

I expect your reply and remain
Your humble servant
Thomas Cromwell."

There was silence for a while as we all took it in. I was aware for the first time of what Joe was so excited about. I was also close to tears thinking of my good friend. My consolation was that his death had really nothing to do with the letter and would have happened anyway. Thomas Cromwell had not struck from five hundred years ago.

Maria was the first to react, not surprising really, she had had the presence of mind and mental acuity to devise the 'hind' clues after all.

"So, Cromwell wanted to make sure that Queen Ann was

219

found guilty of adultery because Henry wanted a new wife, Jane Seymour, who might give him a son. And did give him a son."

Rydal carried on: "So the more rumours they could appear to substantiate the better. They did do this with several men who weren't as lucky as Wyatt. The King's best friend – Henry Norris – was one. Why Cromwell took the decision to use Wyatt and then release him is what we don't know. Why not execute him with all the others, after all they had the testimony, lies of course, of this Coyninge chap."

It was my turn: "I think it was too dangerous. Wyatt might have had some proof that he wasn't guilty. So Cromwell thought of bribing him like this. It was an unnecessary risk as it happened because in the end they had sufficient evidence without Wyatt, but Cromwell didn't know then that his plans would work so well. He must have been pretty sure that Wyatt would go along with it for the reward. It doesn't quite prove that the whole thing was a put-up job but it's the strongest evidence yet of what Cromwell was prepared to do."

We were chastened by the letter. The atmosphere was calm, but solemn really. I suppose we were all thinking what the letters had caused – not all the tragedy by any means – but certainly the death of the Professor (it was clear now that Lats wanted the financial rewards that would come with publication of the letters and Dove-Kemp stood in the way of this) and Maria's ordeal at the hands of Lats, who of course was still out there somewhere.

I couldn't help speculating about the other letter, hidden by Mary or one of her servants:

"Presumably Mary didn't want to publish anything which might suggest Ann Boleyn was innocent since that would reflect favourably on her rival Elizabeth. But why not just destroy it?"

Rydal offered a possible answer: "Perhaps she ordered a servant to destroy it but he hid it instead for reasons we'll never know."

We left the letters with Jethro. If we were ever to set eyes on them again it would be as members of the public looking at them in glass cases somewhere.

I thought back to the night of Dove-Kemp's lecture at the University. How he teased the audience and the journalists by suggesting Elizabeth was not Henry's. When he knew all along she was. He was just whetting our appetites. Poor foolish man, really he was contributing to his own demise.

It was Rydal who broke the news I was expecting, that he and Maria were engaged. I had seen a diamond on her finger though she hadn't flaunted it; that was not Maria's style. What did surprise me was that the wedding was not to be after they had both graduated but in the coming summer.

"How can you both manage, as students?" I said naively.

"No problem" replied Rydal "my parents will pay for it all."

"Oh no they won't" interjected Maria "mine will."

I laughed as they squabbled over who would pay the most. Two rich kids! But I knew there was far more to them than that. I hoped to be at the wedding though much depended on the course of the investigation. If it was over much sooner I would be gone. In fact, the redoubtable Williams managed to drag the whole thing out for a long time. Even with no court case. I managed to make the wedding because it was moved into the early spring. Clearly the lovers couldn't wait or perhaps hadn't been able to!

It was a gloriously sunny day in April. Maria looked wonderful as all brides should. Rydal was the happiest man alive – I could see that. I felt a great warmth and love for my friends. I think what made it the more satisfying was knowing that Leah, who had phoned me the day before, was waiting for me. I was actually angry that she had risked a phone call. If my phone was being listened to who knows what they would do. But that was being far too egocentric. I don't think I was of any interest to the police anymore. I was almost missing Williams' sarcasm!

When I told Sonia and Dad that I was going back to Australia for an extended stay, they were both shocked. I could see the fear in Dad's eyes that given his age I might not see him again. I reassured him as best I could. I would be home for Christmas. It was a lie – what could I do? Leah could never return to the UK and my life was with her now. Dad was far too frail to travel to Australia. Our farewells were tearful. Even Gerald, reconciled at last with my sister who had banned any more au pairs (Carmen had departed, the local bar manager in Marlow had offered her a job), wished me Bon Voyage.

CHAPTER 25

I had sent a letter to Leah – texts and phone calls were too risky – telling her I would be in Adelaide on May 1st. As it happened I got away earlier, desperate to see her. There wasn't time to let her know by snail mail, so I decided to surprise her by arriving a whole week earlier. I changed planes in Sydney and after an evening stop over finally got to Adelaide airport massively jet-lagged and not at all in the mood to surprise anybody. Although it was late April and supposedly autumn in the southern hemisphere, it was still suffocatingly hot in Adelaide. I needed to cool down.

I decided to wait a while before going to Leah's so I settled down in the airport bar for a few beers – I was already getting back into the Oz mindset! That's when I saw him. He walked past me and my mouth gaped open as my eyes followed that oh so familiar loping gait. I told myself, well there must be other people who walk like that, why not in Adelaide airport? But just to be sure, I got up and hurried down the concourse – the man was now some way ahead but stopped at the Auto-quick car hire. There was a long queue. It doesn't matter where you are in the world or at what time, there will always be a long queue at the car hire check-in desks. So I stood, screened by a pillar and waited too, his back was to me throughout the time he queued and several times I told myself – this is ridiculous. This is South Australia not Surrey. When his transaction was complete and he turned, keys in one hand, case in the other, I was looking directly into the eyes of Hugo Lats.

He couldn't see me. I watched him leave the terminal, cross to the car hire park and leave in a blue Ford Focus. I had no means of following him. Stunned, I wandered back to the terminal. Of all the airports in all the world... This wasn't, couldn't be a coincidence, the odds were astronomical and then some. There was only one possible explanation – Lats was here because I was. Goodness knows how but he had found out that I was coming to Adelaide – he must have found out from my family. Perhaps he came across Gerald in his cups; perhaps he put Gerald in his cups in order to find out. If he knew where, he knew when – or at least he thought he did. I had told the family I was flying out on May 1st. But I had come early unbeknown to them and to Lats. He had come early to wait – why? What for? He could have no inkling of my real reason for being here, since none of my family or friends had.

He was here to deal with me! Why? Guildford, Marlow, London were all too dangerous; Australia was safe. What was he looking for? Not the letters surely. It was becoming common knowledge that some important Tudor letters had been recovered and returned to their rightful owners. It must be revenge. I had stolen his fortune from him, hoodwinked him, made a fool of him, put him 'on the run'. But now he was going to turn the tables on me and take revenge. I felt cold at the thought knowing what he had done to Dove-Kemp. But by an amazing stroke of luck I could thwart him again – because I knew he was here but he didn't know I was – I had a week to find him!

I contemplated an astonishing call to Williams – now tucked up in bed with Mrs Williams (was there a Mrs Williams?) and dreaming sweet dreams. But did I want to let the chief inspector know that I was here and make Leah's position far less secure? No. I had to deal with Lats myself.

So I presented myself at the Autoquick car hire desk after the inevitable and interminable wait in the queue. I was met by the beaming smile of – her name badge looked like 'Shark' – surely not!

"Hi, my name's Shar, how can I help you?"

The letter 'k' turned out to be a smudge of make-up or a bit of Shar's dinner – whatever.

Shar's smile was one of the fixed variety that said really:

"I have been working here all day dealing with you mindless idiots but I am determined to smile through it all."

She was a little put-out, even the smile slipped and wobbled ever so slightly at my request. It was all I could come up with.

"Hi, I have a problem. I am in Australia with my brother Hugo. We got separated in Sydney and I had to take a later flight. We were going to hire a car. I just wonder could you tell me if he has already done that?"

Fortunately, Shar (what was it short for – Sharon, Sharmaine, Sharleen, Sarah, Shark even?) was tired and in no mood to start a long rigmarole. She looked up the info on the screen and said:

"Ah, here it is. Mr Hugo Lats picked up the keys to a Ford Focus, S1257 ADEZ about half an hour ago. I expect he's still waiting for you – you should go to the car. You'll find it just outside entrance Z in the car park there. Thank you. Have a nice day" (smile still just intact but wilting at the edges).

Then I asked (the key question) what hotel he had given as his address here in Adelaide in case he had gone. Stupid me I had forgotten the hotel name. She turned to her colleague, Mart (don't ask!) whose answer chilled me:

"Mr Lats, yes I remember the guy, said he was staying out of town, somewhere out in the Adelaide hills, didn't say where."

He knew. Too many coincidences. The Adelaide Hills. How did he know? Leah was in danger. His revenge on me was to start with her. I had to get out there and fast!

You always find, wherever you go, that taxi ranks are end-less and always in the way when you don't want them. But when you need one urgently, never there. The taxi rank at Adelaide airport was nowhere to be seen. I hunted high and low. I scanned airport information boards. I asked virtually everyone I saw. No one knew. Many thought they knew and sent me on wild goose chases to all ends of the terminal. Could I have landed in the only airport in the world which wasn't served by taxis?

I took the only course open to me and took a bus into the centre of town. It was agonisingly slow. So slow in fact that when we were stuck for ages behind an empty taxi, I dashed off the bus, much to the astonishment (and amusement in equal measure) of the passengers, and got into the taxi.

The driver didn't bat an eyelid – well I couldn't actually see his eyelids but I felt there was no batting going on. I told him to get me to Oakbank, where Leah's house was, as quickly as he could. I phoned her constantly but her mobile was switched off. I'm not sure what I would have told her if she had answered anyway. It was blisteringly hot in the taxi. As we drove into the hills it became a little cooler. But I was shaking with fear and sweating with nervousness. I wasn't sure what I should do when we got there. Hammer on the door, creep round the side, I could scarcely remember the geography of the building anyway.

As we pulled up a few yards short of the driveway I saw the grey, not blue this time, Ford Focus outside – there was even an Autoquick sticker on the back window. My heart sank. He was here! He was still here which perhaps meant he hadn't completed his revenge yet. What dreadful things were happening just a few yards away? I was in an agony of indecision – whatever I did would be a mistake! And yet I had to do something.

And then the decision was taken out of my hands as they came down the drive together – Lats and Leah. Hand in hand. They separated to get into either side of the hire car. Leah got in the driving seat. I couldn't make any sense of it. I had little time to try and sort it in my mind. I told the taxi driver to follow them. Maximilian (for that was his name, his badge proclaimed), the driver, was ice-cool as I had already found out. Most taxi drivers at this point might have balked at my request. Not this one – he smiled.

"I've always dreamed about doing this! Are you a detective? Are they criminals, on the run, cheating lovers, drug smugglers?"

His imagination had caught fire. It seemed best to go with it. I became a detective from England, having travelled half the world, to apprehend these two. As we followed at a discreet distance, I fuelled his love for excitement and adventure (there was precious little of it in Adelaide and surrounds by all accounts). We headed back through the hills and into the city. It was all on one main highway with plenty of traffic, so it was relatively easy to stay in pursuit and not be seen. Soon it became clear our journey was a complete circle as we turned onto the road for the airport.

What was happening? What was the conversation, if any, in the car? Did he have a gun to her and was this why she was driving his car? Why were we heading back to the airport? What would happen when we got there?

I was about to find out. The car pulled up outside the terminal, we were hidden a few cars back. And what followed filled me with astonishment. Leah and Lats both got out, he went round to the driver's side and got in. She walked into the terminal carrying a travel bag. The Focus drove off. I stuffed a huge wad of dollars into the delighted Maximilian's hand and thanked him. As he drove off, already planning what he would tell his mates back at the office, I hesitated for a split second. But there really was no choice – I went through the automatic doors into the terminal.

All bets were off now. Until the moment she strolled into the terminal I was certain that Lats had some hold over her, if not actually a gun to her ribs, and that revenge was on his mind. Now everything had changed. For all the world she had behaved like a wife whose husband had gone to park or return the car while she toured the airport stores prior to departure.

But that was impossible for so many reasons. She was in love with me, she was waiting for me! She had chosen not to carry out her brother's plan – albeit at the last second. But most of all there was no possible connection between herself and Lats except me. She had been swept up in her twin's desire to right a World War II wrong; he had been a Kew Record Office researcher who had tried to make a fortune by stealing important Tudor letters. The two separate strands had only been united in Maria's head by the 'hind' idea. They did not, could not, know each other, know of each other.

His hold over her, however, must have been so total that he could allow her the freedom of the terminal. Perhaps he had said that if she didn't do what he said, he would make me suffer as well as her? All this was going through my head as I prowled the building in search of her. I calculated I had perhaps fifteen minutes whilst he parked/left the car.

I started with the shops – up and down the aisles of the various chain stores, peering into the little boutiques – nothing. The Autoquick desk had its customary queue, I even glimpsed the still-smiling Shar but no Leah. The departure desks had snaking queues, I couldn't see her in any of them. The fast food restaurants and coffee shops were doing a roaring trade but no thanks to her. Finally, I saw her thumbing through magazines, as cool and calm as could be.

I tapped her on the shoulder – she turned saying: "Oh you…" (or was it Hu?) and her face registered shock and disbelief. She threw her arms round me and hugged me tightly.

"Oh my darling. I didn't expect you till next week. What are you doing here? When did you land – why didn't you tell me?"

She gave me the most passionate kiss, in full view of busy shoppers. It was what she didn't say that alarmed me. When I asked her what she was doing there, she replied:

"Oh, I'm meeting a friend from Melbourne. Or rather I was supposed to be. She's just texted me to tell me she's missed the flight. Let's get you home. Haven't got a car I'm afraid, Molly was going to hire one and run us both back. Now I guess we'll have to get a taxi. Why don't we go and have a drink in the bar first – it's so damned hot in here even with the air con."

All said in a breathless rush. Was she making it up as she went along? Some of it was lies I was sure, but for what purpose? To protect me or to fool me? I still wasn't sure.

Her embrace had been long and passionate; she had held me in a hug for ages – was she looking at or signalling to someone else over my shoulder? Only yesterday I would have trusted her totally, but now all the doubts were flooding back, remembering what she had been, what she had done or nearly done. Was I wrong about her after all?

The bar was full, but we found a table in a corner and I brought over the drinks, red wine for me, white for her.

"Cheers" she said "what a wonderful surprise!"

If I was going to ask her what was going on and how Lats had been at her home and brought her here – I had to do it now. But I couldn't find the words, so I said nothing. We chatted about this and that. I held her close, we shared kisses. She phoned us a taxi and we strolled to the rank – so there it was, right outside the main entrance – how could I have missed it? For one ghastly moment I thought the taxi driver was Maximilian but no, that would have been impossible.

We were on the way back from the airport; this was the third time I had done this journey inside a couple of hours. In each journey my emotions had been high, on each one very different. Several times I looked behind us, expecting to see a grey Ford Focus, but I didn't. Even Leah remarked on how jumpy I seemed. We passed the race course, and I knew we were in Oakbank and would arrive any minute. I half expected to find the Focus waiting for us on the drive. It wasn't.

It was baking hot inside Leah's home. She was all over me, nonetheless. It was fairly clear we were about to carry on where we left off. She went upstairs to shower and change – pointing me in the direction of chilled beer in the fridge (is there somewhere a fridge in Australia without beer and/or wine in it?). The air conditioning had got going, it was becoming pleasantly cool, the beer was beautifully chilled and relaxing. There was a beautiful, very desirable girl upstairs – showering and changing just for me. I suppose, despite all the chaotic events since I arrived in Adelaide, the moment got to me. So when she called me up to the bedroom I went.

We kissed, cuddled and lay on the bed together. As our excitement built, our clothes were shed gradually. Soon I was on top of her as she whispered in my ear how wonderful it was that I was back to stay. How could I not believe it – she was so sweet – I looked at her and saw just the flicker of a look beyond me. I rolled off her as the steel blade whipped by my shoulder and buried itself, not in my back as intended, but in Leah's stomach. She gurgled blood as her eyes registered the true horror of what Lats had done. Before he could dislodge the knife, I grabbed the marble lamp-standard on the bedside table and swung it with all my might at his head. The crack was terrible. I fled down the stairs, out of the house, naked and retching. I had to get away from that room, that house. There were stares, many of them I'm sure. I paid no heed – I simply ran and ran, until the patrol car found me in the nearby park, crouched, naked and shaking, making no sense.